A SEASON IN EDEN

BOOKS BY MEGAN CHANCE

Fall from Grace
The Way Home
The Gentleman Caller

Published by HarperCollins Publishers

$\mathcal{A}$ SEASON IN $\mathcal{E}$DEN

MEGAN CHANCE

 HarperCollins*Publishers*

 HarperCollins Publishers
10 East 53rd Street, New York, NY 10022–5299

ISBN 0-7394-0603-5

Jacket illustration © 1999 by John Ennis

Printed in the United States of America

Visit HarperCollins on the World Wide Web at
http://www.harpercollins.com

For my grandfather, Kenneth Solt,
who taught me that love can close
even the greatest distances

And for Kany, Maggie, and Cleo,
who fill my own Eden

A Season in Eden

part 1

There's not a joy the world can give
like that it takes away.

—LORD BYRON

1

I used to love this land.

It's been nearly four years since I first looked at these sagebrush-covered hills through the dream-filled eyes of the man I loved. I was sixteen then, newly married. Too young to see the pain in these acres, too young to know the tears other women had cried over this place. I'm not sure I would have believed it if I'd been told.

Now I know that what they say about this valley is true: This land is selfish and unforgiving. It takes your dreams and your hopes.

I know it's true, because that's what happened to me.

The day it happened, I'd smelled the sharp, astringent sage and the sun-baked promise of a sky as blue as my husband's eyes. I'd heard the cherry trees rustling in the wind. The morning this land took my heart, I'd still believed in it.

Its promises haunt me now. I had wanted so much. Prosperity, yes, but more than that. Security, home, the dreams women have of children swinging on porch railings and running through the orchards, of growing old to watch grandchildren playing among the branches of the old oak in the yard—a tree planted and abandoned by someone who had lived here long before. I saw my whole life platted here, in ridges and valleys of a land so empty we could ride the entire perimeter of our claim without once seeing evidence of another living soul.

When I first came here, I saw promise glinting in the windows Eli had brought all the way from The Dalles—seven days each way—driving the wagon slow so not a single pane was broken, just because he said he wanted to see me in the house with sunshine in my hair. I spent endless hours sewing gingham curtains for them, my best tiny stitches and straight, square hems. Those windows became the empty frames for pictures I saw in my head, expectations I had that one day red-checked curtains would border a land green with realized dreams.

I wonder how it is that Eli still sees the future. I wonder how he walks the orchard every day, staring at the trees that froze during the killing winter, replanting them one by one, finding faith in new green leaves. I wonder how it is that he can talk about digging the irrigation ditch deeper, how he can see a time when it will stretch like a thick silver snake all over these acres. He sees the future in forty-dollar words, railroad brochures promising apples as big as fists and cherries the size of plums. A golden land stretching as far as his eyes can see. *Yakima*. To him, simply the word has magic.

That first spring day after the terrible winter, he

told me a story about ancient Indian paintings on rocks up near Selah Gap. Those drawings were older than time, according to the Yakimas, drawn by people not of their tribe, not the Nez Perce. "You see, Lora?" Eli had said. "I'm not the first man to see promise in these hills."

Then, I understood what he meant. I felt it, too. Now, all I know is that those people aren't here anymore, and I wonder why they left, if it was the women who made them go. I wonder if those ancient Indian women had stared out at the dry and endless acres, their fists jammed in their pockets, their eyes focused on places far away, feeling the hopelessness of this place hard in their hearts.

Perhaps it's only women who understand that. I've never met a man who could—not one who ever said so, anyway. Certainly Eli has never admitted it. I suppose it's because men need a promise to live on. For me, those promises have withered away. All that remains is the struggle against details, the never-ending battle with dust and desert. When I look out at the land, I see my garden, belts of green planted between the orchard rows, cabbages, peas, and potatoes wilting in the heat, fighting for every drop of water. My girlish hopes have come down to one simple wish: having enough food for the winter. "I am not a dreamer," my mama used to say. "There's too much to do for that."

I am not a dreamer, either. Not anymore.

It was a day in mid-June—hot in the way that makes men shake their heads and say, "The summer's set to be a scorcher this year," as if it would be different from any other summer—when I first realized what it was Eli meant to do, and how it would change things.

I'd been out in the garden picking strawberries, ferreting through the straw mulch and the broad leaves for ones the birds had missed, the small, bright red ones starting to dry and holding their sugar close. The smell reminded me of childhood, and the green scent of growing wheat and hot weather before it really got hot. When I was a child, strawberry season had always meant shortcake for supper. When the first ones came ripe, I would run to tell my mother, and the whole afternoon my sisters and I would be giggly waiting for that first bite of sweet, crumbling biscuit and pink-stained milk.

But that was a memory from a different time, and I didn't like to think of it now. It reminded me too much of the things I'd wanted, the hopes I'd held like treasures inside me, the wish to give that same memory to someone else.

I had the sudden urge to crush those berries between my fingers, but we could not afford to waste them. When my fingers were red with juice and sticky with little hairs and seeds, and the bucket was full, I took them inside to make jam, and in spite of myself, or maybe just from habit, I set some aside and mixed up sweet biscuits and cut sugar from the cone to sprinkle over.

I glanced out the window to see Eli near the line of dead trees. He wouldn't be at the house for some time yet. He'd been staying away nearly until sunset, every day a little longer, and though I felt his absence and his sadness over it, I waited for those extra minutes, too; I was thankful for them.

Tonight, the jam started its boil just as I heard his footsteps on the porch, so I couldn't talk to him right away—and I'm ashamed to admit I was grateful for it, because just like every other night, I felt his presence as an ache in my head, a strain I couldn't ease.

I kept my back to him as I nodded toward the table and said, "You'd best go ahead and eat."

But he didn't sit, and when I lifted the jam off the stove to pour into the jars I'd set on the old, scarred sideboard near the window, he came up behind me and grabbed the pot full of jam. He could have just taken it from me; instead he wrapped his arms around me so I was trapped between him and the jam, and for just a moment he held me tight enough that I could smell the sweat and dust of him.

"Lora," he whispered into my hair.

I could hardly breathe in the circle of his arms. In the last year, we'd been strangers to each other, and though I told myself it was not how a marriage should be, in a way, it was how I wanted it. I could not explain why even to myself.

When Eli loosened his hold just a little, I twisted away from him, ducking between him and the pan, burning myself trying to escape him.

"Ouch!" I said, sucking my wrist. "Don't sneak up on me like that."

"I'm sorry," he said. "The next time I want to touch my wife, I'll ask first."

His bitterness hurt. I wished I'd stayed quiet.

He looked at the pot in his hands. "Where do you want it?"

"Over there, by the jars."

It seemed that lately I was hurting him all the time, and I hated myself for it. Still, I was relieved when he left me alone and sat at the table.

He only toyed with his dinner. I poured the jam into the jars and sealed them with hot wax, and I took my time about it, delaying the moment when I would have to sit and eat dinner with my husband. The silence between us was strained. He might as well have said, *We need to talk, Lora,* because I felt that much anxiety waiting for those too-familiar words. I tried to concentrate on the jam, to take pleasure in a task I'd always loved, in the way the sunlight died away against the glass, how the strawberries inside glistened. Whenever I made jam, I felt rich. I almost hated to open the jars in the wintertime because they were so pretty.

But this time Eli's tension filled the room, so I was jittery and distracted, and the strawberry smell and the memories it brought with it seemed to grow bigger and fuller until it was a wall between us. When I was done, I wiped at the jars with the edge of my apron, though there wasn't anything to wipe away, and hoped that maybe he'd finish his dinner and go outside.

When I turned to glance at him, he hadn't eaten more than a bite. He'd poured milk on his shortcake, and sprinkled it with sugar, but the biscuit was growing soggy and gray, and he was staring down at the spoon between his fingers as if it held all the secrets of the world.

Finally, he said, "It's going to be a hot summer."

"It's always hot."

"It'll be hotter this year."

I tried to think of some answer to that. Before I could, he said, "The irrigation ditch is too shallow."

I had not expected those words, and so I wasn't ready for the sudden burst of anger that rose in me, the terrible grief. I looked out the window, at the lines of trees, the dead ones looking burnt and crippled, their branches reaching over that ditch like wicked little hands. *It was deep enough,* I thought bitterly. *Deep enough.* But then I looked out at the green vines and leaves of my garden, and I could almost feel their horrible thirst. I told myself it was all that mattered anymore.

"You'd best dig it deeper, then," I told him. "The garden will need the water before long, and the vegetables will have to get us through the winter, I expect."

Then he said the words I'd been waiting for, the ones I hated. "We have to talk, Lora."

"I don't want to talk." My voice sounded so small I wasn't sure he could hear it. But he had. My Eli . . . in that way, anyway, he was not like other men, not like my father. Eli was black Irish, and that legacy didn't live only in his looks, or in the way he felt connected to the land. Eli liked to talk; he liked to tell stories and to say things that embarrassed me, he was quick with *I love you*'s, and he knew how to listen when I had something to say. He understood the feelings inside me the way no one else ever had.

Or at least, once he'd been able to. That understanding had faded until now there was only space between us. I had nothing to say to him, nothing I wanted him to say to me. I wanted silence, and if I could not have that, I wanted idle talk. Tonight, I wanted that so badly I could barely look at him.

"Lora, this is about money," he said, and that impatience was in his voice again, that angry frustration. "I was hoping there might be enough of a harvest this year to get by. But it doesn't look like there will be."

"The trees are young yet—"

"Whatever we get won't make a dent in our account at Ben Schiller's. There won't be enough to put in new trees, and we still owe the cabinetmaker, and Prentiss and Field, and . . . too many others." He paused, looking at me, and his voice grew quiet. "There's not enough money, Lora."

He let that sink in. *Not enough money.* He was looking at me as if he expected me to say something, but I had nothing to say; I had no real idea what he meant. Money had always been short, but we'd made ends meet. Eli had always taken care of things. He'd always told me not to worry. "Why are you telling me this?"

"I was talking to Tom Larsen a few days ago. He said they're looking for men on the Wishkah River. I think I should go for a few months. From what he says, I ought to be able to make enough there to get us through until next year."

He sighed at the end, as if he'd been waiting for days to say the words and was relieved now that they were said. He was staring at me with those fine blue eyes that had once lit a fire inside me. There was a question there that made me wonder what it was he wanted me to say, whether he wanted me to say, *Don't go, please don't go,* or whether he was just hoping to keep his relief from showing if I let him.

And the truth was, I didn't know what I wanted. I couldn't think of a reaction yet. All I could do was say, "The Wishkah? That's so far away."

"It's just for the summer. I'll go into town tomorrow and talk to Ben. I think he'll carry you if he knows I'm good for it when I get back. And John Zimmerman will check in on you from time to time."

"He's busy with his own family."

"He's said he'll look after you, Lora."

That was when I realized Eli wasn't waiting for my agreement. He'd already made up his mind. It didn't really matter what had to say. "So you mean to go."

"The way I see it, there's no other choice."

He looked down at his bowl and let his spoon fall with a soft plop into the milk. His dark hair fell forward to hide his face, and he felt unfamiliar to me then. I wished I knew what he was thinking, what he wanted, but I couldn't bring myself to ask, and truthfully, I supposed I was afraid to know. Instead, I asked a safe question. "When will you leave?"

The question seemed to startle him, and he looked up. Some emotion I couldn't read clouded his eyes. "I don't know. Soon. There's still plenty to take care of before then."

Eli picked up the spoon again and then let it fall once more, and I saw how soggy his dinner was, how the biscuit had melted to pink mush in his bowl. I reached for it.

"You've waited too long," I said. "Let me get you another one."

He looked at me as if I were a stranger—no, more than a stranger, someone he didn't know and couldn't understand.

"I can't eat it," he said. "How can you?"

My guilt then was overwhelming and terrible. For a moment I could not see or think; I could barely breathe. By the time I was steady enough to answer him, he was gone.

He came to bed that night after the lamp had been out nearly an hour, but I wasn't asleep. I had thought to wait for him, but when I heard his footstep on the stair, I stiffened, closed my eyes, and made my breathing come evenly and deep, as though I were already sound asleep. I heard him come into the room, a feeling more than a sound, he was so quiet. His presence filled the loft, and I felt his soft sigh moving the still-warm air.

I listened to him undress: the thud of his boots, the soft *sssshhhh* as he pulled off his socks, the snapping click of his braces. Metal and fabric dropping to the floor, and him picking them up again in the darkness, laying them neatly over the rickety old chair he kept in the corner just for that purpose. His familiar routine, something I knew about him that no one else knew. I had heard those same things over and over through the years; their constancy was reassuring. I thought of how it would be when he was gone, the silence, only the memory of these familiar sounds, and suddenly I missed him before he was even gone, suddenly I wanted to reach for him, to touch him. I wanted to make up for hurting him today. But then he climbed into bed beside me, and I felt the sinking of the mattress, heard the creak of the rope frame, smelled his leather and clean-dirt smell, and the desire withered inside me.

I lay there in the darkness, schooling my breathing, and tried to will myself to touch him. In my head, I did touch him. I moved my arm, my hand, stretched out my fingers, but it was only a fancy. Eli had told me once about mummies they'd found in some desert somewhere, and I felt like that now, encased, wrapped in tight rags, stiff as stone beneath.

He shifted a little in bed, his long-underwear-clad leg brushed mine—soft, overwashed cotton, heat— and the sadness over what we'd had and lost came back to me.

I squeezed my eyes shut against it and kept on breathing until it went away, and I felt calm again, myself, and the darkness was only darkness, not a heavy, suffocating blanket. Eli moved beside me, easing closer, testing . . . and I wished my pretend sleeping was real, that I wasn't awake to feel those things, to regret them.

Finally, he eased away again, and after a time I heard his soft snoring. *Next time*, I promised myself. Next time, I would not feel so untouchable. This fear and longing that tightened my stomach would pass, and I would want him again. That was the thing about life; it was always changing, even when you didn't want it to. Surely everyone felt this way once or twice.

Still, as I lay there, staring into the darkness, I knew I was glad that he was going—if only for a little while. I loved Eli, but it would be better when he was gone.

When he came back, I would make up for tonight, and every other night; I would make things better for him.

But deep in my heart I wondered if that was even possible.

I wondered if I could even remember how.

2

There are times when your whole life seems to be moving forward without you, and that was how I felt the next morning, when Eli left to go into town to take care of things: as if everything was rushing by, racing so fast that the world was nothing but a blur beyond my hand. I was sure that Eli's decision to go to the Wishkah had been long in coming—he was not an impulsive man. Still, it felt sudden to me; I had not had time to think about everything it would mean, and the fact was, I didn't want to think about it. I reassured myself by remembering that he'd said it would be a while yet, that he had things to do, but in my heart, I knew he'd be ready to go within hours. He was delaying only because he didn't want me to think what I knew already: that he wanted to go.

I supposed part of me thought it would all work itself out in the end, that somehow we would find our way back to each other, effortlessly, the way a horse finds its way home after a blizzard melts away. Perhaps absence would do it. He would come home—just like a lost horse—and I would run into his arms, and the past would disappear, unspoken between us.

I was determined to see this separation as something good. As soon as he rode off for town and I turned to the chores that usually filled my morning—feeding the chickens, straining milk into pans—I tried to imagine what it would be like to be alone. I couldn't picture it at first, but as I was fighting off that ill-tempered old hen to gather eggs, and telling her it was just a matter of days before she hit the stew pot, I realized it would be no different than it was now. I was already alone. Eli spent the days in the orchard, and I stayed near the house. I never saw him before dinner, and then I spent hours alone again until supper.

Still, there was an anticipation in waiting for those moments. I was used to thinking about him while I did chores. Sometimes I spent hours figuring out what to make for dinner. I watched the skies, measuring the heat and the sun and the wind, wondering if he had his hat, if I should make a ginger switchel to take out for him to drink. My moments revolved around him, even when I knew he was riding the perimeter of the claim and would be gone the entire day. It was a relief thinking of him, because then I would not have to think about anything else; not of a trunk in the attic that I never touched, or the blankness of my walls and a half-empty whatnot shelf. Those times when guilt and despair rose in dust, and memories wavered in the heat against the bleak ridges beyond, I could turn to doing something for Eli.

Today, all I could think was that he would be leaving soon. Knowing I wouldn't see him for hours, I devoted myself to making his life better. I made him a supper I wasn't sure he'd be home to eat; I oiled his boots.

And then I saw him riding home, coming out of the sunset, a black shadow against the gold- and red-lit ridge beyond him, and my whole body hurt knowing that he would be going, knowing what he would want from me before he left, and I couldn't bear to watch him riding steadily toward me. All my resolutions dissolved, and I turned and went back into the house, putting on potatoes to boil, shelling peas, putting space and energy between us.

That was how I missed seeing that Eli had brought someone with him. That was how I missed the warning of Will Bennett.

I was frying up some salt pork to go into the potatoes when I heard Eli call from the yard, "Lora! Lora, come on out here a minute!"

I glanced at the meat sizzling in the skillet and felt exasperated and frustrated that he expected me to just drop everything I was doing to run out there. So I didn't go right away; I waited for him to call me again, and when he did, when he said, "Lora! Are you there?" I called back, "In a minute!" and jerked the pan off the stove.

I was angry that the greeting I had for him would be irritated now, and that he'd brought it on himself and wouldn't know why, and it would make him angry in turn, and the whole evening would be strange again, and cold. But then I saw the boy standing in the yard behind him, and I forgot all that.

I call him a boy, but Will Bennett was not a child. He was a young man, and that first time I saw him he stood in our dirt yard with his legs spread and his hands tucked into the pockets of a big coat it was too warm to wear. He had a bedroll slung over his back, and his hair was dark gold and fine and rumpled by the hot west wind. The chickens were pecking around his feet as if he were an old and trusted friend.

But the most startling thing about Will Bennett was the way he looked at me, with an open, curious gaze and frank blue eyes and a smile that was at the same time self-sure and disarming.

There are people in this world you don't want to know, whose lives seem to make your own feel nearly burnt out, and Will Bennett was just that kind. I figured him to be sixteen or seventeen, and though I was not much older, I felt the fine wrinkles between my brows and at the edges of my mouth. I saw my youth in the gold of his hair. In those few moments, looking at him, I felt a life span between us, a hundred years at least.

Eli came up from where he stood beside Old Max the horse, and in his worn and frayed clothes, he looked so shabby beside Will Bennett's youth that I was ashamed. "Lora, honey," he said—and that was strange, that sugarcoating, like some foreign language; it had been that long since he'd bothered—"this is Will Bennett. I've hired him to take care of things while I'm gone."

Will Bennett stepped forward, holding out his hand, smiling again, bigger, flashing his teeth. "Miz Cameron," he said. "I'm pleased to meet you."

For no reason at all, I was scared, and the fear made me hard and brittle. Suddenly, I wanted to cry.

The last thing I needed was another mouth to feed, and Eli should have known better. I went back into the house and slammed the salt pork back onto the stove, stirring it around in the pan until it was frying into dust. I heard Eli's booted footsteps on the porch, and the creaking and thudding of the front door as it opened and closed.

"That was uncalled for, Lora," he said in a low, angry voice.

"You never told me this is what you planned."

He was quiet for a minute, and I tensed, expecting him to come over to me, but he didn't. He just said, "I didn't plan it. It just seemed like a good idea."

"Well, it's not. I don't want him here. I don't need him. Send him back."

"He can watch over things—"

"I thought that was what you wanted John Zimmerman to do."

"John has his own family."

Slowly, I looked up at my husband. "That didn't seem to matter to you yesterday."

"That was before I met Will." He took a step toward me and then stopped, checking himself. "Look, Lora, he needs the work. And I'd feel better having someone here all the time."

There was an expression in his face I recognized, that same look I'd seen the day before, when he'd told me he was going, and the desperation I'd felt on the porch came back to me, the inevitability of Eli's will and my powerlessness against it. "He's a boy," I said.

"He's seventeen. And strong. Mac Egan hired him to help move Schull House."

By that he meant that Will Bennett had been helping to move Yakima City to North Yakima, where the
Northern Pacific railroad had determined it wanted
the city to be. The town fathers had spent months
trying to convince the railroad to change its mind,
but in the end, Yakima City had no real choice. Move
or die. So a whole town was rolling across the prairie
on huge timbers and planks. It seemed inconceivable
to me that the golden-haired boy standing outside
had been part of it. For a moment I tried to picture
him bending to lay planks, shouldering burdens normally left to men.

"He's a stranger, Eli," I tried.

He sighed. "I feel I can trust him. I can't tell you
why, I just do."

One of Eli's whims, like the apple trees in the far
field and a homestead claim in the Yakima Valley and
a whole future of plans that only marginally included
me. I felt angry at being at the mercy of this one, too,
and so I fought him much longer than I should have,
than I normally did.

"I don't trust him," I said, though the truth was I
didn't feel anything about that one way or another. "I
don't want him here."

"You haven't given him a chance, Lora. But if it
would make you feel better, I'll send for your sister.
She could be here within the week."

"Dorothy's busy enough with John and the boys."

"Ellen, then."

"They can't spare her, Eli. Not during harvest."

"Either of them would come if you asked. The trip
wouldn't be so bad now that the train's in Yakima—"

"I don't need them. I don't need anyone."

He looked at me with those beautiful eyes, and I saw the pain that had become too familiar. "Yeah, I guess that's what they think, too, isn't it?"

I don't know if he wanted an answer to that, but I couldn't give him one. I couldn't tell him all the things I was feeling; I could barely understand them myself. I wanted Eli, and if I could not have him, I wanted no one, and sometimes I did not even want him. What I did want . . . what I *knew* I wanted was silence, time that belonged only to me, the clock set to my days. "I don't want him here. Send him back."

"Lora, be reasonable."

"Send him back."

Then he did what I had been afraid of, what I suppose I had been unconsciously guarding against. He stepped forward and took hold of my arms, a soft, caressing touch. I resented that touch so much I could barely breathe. I felt his gaze on my face, and then the hush of his breath against my hair, and his hands dropped. I could not help the relief I felt.

"I'm not sending him back. I'll feel better with him here, and I need someone to mind the farm while I'm gone. You can't do everything by yourself."

"How do you expect me to feed him?"

"The same way you feed me, Lora. He'd probably fend for himself if you asked him to. But I did promise him room and board in exchange for work. I thought he could sleep in the barn."

I felt defeated. "I don't want him here, Eli," I said again, softly, though I knew it would make no difference.

"Are you going to dig the irrigation ditch?"

I didn't bother to answer.

Eli sighed—a sound I'd heard so many times, too many times. It was the way we communicated now, words unsaid, lost in breath. "I don't want you alone here. I won't worry so much if I know he's here."

I looked up at him. "Will you worry?" The words felt squeezed from my throat; I almost didn't say them.

He looked so wounded I wished I hadn't.

"You know I will." He stepped back, looked away. "Trust me, Lora, there'll come a time when you'll be glad he's here. Now, it would be nice if you made him feel welcome."

"All right," I said, and relief seemed to rush out of him. The evidence that what I said did matter made me feel light-headed. "Who is he? Where does he come from?"

Eli stood back and motioned to the door. "Why don't you go ask him?"

I eased past him and opened the door to find the boy leaning against the porch railing, staring out at Ahtanum Ridge while the hop vine twining against the house dangled in his hair.

"I'm sorry," I said softly when he turned around. "I didn't mean to make you feel unwelcome. I'm Lora Cameron."

He smiled. He had one of those smiles that wanted to light a smile in me, too, though I didn't let it. "I guess I was a bit of a surprise."

I didn't know what to say, so I just nodded.

"It's no problem, Miz Cameron. I understand," he

said, and that made me feel worse, both his understanding and his "Miz Cameron," as if I were the old
woman I felt I was.

I heard Eli come onto the porch behind me, and
Will Bennett glanced at him and said quietly, to me,
"Your husband hired me to make things easier for
you, not harder."

"Yes," I said. "I know."

"I'll try not to get in the way."

He looked right at me with wide, honest eyes—
blue, like Eli's, but not so striking—and I looked back
at him until the stare between us became a war of
sorts; or not a war, but a boundary. Then, finally, his
smile came back, softer, smaller, and he said again, "I
won't get in the way."

But he was already in the way. He was a hired hand,
and I would be responsible for him, though Eli said it
would be the other way around. My palms felt damp,
and I wiped them on my threadbare apron and turned
back to the house. "Supper's almost ready," I said.

I didn't look at Eli as I ducked past him and went
back inside, but I heard his footsteps when I closed
the door, and I heard him say, "Don't worry. She'll get
to like you," and Will Bennett's quiet answer, words I
couldn't hear. Eli laughed, and there was a little insis-
tence inside me that said, *Oh, no, I won't*, even though
it wasn't in my nature to dislike someone out of pure
selfishness. Will Bennett had seemed nice enough. I
supposed I could get along with him fine as long as
he kept his distance and did what he promised. As
long as he stayed out of my way.

But I was troubled as I ladled dinner onto plates—

potatoes and salt pork, peas and bread with butter—
and took two of them outside onto the narrow porch.
They were already gone, and so I settled the plates on
the thick edge of the railing and called out, "Eli! Supper's ready!"

I heard his answer from the barn, a faint cry
telling me they were on their way, and though I'd
planned to go back inside and let them eat alone, I
ended up just standing there, watching as the two of
them came across the yard.

There isn't much pretty about a dusty farmyard,
but sometimes at sunset the whole place seems
painted with gold, and the hot air limns the edges of
things like candlelight, in soft, dust-filled halos. Eli
and Will Bennett were like that walking from the barn,
Eli's dark head shining beside the boy's golden one as
if they belonged together.

Abruptly, I turned away. There was so much to do
tonight—the dishes, and gathering sage to fuel the
stove, getting things settled for the evening.

"Lora?" Eli said, and I realized they were there, at
the porch. I turned around to see him frowning at
me, that worried look between his eyes, and I shook
my head and motioned to the plates on the railing,
waving away the flies.

"There's your supper," I said. I nodded to Will.
"Yours too. I thought you'd like to eat out here
tonight."

Eli's frown grew a little deeper; I guess he was
thinking that it was strange I was making them eat
out on the porch, since we almost never did. I couldn't
have explained why I was doing it, except that the

house was mine, and I wanted it to stay that way a few minutes longer. I didn't want a stranger finding room within it.

Eli shrugged and handed Will a plate. "Sit down," he said. "I guess you're probably hungry."

Will Bennett sat easily on the edge of the step. He grabbed up his fork, looking ready to devour the whole thing. But then he let the fork go idle and balanced it in his hand. He glanced up at me with a smile. "Thank you for making supper, Lora."

It startled me, that simple compliment, almost as much as the sound of my name coming from his mouth. I wasn't used to being thanked for cooking. Not that Eli wasn't appreciative; it was just that neither of us ever questioned that it was my duty. My mama had always cooked, my grandmother, every woman I'd ever known. People had to eat. I couldn't imagine it any other way. "Well, I hope you enjoy it," I said, turning to the door.

"You're coming out to join us, aren't you?" Eli asked.

I hadn't planned to, but I heard the request in Eli's tone, so I nodded and told them I'd bring out some buttermilk.

Will Bennett made to put aside his plate. "Let me help you."

I was surprised, and I guess I showed it. "It's no trouble."

I was relieved when he didn't argue with me, but sat again and reached for his plate.

I went inside and poured the buttermilk into a pitcher, and I took my time about it, hoping they'd be done eating by the time I came out again. I had the feeling Will Bennett was a talker, and I had grown used to eating in silence, and alone, even when Eli was at the table with me. It was comforting that way; I didn't want it to change, and I didn't want to encourage a companionship with this boy that I didn't expect to keep up once Eli had gone. It was better that we started out the way we meant to go on, and I meant for him to be a hired hand and nothing more.

But when I finally went back onto the porch, they were still sitting there with full plates. I stared at Eli in dumb surprise. "What's wrong? Is there something wrong with it?"

Eli jerked his head toward Will and smiled. "Will thought we should wait for the hostess."

"You do all the cooking," Will explained. "You should be able to join in the conversation."

I had never heard of such a thing, and I was sure I didn't want it. "You must spend a lot of time being hungry."

He gave me a puzzled look.

"Lora grew up on a wheat farm," Eli told him. "The hired hands were like locusts. If you waited for the hostess, you'd get nothing at all."

"My mama ate after everyone was gone," I said.

"Well, that's too bad," Will Bennett said. "That's not living."

Such a strange comment, and it astonished me, brought to mind a memory of Mama bent over the washtub, standing while she ate, bread with jam, or biscuits crumbled under what was left of the gravy—never what we'd been eating for supper, because that

would be all gone—taking a bite between every dish
that she washed. A forkful of biscuits, then wash a
plate, then a sip of coffee . . .

I had the thought that it seemed like the best way
to live—alone like that, separate from everything,
unbothered—but I didn't say it, and the minute I
thought it another memory came to me, of Eli and I at
the dinner table, how I'd ladled stew onto his plate and
he'd grabbed me about the hips and held me close,
and how I'd leaned into him and laughed as I slapped
his hands away, teasing him. It had slipped away from
us, that kind of joy, and it was unbearably sad that
things had changed so much I'd been wishing for my
mother's tired life. I couldn't keep the bitterness from
my voice when I said to Will, "You're still young. You'll
change the first day you work on a harvesting gang."

He smiled that smile again, the one that made me
feel old, but in it, too, was this *knowing*, this feeling I
had that he somehow understood more about the
world than I did. "I've worked as a harvester. Just
came up from Walla Walla a few weeks ago."

"I don't suppose you managed to hold on to your
manners there."

"The world's not a fair place, Lora," Will Bennett
said, "but I do what I can to stay true to my conscience.
Going hungry once or twice is a small price to pay."

"Well, you don't have to worry about going hungry here. We won't be eating together, so you'll have
no reason to wait for me."

I felt Eli's hand on my arm then, a cautioning
touch, and I shook him away and glared at him, dar-
ing him to say something. But my Eli just picked up

his buttermilk and said calmly, "We don't stand on ceremony here, Will. And I imagine Lora'll keep you busy enough that it won't matter."

Bennet looked like he might say something, but then he went quiet and turned to his meal, and I was glad. When dinner was over and I began to take up the dishes to wash, he swooped in before me, grabbing the plates and moving past me into the house.

I stared at Eli, but he only smiled and shrugged. "He's an interesting one, Lora."

When I followed Bennett inside, he was already putting the dishes into the washtub.

"What are you doing?" I asked.

He looked over his shoulder at me. "Where I'm from, everyone helps out. I appreciate the supper, and I can wash dishes as well as anyone."

Such a little thing, a small politeness, something I should have enjoyed because no one had ever thought to do it before. I could see how he might have expected me to appreciate it—there were so many women who would have. But I didn't. When he said, "You go and sit down, Lora. I'll take care of the dishes. Go watch the sunset," I felt nervous and uncomfortable, too idle.

He turned back to the washtub, filling it from the pail on the floor beside, reaching for the steaming kettle on the stove, palming out a glob of soft lye soap from the bucket on the windowsill—he had done this before, many times, by the look of it, and I stood there and watched him, feeling oddly disconnected.

I didn't realize what I was doing until it was already done, until I'd grabbed the towel hanging on a hook in the wall and pushed in beside him. "I'll dry," I said.

And then I wished I hadn't done it, because he gave me that look again, the one that embarrassed me, that made me feel he understood something I wasn't saying. It flustered me so that the first soapy plate he handed me slipped between my fingers, and only his quick dip to catch it saved it from shattering on the floor.

He handed it to me again, and then he looked down at the cup he was swishing in the water. "It's hard for me to think of Eli sitting out there enjoying the evening alone."

The annoyance I felt at that statement was overwhelming, and suddenly I realized what it was that bothered me about Will Bennett. He was trying to change things. I wondered what Eli had told him, if it was pity I saw in Bennett's eyes, and then I decided no. As much as Eli liked to talk and tell stories, he was a private man; he would never reveal our sorrows to a stranger. Somehow, that made Will's attempts to help seem worse. He'd come into a situation he didn't know, and he was trying to make it better when he didn't understand anything about it, or anything about what I wanted.

"He likes being alone," I said sharply. "And I like washing the dishes. I know you mean well, but things are just fine the way they are. There's nothing here that needs changing."

He kept washing that cup, swirling the rag around it until the soap made transparent rainbows on the surface of the water. "The whole world needs changing, Lora," he said softly. "Why should here be any different?"

3

Over the next days, I felt Eli preparing to leave—not overtly, but in little ways, like mending the saddle-bags he hadn't used in years and asking for old blankets so he could fashion a bedroll.

I watched my husband passing the farm to Will, teaching him the orchard, handing down his knowledge the way he would have to a son. With every chore Will learned, Eli's going came another moment closer.

I wanted to hate Will Bennett for that. He was just a hired hand, but I could not watch the two of them together without feeling guilty. I saw in him everything Eli wanted from me, everything I thought he expected. I suppose I pushed Eli away more, because I began to feel his leaving in a growing strain between us, a quiet inevitability. All I was doing was waiting for him to walk away. In his mind, I think, he was already gone.

So I wasn't surprised when one night, after Will went out to the barn and I'd lifted the bucket of dirty wash water to take to the garden, Eli stopped me with his quiet words.

"I'll be leaving tomorrow."

I set the bucket hard on the floor. I'd expected to feel relief. At last, the waiting was over. Instead, all I felt was a fluttery panic. My heartbeat was so loud I could barely hear. "Tomorrow?"

"Now that Will's here, there's no point in my staying around." He paused. "Is there?"

I pretended he hadn't said the words. I felt uncertain, unbalanced. His question frightened me. I did not want to face it. So instead I said, "You think Will's ready?"

Eli's gaze was slow and steady, and I had to look away. I heard him sigh, and there was bitterness in the sound. He went along with my pretense, though I could see by the flexing of his jaw how much it cost him. "He knows enough to get by. If he has any questions you can't answer, you can always ask John. Or you can write to me."

I nodded.

"There are things we need to go over, Lora. You'd best sit down."

I sat across from him at the table and pressed my fingers into the tabletop to keep them from trembling. I did what I could to face my husband with a composure I could not imagine ever feeling again.

"Bessie's starting an infection," Eli said. "I've put some salve on it, but you should be watching it. One teat's already a bit swollen."

"I saw it this morning."

"Take care of it. Don't forget. We can't risk losing her."

"I'll keep an eye on it."

"I'll take Old Max with me and leave Pete with you. He's gentler, anyway, and he does better with the wagon than Max. He should be just fine for anything you need. Now . . ." He cleared his throat and looked at me hard. "I talked to Ben Schiller when I was in town. He says he'll take as much butter from you as you can give him. I guess Ann Robbe's cow went dry, so he can use it. He'll give the money straight to you. He won't put it against the account. Are you listening to me, Lora?"

His face was so serious, his eyes so intent, as if he wanted to brand me with his words, as if he was worried that he might forget something, or that I might not hear him, and I began to feel strange, not quite myself. I pressed my hands into the table until I was sure they would push right through the oilcloth and into the wood. Eli's voice brushed by me like sand in wind.

"I couldn't talk him into advancing you any more credit, but he knows I'm good for it when I get back. You can't put anything else on account, but the butter money's yours free and clear. You can buy whatever you need with it. The cherries are almost ready. I'd say the next week or so. It's going to be a small harvest. The new trees aren't doing much yet, and there were only a few Bings that survived the winter. The Lamberts are a little better. You'll maybe get a couple hundred pounds of the Royal Annes. Beaman's will want those, but I don't expect they'll pay you much. They can't get them to the cannery without bruising, and I haven't heard that refrigerated boxcars help much." He leaned forward, across the table, and I kept my eyes on the three-cornered tear on his collar, the way it was fraying against his throat. "Do you want me to go over the harvest with you again?"

His question unnerved me, called me back to myself, but I felt shaken and anxious. "You don't need to," I managed. "I remember what to do."

"Don't let them cheat you."

"I won't."

"The early Pippins will be ready soon. You'll have to harvest those, too. I've gone over everything with Will, but he'll be counting on you to let him know when things are ready."

He seemed to expect some reply, so I nodded, because my voice was gone.

He reached to the shelf above the table. "The ledgers—"

"No," I said, stopping him, knowing the figures would just run together in my mind, that I could not pay attention. "Just tell me."

He paused, and then he sat back again with a curt nod. "There are bills, Lora. Lots of bills. There's not a one you can pay unless you find some money that I don't know about. When they come to collect from you—and they might—just tell them I'm gone, that I'll take care of things when I get back. I don't know what we'll get for those cherries. I'd think about seven or eight cents a pound, especially for the Lamberts, but who knows what they're paying this year. You'll have to let me know. Then, I guess we'll see what we can do."

He was quiet then, long enough that I looked up at him. Suddenly I realized why the panic was so big inside me; I realized for the first time that he was *leav-*

ing, that after tomorrow morning, he would not be sitting in this chair, that the decisions would be mine, the farm would be mine.

Eli had just handed me his dreams. I was the caretaker of them now.

He must have seen the fear in my eyes, because his gaze turned thoughtful; I saw a tenderness there that made me ache. It frightened me as much as his trust in me. It brought back too many memories, times when he'd looked at me just that way, when his tenderness had filled my days and my nights, when together we'd seen so many possibilities. So when he said, gently, "Are you going to be all right here?" my answer was hard and a little flippant.

"Of course."

"I mean really, Lora."

"I'll be fine."

He took a deep breath and looked across the kitchen to the window above the sideboard, the one that looked out over the orchard. "I'll miss you, you know. I'll miss your pretty green eyes."

The intimacy caught me when I was unprepared, and it stunned me, as if I'd just managed to catch a breath and he had suffocated me again.

"I'll be back before you know it," he went on. "But then again . . . maybe you'd like it better if I took my time."

"It's not me who wants you to go," I said too quickly. It was a lie, and it wasn't, and as always, he saw right through me.

"Lora, it's not that way. You know it. It's just that since—"

"No." My voice rushed out, breathless and fast. "Don't say it."

He closed his eyes, and when he opened them again I saw bleakness there, an anger I'd seen so many times before that I knew what it meant. I said quickly, "I'll be fine. You just tell me when—"

"We need to talk about it, Lora. It's been a year."

"No. No, not yet. I need more time. Eli—"

"There is no more time," he said softly, but there was a command in his words that made me stop. "Lora, I won't lie and say that all this hasn't got something to do with my leaving. This last year . . . it's destroying us, can't you see that? I want to stay, but not . . . not if things keep on this way. I can't keep doing this. If you wanted to talk it through, if you wanted to try to make things better, I'd stay. We need the money, but if you were willing to try, we'd figure out something."

I heard his question, I knew what he was asking me, I knew it was my choice. I wanted to say, *Yes, stay,* but I could not say the words.

He pushed back from the table so hard it shook. He raked back his hair and turned away with a curse, sweeping the room with a motion. "How long do we have to live this way? Doesn't it bother you, all these blank spaces? It's been a year, Lora. A year, and I can't even touch my own wife, for Christ's sake! It's like a wound that won't heal. You just keep it open between us. If we don't talk about this—"

"Oh, Eli," I said, and I heard my voice as if it were far away, breaking on tears. "What good would it possibly do?"

He sighed then, his anger already gone. "I don't know. I don't know. But this—this isn't living. I miss the sound of that damn contraption of yours. I miss your threads hanging all over the place. You aren't happy, Lora. I'm not happy. And I've been thinking—"

"I don't want to think. I want to forget. It's best to forget about it."

"I can't forget," he said quietly. "And neither can you."

There was nothing to say to that. This farm, this life, had shrunken down to nothing for me, nothing but a day-by-day need to go on, to survive, to *do*. The reasons for that were in the past, and I wanted them to stay there. I wanted nothing to shake me, and so I grabbed the bucket of wash water and skirted past my husband when he was despairing, passing him the way I'd passed him nearly a year ago—a journey that kept taking us farther and farther apart.

"I have to water the garden," I said.

"Lora," he said, and when I stopped to look back at him, he said, "I love you."

I could have said it back to him. I knew he needed to hear it as much as I needed to say it. But the words locked up my throat, and when I opened my mouth to say them, they came out as, "I have to go."

I had no idea how he looked as I left him. I was afraid to wonder. He didn't follow me as I lugged the bucket across the porch and down the stairs, racing for that garden of mine as fast as I could. The handle cut into my palm, the water splashed onto my skirt, and I was breathing fast with panic, my thoughts and my heart racing so I thought they would never be still. I wanted to be in that garden, I wanted the peace of beans bending in the heat and the leafy potatoes waving in the breeze. I wanted to see something green now, when my soul felt brown and wilted.

This garden was everything to me now, the only thing I could keep alive in this desert prairie, the one thing I hadn't failed. In the spring, I'd planted until Eli told me to stop, that the vegetables would overtake the trees. Peas strung on poles, potato hills, cabbages in straight rows, bush beans, turnips, carrots. They grew beneath my touch, they spread their leaves and their roots and drank up the kitchen slops I fed them every night. Eli had teased me once that he thought the only thing I cared about anymore was this garden, but I didn't laugh with him. Sometimes it felt like the truth.

Thinking of that now brought a hard ache behind my eyes, a wave of loneliness and pain that weakened me so I could hardly stand. The world wavered in front of me suddenly, everything shifting and changing, wet now behind a veil of tears I wouldn't admit to, hills and valleys leveled out, colors blurred. I was jerking and off balance, and when my foot caught, I wasn't ready for it.

I was just on the edge of the garden when I tripped, and in horror I grabbed for the bucket. But I hit the ground hard, and the bucket went flying. I scrambled up as quickly as I could, but the water was already spilling, tumbling, racing across that dry ground like a flash flood, lapped up by scrub grass and dust, disappearing into the soil until there was nothing left but a soft lye scum, and it seemed then that the water was like my life, disappearing into nothingness before my eyes, spilling from my clumsy hands.

I sank onto the ground and stared at the wet fading patch as though it had never been, swallowed by that parched and greedy land, and suddenly I was sobbing, and there was nothing I could do about it, no way I could stop it. I cried because my garden would go without water, and I cried because I hated this place, and I could not forget what it had done to me. But mostly I cried because my loneliness had never seemed as vast and endless as it had the moment I looked in Eli's eyes and realized he wanted to stay.

And that I could not say the words to keep him.

The next morning was like a dream. Everything moved slowly; the colors seemed hazy and not quite real. When the morning light eased past the curtains and I woke up, Eli was already gone. The bed felt empty where he'd been, and in those first waking moments, it was as if he'd never been there.

When I went downstairs, he was sitting at the table, dressed to leave in clothes so tattered and worn he looked already like a hobo, and I felt guilty for that, too—one more thing to add to my list of fail-ures. He was so quiet and still he could have been cut from paper. When he brought his coffee to his mouth, I was surprised at the movement. I had the thought that it might be the last time I saw him do that, and I had to turn away.

We barely said two words to each other as I made him breakfast. I wondered what he was thinking as I cracked eggs and sliced salt pork. I felt his eyes on me when I walked out the door to go to the icehouse—our own name for it, since there was no spring for a spring-

house, only a lean-to built onto the barn to hold ice—
and when I came back with a bowlful of butter dripping condensation and a jar of milk, he was still
watching me. He ate without comment, but I felt he
was holding on to me with his gaze, that he was imagining things about me—perhaps the kind of life he'd
wanted, or maybe a life without me altogether. In any
case, he didn't tell me, and when he was done he only
sighed and pushed back his chair and went to the
barn. It seemed only moments before he was back
again, though I know it was longer, and he had Will
Bennett with him—bright-eyed, energetic, too young.

"I'll be leaving," Eli said, and then he gave Will a
look that told me they'd already discussed me in the
barn, handing me over, the trade of a prized horse.
"I've got to get going. Can't waste the light."

I followed him out onto the porch, and Will Bennett stayed behind, in the house, giving us privacy for
our good-bye.

Eli paused on the steps, and I on the landing, and
we looked at each other like strangers. Strangers after
five years of marriage, too far apart to touch.

I thought he might leave like that, just walk away,
without a kiss good-bye or an embrace, and I was so
unbearably lonely thinking of it that I could hardly
look at him. But I remembered his *I love you* with
some comfort, and when he stepped up the stairs
toward me, I was waiting for him.

Still, it was an awkward embrace. He reached for
me and I went into his arms too hard, bumping my
chin on his breastbone. He tilted my chin up to kiss
me, and I looked up into his eyes and was unsettled by

the distance I saw there, as if his thoughts were already far away. It hurt more than I wanted it to. I barely felt Eli brush his lips over mine in a halfhearted kiss. It was not the memory that I wanted to hold close while he was gone, but when he stepped away from me, that final kiss settled inside me in a hard little knot.

"You take care," I said nervously.

"I'll write," he said.

"I'll write back."

"You'll be fine without me," he said.

And that was it, that was good-bye. Eli stood there for a minute longer, as if the standing would give him something more to say, but the silence between us just grew awkward, and this lingering was too hard to take.

"Good-bye, Lora."

Those were the last words he said to me before he went down the stairs and mounted Old Max. I thought to watch him until he was nothing but a black speck on the horizon. I imagined how I would wave so hard my hair would fall and stick to the tears on my cheeks, and how Eli would keep that image in his heart while he was gone. But the truth was, there were no tears, and I heard the kettle boiling before he rode out of the yard, and went inside to check it.

In the end it was Will Bennett who stepped out on the porch to see Eli evaporate into the scorched ridge, not me. I didn't see him go, so it was easier somehow to pretend nothing had changed, that the worry I felt over his leaving was not this living, breathing thing inside me.

By the time I'd finished the breakfast dishes, Will was gone from the porch. I saw him a few minutes

later, coming from the barn with a shovel and a pair
of Eli's heavy work gloves that looked too big on his
hands. His shirt was partially unfastened, sloppy,
trailing from his pants.

"I'm going to start on the ditch," he told me as he
neared the house. "Anything I can do for you first?"

I stared at him. The cursed ditch. I wanted to tell
Will no, to let it dry up, to let the earth have it back,
but there was Eli to consider, and my garden, so I
turned away and shook my head, unable to say a word,
and Will went off whistling, his boots crunching. It
was strange, but I felt truly alone then, I felt Eli's going
like a presence all around me. When he was home,
there was always the chance that I might pass him on
the way to the barn or the orchard, and it was odd
thinking that I wouldn't, that I had time to myself,
and this boy he'd left behind was nothing but a hired
hand that I could direct as I would, with no rights to
my thoughts or my hours.

I had wanted this freedom, but now that I had it,
it sat on me uncomfortably, like a stiff new dress I
was afraid to soil.

That first day, the things I did were my own
chores, the tasks that normally took up the hours:
sweeping the ever-present dust from the house, weed-
ing the garden, chasing jackrabbits from the potatoes. As the hours passed, my panic over Eli's leaving
eased somewhat; I began to think that nothing had
really changed, that his absence would be easy to get
used to, that my days would be the same.

I had myself believing it, too, as I made supper that
evening. The only thing that told me I wasn't the only

person on this farm was the evidence I kept seeing of Will—a shovel left leaning against the barn wall, a ball of twine tossed on the porch step, buckets where Eli would not have left them. I'd simply let myself forget Will was there, and so those things were little surprises—and when I was on the porch that evening, shaking out a towel full of bread crumbs for the chickens, and I saw him coming from the barn, he was a stranger to me; it took me a moment to remember who he was, what he was doing there, why he wasn't Eli.

Reluctantly, I waved him over. "Supper's ready," I called as soon as he was close enough to hear.

He had washed before he came from the barn—the dirt that had been on his face was gone, and he had that freshly scrubbed look about him, wet hair at his temples, the collar of his shirt darkened with water. I motioned for him to follow me into the house.

Will Bennett sat at the table and waited for me. I was not comfortable with him, and so the meal was strained and quiet. I guess he was hungry, because he ate with single-mindedness once he saw I was going to eat, too, and I found myself watching him, because, as ravenous as he had to be, he had pretty manners—quiet chewing, no slurping, balancing his butter knife on the edge of his plate instead of just laying it down to stain the tablecloth. I'd never seen any man as polite as the boy sitting across from me.

"This was good," he said finally, setting aside his spoon and looking up. "Thank you."

"Hunger makes the best sauce," I told him.

It was quiet for a minute now that our polite small talk was exhausted. Then he said, "When I was out in the barn, I noticed the stable door is loose. Looks like it needs new hinges to me."

It took me a minute to realize he was asking me a question, *What do you want to do about the stable door?* and that I had to have an answer. A loose stable door would have been left to Eli, I would never have known about it, and it occurred to me that I didn't know what to do. Eli kept his tools in a wooden box in the barn, along with a jar full of loose things like nails and screws and little mismatched bolts. Maybe there were old hinges in that jar. Or maybe he would have fixed the hinge with something, or repaired it. How much were new hinges, anyway?

Will was looking at me expectantly, and I stared at him blankly until he said helpfully, "Hinges are pretty dear these days. If you can find me some leather, I'll see if I can fix it, if you like."

I was embarrassingly relieved. "That would be good."

"That old horse isn't much of a kicker, is he?"

"I don't think so."

"I can probably make it hold a few months, anyway." Will gathered up his bowl and his cup and took them to the sink, and then he took mine, and I was still thinking about the hinges. It was not that they were important; it was just that they made me think of everything Eli wanted, the promises he expected this land to keep for him, the hopes he wanted me to make real. Those things consumed me. It was a minute before I realized Will Bennett was standing before me. He'd already washed the dishes, I saw, and when I looked at him blankly, he shook back the hair falling into his eyes and smiled at me. "You want me to stay around this evening? I imagine it'll get lonely up here without Eli. I could stay for a while. Keep you company, if you want."

"No," I said, and though I hadn't meant it to be so curt, it sounded that way, just a plain no, so I hastily added on a "Thank you" to ease it.

He didn't seem to take offense. He was still smiling when he nodded and walked past me out the door and into the sunset falling across the yard.

And though I'd thought I would sit there in my house and breathe in the silence and spend the hours until dark relishing having no one but myself to answer to, the empty spots on my walls mocked me. I heard the sounds that had been missing from inside this house for too long, the sounds that Eli's presence muffled for me.

I hurried onto the porch. It was too narrow for the rocking chair to make a complete arc, so I angled the chair toward the orchard and sat down.

But without Eli there to distract me, I saw the memories there, too: a thick, high railing that Eli had spent days on, anchoring it with more nails than it needed, using heavy pieces of lumber to make it safe. I remembered him standing back from it, the pride in his eyes. "No child'll fall through that," he'd said, and I'd laughed at him and told him no, that he was just the man to keep one safe.

I looked away from it, past the bright green of the hop vine fluttering tentatively against the rails, staring out at that orchard I hated, at Eli's dream and the way the trees looked golden in the light, just as those railroad brochures had said they would. Golden and hung with apples so large it would take two hands to hold them, children sitting beneath the branches. Children with sunlight glinting in soft blond hair . . .

The image was so strong I caught my breath at the pain of it. It was a moment before I realized it wasn't a memory I saw, but Will Bennett sitting there, his back to me and his knees drawn up and splayed out, bolstering himself with hands planted in the coarse grass. He was staring out at the trees and the faint dark outline of the mountains beyond, and I could not tear my eyes away. As much as it hurt, my soul was hungry for that sight, my heart ached for it.

He was so still it seemed he might be listening, or praying—he didn't move when a crow landed in the tree above him and shook the branches with its raucous caws. The sun faded, the brightness gave way to dusk, turning everything the same color as the hills, that soft grayish purple. The crickets grew louder, and still Will Bennett sat there—and it was so peaceful, so much like the evenings I'd thought I would have forever, that I found myself reaching for my embroidery hoop, for my basket of colored threads, for the relaxation of something I'd loved to do.

But they weren't there, and I remembered that those evenings were long gone. Hastily, I went inside, but the house was unbearably quiet; there wasn't anything I saw that didn't remind me, that didn't hurt to look at, and I wished for Eli so much that I went upstairs to our bedroom in darkness, and I breathed in his scent as I climbed in between our flour-sack sheets, and pretended he had not left me.

4

In the week after Eli left, Will Bennett and I settled into a kind of routine. He would wake early—earlier than Eli had—and he would be waiting on the porch when I came downstairs, even if the sun was nothing more than a faint pink line on the horizon, and there he would stay until I invited him in for breakfast. Those first days, I would go out to the barn to milk the cow only to find he'd already done it and there was a pail of milk on the back stoop, and after that, I never checked again. He must have heard me go to the icehouse each morning, too, because suddenly one morning, beside the milk, was a bowl of butter, still cold and wet from the ice. No matter how early I woke, those things were there, as if he somehow knew when I was coming down, when I would need them.

I began relying on him in spite of myself. It was disturbing in a way, and nice in another, because though I considered Eli to be a thoughtful man, he had never done these things for me. I'm sure he considered them women's work, if he ever thought about it. There had been times in months past when I would lie in bed and think of what he would do if one day I disappeared, how long it would take him to notice the dirt collecting on the floorboards, the laundry piling up, the eggs hidden under the back step growing rotten—or if he would notice at all. Now that game only made me realize how much expectation there was between us, all the little things I did to keep the household running—things he had no idea of—and all the things he did to keep us afloat that escaped me.

In a way, I wanted to fall into the routine; I wanted to pretend Will Bennett had always been there, that he always would be. He filled the spaces around the farm, though he didn't say much and was around even less. Still, he was *there,* and though I did not want to have conversations with him or get to know him, I liked having someone to do things for, to give form to my days.

Truthfully, I suppose I wanted him to take some of the responsibility from me, and as long as he was there, I could pretend he was doing that. But Will didn't know the rules to this game of mine, and there wasn't a day that went by that he didn't put the full weight of that responsibility squarely on my shoulders, not a day that he didn't want a decision about something. Should he get some oil for the shovels? How deep did I suppose the irrigation ditch should go, and should it be deeper near the creek or the same all the way? He needed the broken hoe handle—could he use it, or was Eli saving it for something else?

That Monday morning a week after Eli had gone, Will sat down to breakfast while I cleaned the lamps, and said, "I don't know anything about cherries, but they look pretty ripe to me. Should I hire someone in town to help us pick? Or do you think the two of us can do it alone?"

I paused in trimming a wick and glanced out the window at the fruit on those trees. Every other year, we'd hired a few pickers, but Eli hadn't told me what to do this year, and though I knew there wasn't much money, I wasn't sure exactly where we stood. I still hadn't managed to pull out the ledgers and look at them, but that Monday morning, I said, "I'll have to check the ledger."

When Will left to go work on the ditch, I went out to the orchard to look at the fruit hanging fat and heavy on the trees. Will was right, the cherries were ready to pick. In a few days they would be past ready. Whatever I did—hiring pickers or not—it had to be done soon.

I hurried back to the house. The ledgers were right where Eli had left them, heavy and dusty on the shelf above the kitchen table, and reluctantly I took them down and laid them out.

Those account books held the record of my life with Eli, the record of this homestead. Their covers were faded, oiled with sweat from daily handling, their pages thick and dusty-smelling, scrawled in Eli's cramped handwriting, scores of figures, lists of names and numbers and reasons, success or failure written in lines slanting unevenly across the paper. *Sulfur .80, lime $1.70, dry goods $3, groceries Ben Schiller's $6.80 on account, lumber and 5M shingles, $7.75, 1M shingles, $2.30—Prentiss & Field on account, cherry trees: Lam-*

berts, Bings, Republicans, Royal Annes $35.00 . . .

The numbers seemed manageable at first, a few dollars, eighty cents here, a dollar ten there, then suddenly they swelled and fed upon each other, and I had to stop adding because they jumbled impossibly together. I looked at the income column, and the numbers there were worse than I could have imagined: *500 lbs strawberries @ .06 $30.00, 500 lbs raspberries @ .07 $35.00, 2,000 lbs apples @ .02 $40.00 . . .*

Eli had explained how bad things were, but I realized then how little stock I'd put in it. I'd trusted everything to him; Eli had a way of making things work, even during hard times. Now, without him, I felt helpless. Eli had hayed before he left, but there wasn't much that the sage rats hadn't got to, not enough to sell. The strawberries had already been picked, and most of the raspberries. There would be no more to market.

We owed over three hundred dollars at Ben Schiller's, and that number shocked me—I thought of how Ben had told Eli that the butter money was mine to use, and his generosity made me want to cry. The Feed and Seed we owed for last year's trees and the seed Eli had bought this year, over five hundred dollars. And the cabinetmaker . . .

I put my head in my hands and closed my eyes. I wanted those ledgers to disappear; I wished I had never opened them. Now I knew why Eli had to go to the Wishkah, and I knew just how much charity I would be begging off Ben Schiller on Saturday when I went into town to buy the things I needed and put those trays of butter on the counter. It made me want to curl up in bed, to hide. Eli had kept me so blissfully ignorant—perhaps he knew how I would feel, how the knowledge of this enormous debt would make me cowardly. If I had known before, I would never have been able to go into town with him, to smile at my neighbors as if we were all equals. There were people there who knew how much we were struggling. I could not bear them talking about us in that sad and pitying way: *The poor Camerons, you know what they've been through. I expect they'll be starving out before long.*

I could not understand how Eli managed to face those people every week knowing what he did, and in that moment I almost hated him for letting me find out, for leaving me with this ugly knowledge and no defenses.

I slammed the books shut and rested my elbows on them and stared at the wall, at the chinking loosening and cracking between the roughly squared logs. Three winters ago, Eli had built an addition on—all frame and planed lumber—and I had chastised him, saying that it made the house look lopsided, like a crippled old man. I had wanted everything new, a two-story frame house with gabled windows and a pitched roof and a wide porch for children to play on. But Eli had only said, "In a few years, Lora." And I'd waited for it; I'd thought, *Soon, soon.*

Now I thought of the notations on the ledger for Prentiss & Field, and it shamed me to realize that the addition I'd complained about was still not paid for, more than we could afford. He had done that for me, I knew. He had wanted me to be happy.

I did not want a frame house anymore. To me, it

meant permanence; it would have been an admission that we belonged to the land. But I realized, looking at those ledgers, that we were already its prisoners. We thought we were free, but this land held us firm in its grasp. It held the best of Eli and me already.

I put the ledgers away and went about my chores, but those numbers churned in my mind so that when dinnertime came and Will trudged up from the ditch, dusty and hatless, the shovel over his shoulder and his boots heavy with mud, I met him halfway through the orchard.

"We'll have to pick ourselves," I said. "I can't afford someone to help."

If he was surprised, he didn't show it. He acted as if it were every day that I met him coming back from the ditch, blurting out answers to questions he'd asked hours earlier. He only looked at me for a moment, and then he nodded.

"Do the cherries look ready to you?"

"We'd better start tomorrow," I told him.

And we did. The next morning, just after breakfast, I brought out the baskets for cherry picking and set them at the corner of the porch. They were juice-stained, and littered with dead, dried leaves from two years ago—the last time there'd been a harvest decent enough to pick, before the killing winter—and unexpectedly the memories of that harvest came back to me, startling and tender; the sun blinding and hot, reflecting off Eli's white shirt, the sweat on his face as he whistled. Hope and cherries glistening in the sun, bursting between chubby fingers that held them too tight . . .

In that second, those trees and those cherries stole my will. I had to force myself to think of Eli, to remember the desperate hope I saw every day in his eyes. It gave me the strength finally to walk with Will to the orchard, but it wasn't until we got there and I was looking up at the cherries gathered beneath dusty leaves that I could lock that grief away. I was ready now; the memories would not be able to surprise me again.

But still I was shaky as I reached up and took a ripe cherry from the branches and held it out to Will. "Take the ones like this," I told him, and then I picked a Royal Anne to show him how, taking a cluster by the stems, twisting with gentle pressure. I handed him a large graniteware bucket to hang around his neck. "This lets you have both hands. Drop them in easy, so they don't bruise. The Royal Annes are bad that way. You need to be careful."

He looked up at the trees, and I wondered what he was thinking, if he thought what I did, that a harvest this small was hardly worth the trouble.

But he said only, "I'll start here."

We had a short ladder and a step stool, and he took the stool and reached easily into the branches. Before I started to climb the ladder for my own tree, Will was halfway done with his.

That morning, I'd tied up my hair beneath a scarf, and worn a wide-brimmed hat to keep the sun from my face, and I was hot and sweating as I worked. It was tedious, dusty work, but once I'd liked it. There had been a time when every fat cherry had been like gold to me; like Eli, I had seen dreams in them, sweet and wonderful, tasting like the sun. I had hardly believed we got paid for growing them, because I would have raised them on my own, simply for love. But now I looked at this harvest and saw failure all over it.

Will finished the tree beside me and then went on to the next. He was much faster than I; he picked with an economy of movement that made him look too experienced for his claim that he knew nothing about cherries, and he was tall enough to reach the highest easily.

"Are you sure you've never picked cherries before?" I asked him finally.

He shook his head. "I've picked almost everything but cherries. Even picked strawberries once, but that was in the early days. Before I learned to trust the land. I don't think I'll be that desperate again."

His voice spoke of faraway times, of distance that seemed strange for someone so young, and I stopped my picking and sat on the top of the ladder, wiping the back of my hand across my sweaty face. "The early days," I repeated. "What do you mean?"

"When I first hit the road. I guess it's been . . . oh, about five years now."

Longer than I'd been on this homestead. As long as I'd been married. The years I'd grown from a girl into a woman. It seemed I'd lived a whole lifetime in five years; I'd been just a child at the start, and he was younger than I was. I did the math in my head—he'd been twelve when he first left his family.

"So young," I murmured, and though my voice was low, he heard me.

He laughed. "Young for what, Lora? What does age matter? 'Time is but the stream I go a-fishing in.'"

"I can't believe your mama let you go."

"She encouraged me. My parents were . . . I guess you'd call them freethinkers."

I could not imagine a mother sending her twelve-year-old out into the world alone. A world as dangerous as this one. It made me cold. "Wasn't she afraid?"

Will stopped picking. He turned to look at me, and there was a puzzled look on his face. "Of what?"

"Of . . . everything."

"I didn't see anything to be afraid of," he said slowly. "I don't think she did, either."

This made me laugh; it was too ridiculous to be real. "Where are you from? Paradise?"

"Massachusetts," he said.

I laughed again, and stepped down the ladder. I bent and tilted the bucket around my neck so the cherries tumbled gently into the basket.

"'The universe answers to our conceptions,'" he said softly. "'Whether we travel fast or slow, the track is laid for us.'"

It was as much a riddle as anything I'd ever heard. I turned to stare at him. "What did you say?"

"Henry David Thoreau. It was a quote."

"Well, I don't understand it," I said, and I felt impatient as I turned away again, I had again that sense that he knew more than I did, that he was making fun of me and trying to change me at the same time.

"It means that we make our own world, Lora. Whatever we see in life, that's what it becomes."

It was amazing to me that anyone could say such a thing, much less believe it. That we had the power of God, that we could somehow make life what we wanted it to be instead of accepting His will . . . I felt a quick anger at the assumption, at what it meant, at the power it gave us. To be responsible for all the terrible, meaningless things that happened in a life, to know that failure was your fault, that there was nothing to believe in but yourself . . .

I could not help it; I started to tremble. Such an unbearable thought, too unbearable to contemplate. My own failure spread in me like a disease, and I felt that cold little place where it never went away shoving at me, growing. "You haven't lived long enough if you believe that."

"You haven't lived much longer than me. How old are you, Lora? Eighteen? Nineteen?"

"Twenty."

"There're only three years between us."

"No," I said curtly. "There are a hundred years between us. You don't know anything about the world. You can't even imagine the things I know."

"Oh? Like what?"

I could not answer him. It took all my strength to find forgetfulness, to keep the memories away. "We'd better get back to picking."

I didn't look at him as I climbed the ladder again, and so I didn't see his misstep, I didn't see him fall. I was halfway up the rungs when I heard a heavy thud, and a cry of pain, and when I turned around it was to see him lying on the ground.

He was still, and for a moment I saw someone else,

a smaller body, gold hair against dirt. I jumped off the ladder and raced to him.

"Will," I said when I got to him, and my voice sounded high and strung tight. "Will—"

He sat up carefully, holding one hand with the other, grimacing, and it was a moment before his words came to me, before I heard them muffled in my head.

"My hand. I think I hurt my hand."

I knelt down beside him. He didn't move when I leaned closer. He just stared at his hand; I suppose he was in shock, because I could see how much it must hurt. It was swollen already. Carefully I pried his hand away from his too-tight grip and took it in mine. When I moved it gently to look more closely, he groaned between his teeth.

"It's sprained," I said to him. "We'll have to splint it, I think. Are you hurt anywhere else? Can you walk?"

He looked at me and nodded. Gingerly, he took my elbow for balance and tried his feet. "I'm fine," he said, pulling away again.

When we got to the house I made him sit on the porch, in the shade, and then I went inside and stoked up the stove fire to put water on to boil. I grabbed one of Eli's old shirts from the full-to-bursting rag bag and tore it quickly into strips—the fabric was so worn from washing and wear that it split easily—and I piled them on the table and went out to the barn, where I found some beanpoles gathered in the corner. Then I paid a visit to the icehouse.

Will was sitting in the rocker, cradling his hand,

staring out at the ridge, when I came back out. I handed him a cup of milk and he took it cautiously, as if he were afraid he would injure his good hand as well.

"Drink it," I said. "It'll make you feel better."

I waited for him to drink it, and when he did he gulped it down, and I could see he was surprised by how thirsty he was. It made me wonder how many hours he'd spent out there at that ditch, sweating and light-headed, thirsting without knowing it, and I made a promise to myself to take him out a jar of water twice a day and make him drink it. He was courting sunstroke anyway, the way he never wore a hat.

While he was drinking the milk, I went inside and took the boiling water off the stove. I poured in a good amount of salt, and added water to cool it, and then I grabbed a jar of vinegar and went back onto the porch again.

Will looked at me warily as I stepped out the door. "I don't need any of that."

"Yes, you do." I set the pan of warm salt water on the bench and motioned for him to come over and sit beside it. "Put your hand in there for a while."

"What is it?" He looked down at it as if I were trying to trick him into drinking poison.

"Just sit down and put your hand in it."

Finally he did. I went over to the railing and broke the beanpole until it was the length I wanted. Then I opened the jar of vinegar.

Will's nose wrinkled. "Not vinegar."

"It'll take the swelling down."

"That's what my mother used to say, too. It just means I'll be walking around smelling like a jar of pickles for a week."

I couldn't help smiling. "I'll add dill to it if you like."

His hand must have been feeling better, because he laughed a little. "I've always wondered—is there some book women read to know all this? How is it that all mothers know the same remedies?"

All mothers. The words struck me hard. "I'm not a mother," I said stiffly.

He didn't seem to notice. "Women, then," he said. "All women know the same things. Why is that?"

I could have said that it was something I learned from my mother, who learned it from her mother, who learned it from her mother. I could have told him that my knowledge went back forever, that it didn't matter if vinegar didn't take the swelling down or salt water failed to work its magic, because the secret was not in the ingredients. The secret was in the touching and the soothing, in the instinct to hold a baby close and pat her back in time to the beating of a heart, in the comfort of smoothing back hair from a hot, sweaty cheek and rubbing vinegar into pain with a light caress.

But I didn't tell him those things, because his words brought my own sorrow back to me again, and it turned out that as I took his hand from the water bath and dried it carefully and began to massage the vinegar into his skin, it was me who needed solace more. His pain was gone, or fading. Mine was as strong as my heartbeat.

And I took comfort in soothing him. Injured, he was like any other man, like a child, really, depending on me, needing me, and my soul drank it up. That need to comfort came as strongly to me as it ever had—stronger, perhaps, because there had been too long when I had had no one to comfort, no one to take care of. And I realized then, as I soothed this man, this *boy*, who had seemed decades younger than me, that I had missed this, the touching, the caring. I had missed it more than I could have imagined.

All mothers.

Perhaps that was when it started, when he'd so innocently seen a mother in me.

Later, I was to think of it as the day everything changed.

5

"I'll get Boyd" was the first thing John Zimmerman said when he came by the farm the next morning to "see how you're doin' now Eli's gone." I was in the orchard, perched on the ladder, and Will was trying hard to pick with one hand, and not succeeding too well, because the splint on his other hand made him clumsy and unbalanced. I don't know how long John had been watching before I turned to see him standing on the edge of the orchard, but there was already a frown on his face, and that was when he told me he was going to get his son.

John Zimmerman had settled on the bottom a few years before Eli came up to see if this land had anything to offer, and they had become friends quickly. Like Eli, John was a farmer clear into his bones, a man who liked watching things grow, who believed that he could beat the sun and the desert. He was stocky and short, and though he was still a year away from thirty, his hair was already fully gray, and I never looked at him that I didn't think he was an old man, though he was only a year older than Eli.

John had started his family when he was still a boy, really. He was one of those men who went around saying things like, *Lizzy and I been together so long I can't remember a time when I was without her.* Their families had been close neighbors in some little town in Montana, or at least as close as families on quarter-section homestead claims could be, and when Elizabeth's family had starved out and abandoned the claim, fifteen-year-old John had stepped forward to take her away. She was thirteen, and her parents let her go because, though the Zimmerman farm was failing, too, John had plans for something bigger, something better.

To hear Elizabeth tell it, that something "bigger" was moving farther west, working on wheat farms and in logging camps, dragging four bedraggled, hungry children with them until they finally got to Yakima and the better life they'd waited for. They raised sheep and a small amount of wheat, and the way I saw it, they'd only traded one arid, failing farm for another, but the Zimmermans were like Eli—to them, the land was everything. And if sometimes I thought I saw a distant, sad look in Elizabeth's eyes, she made me doubt it the minute she turned back again. She was the most cheerful person I'd ever known, and that cheerfulness was hard to understand because, like John, she looked old already, thin and bony and land-ravaged. But she was always smiling, and she was easy to like. We'd been good friends when Eli and I first came to the bottom.

But now I couldn't look at her without remembering how she'd taken me in her arms that one terrible day, and held me and soothed me though I didn't want either, and through dry eyes I'd seen an understanding and misery in her face that was unbearable.

Eli had never understood how I could turn from her so easily, when she was my closest neighbor, and as near to a friend as anyone had ever been. But I think Elizabeth understood, and it was that understanding that made me put more and more distance between us. It was why we were strangers now, and why this day, when fourteen-year-old Boyd came back bearing a round of sheep's-milk cheese, he simply put it on the rocking chair on the porch without saying that his mother had bade him bring it over.

"We've got a few hours to help you out," John said, pointing Boyd to a nearby tree. "Wish it could be more."

"Well, I appreciate it, John," I told him. "We'd have been fine but for Will's hand."

At that, John gave Will a chiding look, as if somehow Will had hurt himself on purpose—or at least been so irresponsible he'd got himself hurt—and it raised a sharp irritation in me; I had to bite my tongue to keep from making some kind of comment.

"Can you pick at all, boy?" John asked Will, who gave him a quick smile. I thought, *This boy of mine can hold his own,* and the thought startled me. I stared at Will and wondered where it had come from, why when I looked at him now I felt a strange protectiveness.

"I can pick," he said with quiet assurance. "Just not as fast."

I could see that smile of his was working its magic.

He harrumphed a bit, and pulled at his braces, and then he said gruffly, "Well, pick, then. We haven't got all day."

John started picking himself. I caught him constantly looking back at me, checking, as if he wanted to tell me to go to the house and do the wash or cook dinner, but couldn't quite bring himself to do it, because with or without Will's being injured, I needed to pick, too, if we were going to get these cherries before they got too ripe—as small as the harvest was.

When it came near to noon, I left my ladder and went to the house to put together something for dinner. But as I started to the house, I passed the garden. It had been two days since I'd been able to work in it, and when I saw the weeds struggling through where they hadn't been before, and the pea vines wilting in the sun, I felt a hatred toward those cherries and Eli that made me walk over and stamp on those weeds with a vengeance. They only pushed back—those plants were accustomed to this arid prairie, it was the beans who were strangers. I tried yanking them out, but without a trowel they were stubborn and mean, and I felt guilty and helpless when I finally had to give up. I pulled some carrots and picked some beans, and I had to force myself to leave it. I would have to get to it tomorrow.

The will to keep the garden alive was with me all the time, a faint desperation I couldn't ignore. Today I found myself hurrying, trying to save seconds, to somehow create spare moments when there weren't any to be had. I strung only half the beans before I put them on, and I cut my thumb in my rush to peel potatoes. But I was feeling better as I went to the ice-house. I felt as if I'd managed to make some time. Then I opened that door, and as the cool air rushed out to dry the sweat on my face, the first thing I saw were those pans of milk sitting there, the cream heavy at the top. It overwhelmed me where I stood. I just stared at those pans, and they reminded me of all the things that still needed to be done: the butter to make for Ben, the cherries finished and crated and sold, picking the summer apples. There were not enough hours, and yet there had to be, and I had to find them. What kind of a woman would I be if I let a garden die?

The answer came back to me. *The kind of woman who would rather sew ruffles and pretty birds on a pinafore.*

I turned away and shut the door. I stared at the house, at its lopsidedness, the squinting cripple of those heavy logs and the dead and dusty yard around it, and I felt how much I belonged to this mean ugliness with every breath I took.

Then I saw John and Boyd and Will trudging back from the orchard, and the sight of that golden head gave me something else to think about, something else to do. I hurried across the yard, relieved and grateful, and when I thought of how I'd wanted Eli to send Will away, I started to run.

I was breathless when I reached them, and Will looked at me oddly. When John and Boyd went inside to fill their plates, Will asked, "Are you all right?"

I went up onto the porch. "I'm fine. Come up here so I can check your hand."

"It's all right, Lora," he told me, but I took the bandages off anyway, and he only sighed and sat back until I was finished.

"A few more days, and you'll be good as new," I said.

"I'm sorry," he said to me in a low voice. He glanced up, as if he was looking for John, and then he said, "I'm not much help to you like this."

"You're help enough."

"It's good of you to say so, but I saw the way John looked at me. A real man wouldn't be wearing a bandage right now."

"You're not a man, you're a boy," I reassured him. "You didn't hurt yourself on purpose, and besides, any man who didn't wear a splint on a sprain like this would be a fool."

He went so still I thought I'd hurt him, but then he relaxed again, so I just patted his shoulder and said, "I'll get you a plate."

John and Boyd came out from the house. It was too hot to eat inside, so they sat on the porch steps, balancing their full plates on their knees. For a while, there was nothing but the sound of eating and the frustrated calls of robins circling those baskets of cherries, frightened away again by the fluttering rags Eli had tied to the tree branches.

"So where d'you hail from, Will?" John asked finally. Though his voice sounded friendly enough, I heard the questioning below it, and I knew John was trying to figure out if this boy was likely to steal from me and run off in the night. It irritated me, but I said nothing. He wouldn't listen to me anyway. There wasn't a man on this prairie who had respect for a woman's opinion about anything. As much as John loved Elizabeth, I'd seen him turn away in the middle of her talking as if he'd suddenly stopped hearing her.

"Massachusetts," Will said. "North of Boston."

"An easterner, huh?" John shoveled a forkful of potatoes into his mouth. "What brings you out this way?"

"Simplicity," Will said.

John stopped his chewing. "Huh?"

"Simplicity," Will said again, and there was that confidence in his voice, that well-read tone that made me think of suffragettes and preachers. "Self-reliance. Thoreau said, 'The mass of men lead lives of quiet desperation.' In Massachusetts, that's true enough. I didn't want to be one of them."

Boyd snickered.

"That sounds like fancy school talk," John said. "There's not much use for that out here."

"You mean there's no place for philosophy here?" Will asked. "Or poetry? What about politics?"

"How old are you, boy?"

"Seventeen."

"What does a seventeen-year-old know about anything?"

"What did you know?" Will asked quietly, "when you were seventeen?"

John flushed. By seventeen, he'd had a wife and two children to feed. He'd lived already in a dozen places.

Will leaned forward, bracing his forearm on his

knee so his splinted hand was between his legs, and at that moment, with his hair falling forward into his face and his eyes lit up, he looked so young. "I've been all through this country. I've worked on cattle ranches and wheat farms and picked fruit. I've done just about every job a man could hire me to do, for just about every kind of man you can imagine. But I'll tell you one thing: I'm richer than anyone who's ever paid me to bring a harvest in." He tapped his fingers against his chest. "I'm rich in life, and the freedom to live it."

John snorted. He reached again for his plate. "That's easy enough to say now. But I never heard of a family yet that could survive on freedom."

"My family did," Will said quietly.

"Oh? How's that?"

"My father lived the words he spoke. He's an orator. Robert Bennett. Maybe you've heard of him. He's written newspaper articles on transcendentalism."

I'd never heard the word before, and John's blank look told me he hadn't, either. I imagined Eli might know what it was. Eli was a reader and a thinker. He was always throwing ideas out to me that he'd read in the latest *Washington Farmer*, things I barely understood and had no interest in, in any case.

"A what?" John asked.

"He and my mother founded a society outside of Boston."

"A society?" Now John was looking suspicious. "They started their own town, you mean?"

Will shook his head. "A utopian society. Based on the idea that everyone is free. There's no ownership, everything is shared, and everyone works equally according to their talents." He said the words as if he'd said them many times before, and then, as if he'd had to defend them, too, his face took on a wary look that wasn't needed. John was a farmer, and his battles were with the land, not people. I think if you'd told him the Mormons were taking over Yakima, he would have just picked up his hoe and said, *As long as they don't bother me,* and trudged off into his fields.

Now, he only shook his head and shrugged and took a bite of beans. "Don't seem like much of a life to me. I'll take a piece of this desert any day. At least then a man's got something to pass down."

"But why should you have to work so hard?" Will insisted. "What gives your children the right to more happiness than you?"

"Because they're my children," John said. He picked up his fork and pointed it at Will. "You're young yet, boy. Someday you'll see what life is about— and it ain't freedom."

Will made a soft, disbelieving sound and sat back in his chair. I reached for his plate, meaning to take it inside and refill it, but he shook his head and took it back from me. "I can get it, Lora. Sit down yourself. You need to eat. It'll be a long afternoon."

I was surprised again, the way I always was when he did something like that. It flustered me, and I sat back in my chair and reached for my plate, and that was when I saw John Zimmerman's strange look.

I had the sense he saw something that I should be afraid of, though I had no idea what it might be. Then Will took his plate inside, and John set his on the porch step and got to his feet, clapping his hand on his skinny, dark-haired son's shoulder.

"Come on, Boyd," he said. "We got to finish this and get back." Then he looked at me. He jerked his head toward the house where Will was, and said quietly, "He's a drifter, Lora. He'll be moving on."

I didn't know what to say. But as I watched him and Boyd turn away and go out to the orchard, the warning of those words left a taste sour as vinegar on my tongue, and I felt sad already, as if things were ending, when they had barely only begun.

We picked cherries until it was too dark to see, too dark to go to the garden. All I could do was water it, and I didn't sleep well thinking of it. It had to wait the next morning, too, because Will and I were in the barn by sunup. On the big worktable just inside the door were piled cherry crates that Eli had fashioned. He'd worked on them throughout the winter—whenever he had a few spare minutes, he made one—and when I looked at them now, stacked, all the same size, all expertly made, I thought of him out in the unheated barn while the wind howled around him, pounding nails into splintering wood with hands clumsy from heavy gloves. He'd made hundreds, it seemed to me, and his faith nearly made me cry. I could not have built even one without remembering the trees popping and splintering in the freeze the winter before. I would never have had this kind of trust in the future.

And now, looking at the tall stacks of them, his hope was heartbreaking. We wouldn't fill a quarter of them with this year's harvest. But even a quarter would help, so I helped Will bring the crates down and set them on the barn floor, and with the barn doors open for light and air, and the smells of dusty hay and cows and oil around us, we began to sort through the cherries we'd picked, culling the small and cracked ones. Row after row of gleaming reds, laid out in uniform size, blushing yellows. It was hard work, and before long the muscles between my shoulder blades began to ache. I looked up at Will, who was bent over his own crate, slow because of the splint on his hand, slow because it took a while to know the size of a cherry by feel, until you could reach into the bushel and pull out a handful all the same.

He looked studious, and though this work was boring, he did not look bored. I thought it was strange, that I never saw Will Bennett look anything but intent on whatever he was doing, and that made me wonder what kinds of things he was thinking, where all those strange ideas of his came from.

I was thinking of that, and of the day before, how young and eager he'd seemed, how excited when he talked of his freedom. I must have smiled at the thought, because he said, "You look happy. What are you thinking?"

I looked up at him in surprise. I felt myself flush, and I looked down again, embarrassed by the intimacy of the question, by the fact that I'd been thinking of him and was reluctant to admit it. No one in Yakima ever asked questions like that. "Nothing."

"Must have been something. Just a few minutes ago I was thinking that you didn't smile enough."

That unnerved me again—the idea that he thought of me at all, that when I'd been looking at him and wondering who he was, he'd been wondering why I didn't smile. I remembered a long time ago, years ago, it seemed, when Eli had been courting me, and he helped me carry a basket lunch out to the harvesters and told me he'd been thinking I had a pretty smile, and how I'd been flustered then, too, and flattered, and shivery inside knowing that he'd been thinking of me.

But this was different. I wasn't sure how I felt about it, whether it was nice that he cared enough to notice things about me, or whether I thought it impertinent and a little disturbing. I looked down at the cherries and kept sorting.

"What do we do with these, anyway?"

"Take them into town. There'll be buyers from Beaman's waiting."

"When are you planning to do that?"

"As soon as we're done here. And I've promised to make some butter for Ben Schiller. I'll do it tonight, when it's cooler."

"When do you plan to sleep?"

His words were joking, but all I could think about was my garden withering in the heat. "Maybe never again."

"It must be lonely for you without Eli."

I concentrated harder on the cherries, and they blurred beneath my eyes, reds dashing into each other. "It's not so bad."

"You've been married a long time."

I nodded.

"It must be something," he said, "to be with someone that way."

I kept counting cherries. There seemed to be nothing to say without revealing things too private for Will Bennett to know. A person went into a marriage with so many dreams, expecting so much. Eli taught me things about the world I'd never known, and I think for a little while I almost thought of him as God. I thought it would go on forever, my loving him that way, my hanging on his words.

"I can imagine it, you know. I can imagine how lonely it must get here for you, especially with no children around."

He said it as if it were a natural thing to have no children, as if there weren't children running about on every farm in Yakima except this one, and his words hurt so much I couldn't bear it. I felt loss like a hole in my body, something you could see right through, a silence in my soul so loud I could not hear my own heartbeat.

But for Will Bennett, the word *children* was not the point. I could see that it didn't occur to him to wonder why we had none, because he was moving on; his point was my loneliness. His point was this: "I've been thinking you might like to do some visiting when we go into town. I'd be happy to take you there, if that's what you'd like."

I could barely speak. "I don't think so."

"Oh, now, Lora," he said chidingly. "You've been on this farm alone for the better part of two weeks. Taking a day to visit can't hurt. I've watched you. You spend every night in the kitchen doing something.

You never sit down. I've offered to stay around and talk awhile, but you've never said anything but no. It gets dark, you go to sleep. I've never seen you read a book or write a letter. You work too hard, Lora. Seems to me that's all you ever do."

"This is a farm, Will. There's nothing but work."

He shook his head in that slow, sad way he had. "You could use some fun, Lora. You could smile more."

I finished another box of cherries. I set the crate on the dirt floor so hard that the cherries shuddered. My hair was falling into my face, and the straw dust itched in my nose, and I felt a desperation I could not control. I wanted nothing more than to be out of that barn.

I looked at Will. "A smile won't get the cherries packed, will it?" Then I turned and marched back to the house, meaning to get dinner ready, needing to leave him alone there in the barn, but when I got outside that crooked door and stepped into the dirt yard, a dried-up tumbleweed spun by in front of my boots, blown by a hot, dusty wind.

I looked out on the purple cloud shadows racing across the parched ground, and the skinny, starved chickens scattering in the dust. I saw the wilting green of my garden, and in my head those weeds were pushing up, wrapping around the peas and the beans, strangling them, and there was nothing I could do, because the cherries demanded everything.

When I realized I was crying, the tears were already gone, drying up the moment they hit my skin, leaving nothing but salt on my face.

6

The sun was setting fast behind the ridge when I finally left Will to finish the last of the sorting. I felt restless and ill at ease, and there was still so much to do. I made the butter to take into town the next day, and as I patted it into molds and turned it out onto trays, I worried about those cherries in the barn. Eli had always sold the fruit before; although I'd gone with him each time, I'd never paid attention to the talk between him and the Beaman's man. Mostly I'd looked in shop windows and smiled at our neighbors. Now all I could think of was our ledgers and our debt, and the thought of seeing those people left me feeling sick and ashamed.

I wasn't sure where to take the cherries now that Yakima City was scattered all across the prairie. I could ask Ben Schiller when I took the butter in, I supposed, but that thought didn't reassure me. Not because I didn't really know which Yakima he was in, though that was part of it, but mostly because I wasn't sure how I would face him. My grocery list was pared down to necessities, and though he'd promised Eli that he

would let me buy whatever I needed as long as I
brought in butter, I could not forget the huge account
we had there or the charity he was offering. When
dawn finally broke between the red gingham curtains
at our tiny bedroom window, I was exhausted.

Before, I had always looked forward to going into
town. Then, I would dress in my second day gown—in
the summer it was a twilled surah of a color called
invisible green, decorated with bands of silk pat-
terned with pompadour roses. It was a dress I'd loved,
because there were layers of fabric and ruffles over the
bustle and lace trim everywhere there could be, and it
had been bought in Walla Walla as part of my
trousseau. The fabric still shimmered with anticipation, with youthful dreams.

I hadn't worn it in a long time, and today, too, I
passed it by. I paused at the open door of the armoire
Eli had fashioned for me from leftover lumber, and
stared into the darkness, to a dress hidden in shadow,
a dress I had not worn for almost a year. I should have
burned it. I had wanted to burn it, but we could not
afford it, and so I told myself that a married woman
should have a black dress, and I buried my resentment and my hatred for its necessity in this place that
demanded such sacrifice, that required grief to survive.

It was the dress I'd been married in, but it had
been blue then, a blue the color of innocence. I
remembered how I'd watched that pale color billow
up in a vat of black dye, like clouds in an angry sky,
and how my guilt deepened with the hue until I'd
vowed I would never wear that color of blue again.

Now, I pulled that dress from its hook. The black silk caught on the splintered edge of the door, and I unsnagged it with trembling hands, because the feel of it brought back the memory of when I had worn it last, and what the wind had sounded like whistling through the barren valley, the feel of the silk damp with sweat between my shoulder blades, the stain of dye leaving purple bruises on my skin.

But it was the dress I needed today, a dress for an older woman, no frivolous lace or rose-patterned trim, a dress to make everyone remember who I was, what I had been through, to remind them that although I was not a widow yet, with my husband gone, I might as well be. To remind them of dignity and kindness when it embarrassed me to need either.

I took off my ragged gingham and dressed carefully in petticoats and my best boots, scuffed as they were from five years' wear. I pinned up my hair as severely as I could, though it was too fine and straight to stay that way long. By the time I reached the bottom of the stairs, strands were already falling into my face.

Will was waiting for me on the porch. I had not heard him that morning, but he must have been up earlier than usual, because Pete was already harnessed to the wagon, and the bed was filled with boxes of cherries.

"The butter's not in yet," Will said, following my gaze. "I'll load it now, if you're ready to leave."

I motioned to the kitchen—not very enthusiastically—and said, "Let me make breakfast."

He shook his head. "Let's just grab some bread and go. I know you're anxious to get started."

And I was. Anxious. Nervous. I don't think I could have eaten a bite. I wondered if there was something I could do to keep from going. I thought about feigning a sudden illness—and that wouldn't have been far from the truth, because when I thought of facing Ben and selling those cherries, I felt like vomiting.

But I had to go, and I knew it. When I thought about the faith in Eli's clear blue eyes, I couldn't stand myself for wanting to fail him. So while Will loaded the trays of butter into the wagon, I wrapped a loaf of bread in a cloth and grabbed a handful of cherries from a bowl on the counter. When I went outside, he was just setting the cheesecloth-covered trays in the front, beneath the seat to protect them from the sun, though I wondered if that would help, or if I would get to Ben Schiller's to find the cakes I'd so carefully molded melted into blobs of grease.

I tried not to think about it as I climbed onto the buckboard seat and waited for Will to sit down and take the reins. He moved around the wagon, checking things, tightening things, and my heart seized a little, because it was just what Eli would have done, and this trip was one that he should have made, and if he were there, I would have had the innocence to wear an invisible-green dress and meander through town checking windows for something to yearn for.

Finally, Will climbed up beside me and took the reins in his good hand, slapping Pete's rump a little with the lines until the horse started to move. The wheels creaked up into my spine, and that seat bounced on the rough ground until I had to grab the side to keep my balance. The road was no better.

Before we'd even gone a mile, my teeth had rattled into a headache and my arms hurt from holding on. I perched on the edge of the seat, and Will Bennett leaned forward, the reins hanging loosely from one hand where it dangled between his legs, balancing his elbows on his thighs and looking for all the world as if he'd driven wagons since he was six. Which he probably had, I realized; every boy I'd ever known had. I tried to understand what it was about Will Bennett that made me think his driving a wagon was unusual and decided it was because of the way he'd looked the first time I'd seen him, standing in the barnyard with his hands in his pockets and a smile on his face as if he'd never done a day of hard work in his life.

First impressions are hard to get past, I suppose. I was quick to make judgments about people—I always had been, from the time I was small. Eli had tried to break me of it; he was much slower to form an opinion, more ready to believe the best of a person. I'd never been that way. I viewed people with distrust—a lesson my mother had passed on to me. My older sister, Dorothy, once told me it was because Mama had spent her whole life moving from place to place. Her father had been a drummer who went from town to town, selling pots and pans, toilet water in cheap little bottles stoppered with wax, ribbons and writing papers and shawls he said were direct from India but which were really knitted by my grandmother at night when they camped around a fire.

Dorothy said that being raised as a drummer's daughter made Mama believe that everyone would take advantage if they could, and so whenever Mama saw a stranger riding up to the farm, she put on a grim face and her blue eyes grew dark and distant.

Dorothy was twenty-five now, and married to the son of my father's nearest neighbor, and so she and Mama spent hours and hours in each other's company, and I suppose they talked about living as a drummer's daughter and not trusting people, and things like that. All I knew was the distant face of my mother, and how hard drummers always had to work to sell her anything at all, how she would watch them with faraway eyes as if she expected them at any minute to try to swindle her. I wondered once just how much swindling she'd done as a salesman's daughter, but I couldn't imagine Mama ever telling a lie, because her bitterness was so hard and honest.

My father was not like that, and—unlike Mama—he had plenty of reasons to be bitter. He'd been a farmer all his life, with all the failures and hardship that meant, and he'd lost a leg in the war, too. He never spoke about it, and I was ten before I really understood why he walked so funny—he brought his wooden leg into line by rotating his entire body, so he had this rolling, jerking way of moving. Until I heard some schoolchild taunt that he was a cripple, I'd never realized that he was.

My father had a way of facing things head on, never flinching. He was open and direct, and I'd heard the neighbors speak of him with kind respect. Eli used to say that though Theodore Downey was a hard man, he was always fair.

"Where're we going to?" Will asked. His voice startled me, breaking into my thoughts that way, and I must have stared blankly at him, because he said gently, "Yakima City? Or the new town?"

I didn't know. It had been a long time since I'd come into town; Eli had said there was no point, that the businesses were so loosey-goosey, half of them rolling across the prairie, the other half insisting on staying right where they were—planning their demise, Eli said. I didn't know if Ben Schiller had decided to take Northern Pacific's offer of a free lot in the new town they were calling North Yakima.

"Most places are already moved by now," Will told me. "They've got the railway station up. My guess is they'll be buying fruit close to there."

"Let's go there, then," I said, unable to hide my relief at his decision. "I—I don't suppose you know where Ben Schiller's store is?"

"New town," he said. "Eli and I went there after he found me."

That reminded me of what Will had been doing before he came to our farm. Again, that picture came into mind, strangely irreconcilable, a boy helping to move a building. I was thinking about it when we got closer to the new town they were calling North Yakima, and I saw what Eli meant. Buildings dotted the prairie, helter-skelter, defenseless. I was used to towns huddled together, houses built so close you could imagine the fortress walls around them, protection against Indians first and prairie fires second. These vulnerable buildings made me nervous and uncomfortable, floating alone that way, wrong somehow.

Then we drew near to Schull House—still moving, still a mile from the new city two weeks after Will had stopped working there— and it looked so strange that at first my eyes would not reconcile it. The boardinghouse looked the same: two stories with windows and a boardwalk fronting it, but there were guards at the doors, and it was sitting in the middle of a field of sagebrush instead of on Main Street. There were men hitching their horses to the porch, which wasn't unusual, of course, but what was unusual was that the big hotel was on huge rollers that creaked against planks laid beneath them, and it was moving, long and slow, so the horses hitched to the poch had to walk along beside it until it stopped and waited for the planks to be laid again.

That was what Will had been doing—laying those planks down, one after another, to keep those rollers from sinking into the loose soil—and as Will directed the wagon around the boardinghouse and we left it in the distance, I turned around to look at those thick-armed, broad-shouldered men laying the planks and urging the team of horses pulling it forward, and I could not imagine him there.

It took my mind off town, thinking about it, so that by the time we reached North Yakima, I had almost forgotten why we had come. But the minute I saw the new town, my palms began to sweat beneath my black gloves. It was Yakima—I recognized Weed & Rowe hardware and Allen & Chapman's Drug, Ward Brothers grocery—but it wasn't really the same. The streets were laid out in nice, neat lines, the main street bordered on each side by an irrigation ditch bringing water from the Naches right into town. There were new buildings and some old ones. Tents had been erected along the west side of the railroad tracks; they were flapping in the wind, their taut lines shivering.

The new town was noisier than the old. There was a train in, chugging smoke, clanging engines. From the saloons came music, and the crack and roll of roulette balls, and besides that there were hammers pounding, men carrying lumber and shouting across the street, shoveling, digging, workers laying plank sidewalks, wagons creaking, drivers yelling and careening through the narrow streets, and Indians lurking about everywhere.

The only truly familiar thing was the dust. It was in my eyes and my mouth and my nostrils, dry and tickling, and I had to blink my eyes and swallow—or perhaps that was only my nervousness, because looking at this new and unfamiliar town, I was so nervous I wasn't sure I could speak. The cherries and butter in the back of the wagon suddenly felt like hundred-pound weights around my neck.

We were stopped, and I turned to Will and found him looking at me, waiting for direction. I swallowed again. "Ben Schiller's, first," I managed to croak. Will nodded, and we started off again, jerking and rolling, trying to work our way through the chaos. Finally, Will pulled the wagon up in front of a building I didn't recognize. Ben Schiller had built a new general store with fancy glass windows in the front and a painted sign. No doubt he expected the railroad to bring him riches. I was sure he wasn't expecting them from us.

I got down from the wagon and held up my head as I went inside, leaving Will to follow me with the trays of butter held awkwardly in place against his hip with his one good hand.

There was another woman in the store ahead of us, Irma Peavy. Her husband was an attorney who had come from Walla Walla to Yakima only three years ago. He'd built her a lovely two-story frame house just outside Yakima City, with windows that sparkled in the sun and white lace curtains that peeked from the edges. He'd had a ditch dug from the Naches to the house, because she loved gardening, and Irma had a garden that must have rivaled those in any other city in the country. The pride of that garden was a big bed of huge, fluffy yellow flowers the likes of which I'd never seen before. Though I hadn't been to her house for a long time now, I still remembered the teas she'd given there, with cakes and sandwiches and lemonade. Irma Peavy was a woman who liked to live in luxury—Eli used to say she'd been lucky to find a man like George, who could afford to keep her that way.

Now, she smiled when I came in, and rustled over in a bustling mound of lace and ribbons and flounces, patting at the hat that covered her dark hair.

"Lora!" she said. "Lora Cameron! It's been ages since I saw you." Her eyebrows rose when she saw Will behind me. "And who can this young man be?"

"Will Bennett," I said. "Our hired hand."

I thought I saw her calculating, *How can they afford a hired hand?* and I felt myself go hot. Then she grasped my arm, a little squeeze, a sympathetic look from her quick brown eyes. "How are you doing, Lora? I heard from George that Eli's gone to the Wishkah. How hard it must be for you. I daresay, I don't think I could manage it."

"We're getting along just fine," I told her.

"Have you heard from him yet?"

"He's only been gone a few weeks. I didn't expect to hear so soon."

"You will, dear, you will." Irma patted my arm again. "Now, you be sure and let me know if you need anything."

"I'll be fine."

"Of course you will. By the way, dear, I'm having a little tea party next week—Saturday—if you'd care to come. The girls have all promised to be there—such a busy time of year, I know, but everyone needs a few hours of rest, don't you think? I know they'd be delighted to see you. We can take strength from each other. You mustn't isolate yourself out there on the bottom."

Isolation was what I wanted, but I nodded and smiled and said, "I'll think about it, Irma. It sounds lovely."

"Good. You just let me know." She drew back and wiggled her fingers at me. Then she called up to Ben, whose other customer had just walked away, "Send it over to me this afternoon, Ben, won't you? Or should I have George pick it up?"

"I'll send it over," Ben said.

"Good, good. Excellent!" Irma smiled and winked at me. "Now, I really must be going. I expect to see you next week, Lora—don't forget!"

Then she was gone, out the front door in a cloud of scent—rose toilet water—and I was left there alone with Ben waiting for me at the counter.

"Hello, Ben," I said.

"Hello, Lora." He nodded at me. Ben was a darkly handsome man about Eli's age. He wore his hair short and had a full beard that bushed out from his face so that sometimes you had to search for his mouth within it. Today, he was smiling, but I saw the strain in his expression when he saw me, and I wanted to be gone so badly I could hardly make myself walk up to the counter. But I did, and I heard Will behind me, his solid footsteps. When I reached the counter, he put the trays down beside me, and I smiled a thank-you to him and turned again to face Ben.

"Eli said you'd buy some butter," I began hesitantly.

"Miz Robbe's cow went dry," he said. "I can sure use it."

He lifted the cheesecloth from one of the trays, and my heart stopped as he looked it over. I imagined it was nothing but a runny, greasy mess, the fine heart-and-flower design pressed on the top from the butter mold melting into some formless lump. But Ben nodded soberly and I saw him counting in his head.

"They look fine, Lora," he said. "I'll pay you ten cents a pound, if that's all right by you."

I had no idea if it was all right. I didn't know if he was taking advantage of me, or—worse—if he was overpaying me because we needed the charity. "Sounds fine," I said quietly.

"So that's four dollars even," he said. He took out a pad of paper and scrawled the number down. "You need anything today?"

I swallowed. Four dollars. It seemed so little suddenly, not enough for anything. "Do you . . . do you need eggs, Ben?" I asked him. "I could bring some eggs. . . ."

He gave me a look that told me he didn't need eggs, but he nodded anyway and said, "Sure. Bring in some eggs next time. I'll take any extra off your hands."

I could barely meet his eyes, I was so uncomfortable and embarrassed by his generosity. I turned to look at the shelves behind me, and in the loudest voice I could muster—which was nothing more than a whisper—I said, "I need five pounds of sugar, Ben. And two sacks of flour. Two pounds of coffee."

We needed so much, but until I had enough money in hand, I was not applying to Ben for more. These were the things I had decided I must have. We were low on kerosene, but I had candles for now. Castile soap was a luxury. I could do without.

I waited while Ben put everything together, and watched him write it down on the pad, balancing the number against the meager four dollars I'd earned with the butter, and then I said, "If you could apply what's left against our account, I'd appreciate it."

He looked up at me, and he looked as uncomfortable as I felt. It occurred to me that Ben was not used to talking to a woman about money, and that it was something he would rather not do. "You sure you want me to do that, Lora?" he asked quietly.

"Yes. There'll be more butter. And eggs. I'll . . . get by." I hesitated then, and said, "Eli's left me to sell the cherries. I'm just . . . not sure . . ."

"Where are they buying cherries today?" Will asked outright, and I was grateful to him for taking the matter into his own hands. I didn't want to so plainly admit my ignorance.

Ben looked at him in surprise, and then he looked quickly at me before he nodded and said to Will, "Just off the station there, you can't miss it. Must be a line of eight or ten wagons waiting to unload."

"We'll be going, then," I said. "Thank you, Ben." I turned to walk away, and Will shouldered one bag of flour to take to the wagon.

"Lora?" Ben called softly before I'd taken a step. When I turned around, he squirmed; I thought I imagined a red flush on his cheeks above the beard. He held out a piece of folded paper. "Mason Albright dropped this by to give to Eli. I could hold on to it for him, if you like."

I stared at it, feeling a sudden dread. Mason Albright was the cabinetmaker, and that folded piece of paper could be nothing good. "You'd best give it to me."

I felt my cheeks burn as I took that piece of paper and flipped it open. It was a bill for $20, nearly a year old. Still unpaid. With interest. Scrawled at the bottom, in Mason's distinctive, fine hand, were the words *I've held out as long as I can, Eli. If I don't see a payment by the end of the month, I'll have no choice. I'm sorry.*

Quickly, I folded the piece of paper and shoved it into my pocket. When I looked up, I saw both Will and Ben looking at me—Ben with a look that told me he knew exactly what that note said, and Will with concern. I shook my head at him slightly and tried to smile at Ben.

"Thank you, Ben," I said, and my voice was a whisper. I motioned for Will to follow me, and then I walked out of that store with a smile pasted on my face.

When we got outside, I felt Will's soft touch on my arm. "What is it?" he asked. "Can I help?"

I shook my head mutely; I could not summon words, especially when I looked across the street to the tents, their canvas sides alive, breathing in and out with the wind. I saw the line of wagons leading from one of them, cherries gleaming in the hot sun. I could almost smell their sweetness through the stink of dust and sage, horse manure, warm beer. None of the wagons was piled full—we were not the only farmers who had suffered a loss during the killing winter. We were not the only ones struggling. I tried to remember that as Will loaded everything into the wagon and we drove over to the line.

I saw the other farmers look at me as we drove up, and I saw something like pity on their faces as they tipped their hats or nodded or called out hellos, but they were wary greetings, as if they expected that somehow my being there would hurt them. They were lounging on their wagon seats, hats tipped forward, waiting. On the bright new sidewalk next to the railway station, a group of businessmen had split open a watermelon to eat there in the sun. They were in their shirtsleeves, laughing and spitting seeds while the juice dripped on the sidewalk and burned away to stickiness in the heat.

They were carefree and rich-looking, and for a moment that was what I wanted to be, a man with money and no worries. A man who could take time off in the middle of the afternoon to suck on a watermelon, instead of what I was—a makeshift widow with a boy at her side trying to do a man's work.

"Lora!" The call seemed to come from everywhere. I twisted on the wagon seat, trying to place it, and saw Sarah Laughton, the postmistress, waving from the door of the post office on the bottom floor of a building that bore the sign *Milroy Bros.—Attorneys at Law.* "Lora Cameron!"

I shielded my eyes with my hand and looked in her direction. She was motioning wildly, her whole body shaking.

"Go on, see what she wants," Will said. "I'll stay with the wagon."

I hesitated, then I got down and walked across the dusty street to Sarah, who smiled when she saw me.

"I've been waiting for you to come into town," she said, gesturing for me to follow her inside. The post office was small and hot, and the windows were open, so dust coated the new wood floor and filmed the narrow countertop. Sarah bustled to the rows of tiny boxes against the wall. "There's your usual letter from your ma, and I've got a letter from Eli that's been sitting here the last two days—I would've thought you'd be in here every day asking for something from your husband!"

She reached into a small cubbyhole in the wall

behind her and pulled out a letter. When she handed it to me, I smelled my mother's smell in the paper, that castile soap scent that clung to everything she touched, and it comforted me for those few seconds before Sarah held out the thin, folded sheet that was Eli's letter. I saw my husband's writing on the outside, my name in his hand—the backward slant of the L, the looped o. The paper was dirty, and there was something sticky on the side of it that had gathered lint and dirt.

Sarah held out that letter. I must have stared at it a long time without taking it, because the smile faded a little on her face, and she gave me a puzzled look. Finally, I took it from her, and I think she was more puzzled when I shoved both envelopes into my pocket beside that bill from Mason, but I wanted Eli's letter out of my hand, out of sight. I remembered the words between us before he'd left, the questions he was always asking me, and now I was afraid of the words the letter held, of what distance would allow Eli to say to me. I was afraid of what it would make me feel.

So I gave Sarah the best smile I could muster— which was not very much—and murmured, "Thank you," and I think she was a little bewildered, because we had always been friends, and I had never made a visit into town without stopping at the post office to see if there was a letter from my mother or one of my sisters or to share gossip with her.

But today I didn't. I turned to leave. She reached out and stopped me with a soft touch on my sleeve. "You doing all right out there alone, Lora?"

"I'm fine."

"Eli stopped in the other day to ask me to keep an eye on you. I've meant to come out, but you know how it is. This time of year is just terrible."

Gently, I pulled away. "I'm fine, Sarah, really. There's no need to trouble yourself."

"Well, I told Eli that I thought you'd be able to take care of everything just fine, but he seemed worried."

"He needn't have been."

"I suppose not." She let me go then, but I felt her reluctance, and I was embarrassed and uncomfortable when I left. I wasn't sure which bothered me more—Eli's asking her to look in on me, or the fact that I wouldn't have thought to go to the post office today without her call, that I had forgotten there might be a letter from Eli waiting. Or maybe it was just that I'd wanted to forget. It was disturbing to think such a thing. I think Will saw it as I went over to him again, because he frowned a little and studied me carefully before he said, "What did she want?"

"There was a letter from my mother," I said. "And one from Eli."

"Oh? What does he have to say?"

I felt that letter pushing at me, insisting. I heard its little voice: *What's wrong with you that you don't want to read a letter from your own husband?* But I didn't pull it out. I looked straight ahead and said to Will, "I haven't opened it yet. I'm waiting until we get home."

He looked at me for what seemed like a long time; I felt his gaze on the side of my face. I waited in burning silence as the wagons in front of us moved up to the tent, one and then another, until finally we reached the wooden loading dock.

The man waiting there was not someone I'd ever seen before, but I was not sure I would have recognized him anyway, given that Eli usually took care of this. This man was tall and thin, with a thick mustache, and he was chewing tobacco as we pulled up. He looked at Will and ignored me completely as he lifted his clipboard with a list of names and said, "Which farm?"

"Cameron," I said, before Will could answer.

The man looked at me in surprise.

"Elijah Cameron," I said, and though I meant to say it firmly, there was a catch in my voice. "I'm his wife, Lora."

The man looked at me thoughtfully, but it was not a nice look. It was obvious he didn't like dealing with a woman, and as he went to the back of the wagon and ran his hands over those boxes of cherries, I felt his distaste filling the air around us.

"They don't look too good," he said. "Lots of cracking. They look small, too."

"There's hardly any cracking," I said quietly.

The man didn't seem to hear me. He picked up a cherry and held it between his fingers, then let it drop with a contemptuous plunk back into the box. "No, no, they don't look good at all."

"They look fine," I told him.

He took a deep breath, leaned on the edge of the buckboard, and looked at Will. "Boy, you know anything about cherries?"

"I know they look fine," Will said.

The buyer laughed a little and tugged on his mustache. "Well, boy, I'm sorry to have to tell you this—"

"Talk to me," I said quietly. "He's just my hired hand."

The man seemed surprised, but he nodded slowly, and a meanness came into his face that made me wish I'd been quiet. "Miz Cameron," he said, and his tone was smooth and well-practiced; he acted as if talking to me, and telling me this in particular, was a special kindness. "I'm sorry to say these cherries aren't the quality that Beaman's expects. But I'll tell you what, I'll do you a favor. I'll take 'em off your hands anyway. Say, four cents a pound? I'd say you have about eight hundred pounds here, does that sound about right? That gives you thirty-two dollars. A nice profit, I think, given what you've got here."

Thirty-two dollars. I thought of the bill from the cabinetmaker folded in my bag, of a year's harvest already more than half gone. I was being cheated; I'd heard him give the man in front of me twice that. I knew that Eli would have insisted on the fair price, and that these cherries were as good as any others there—or at least, I thought I knew that. I hadn't actually seen any other cherries; perhaps the man was right. Perhaps they weren't quite good enough.

It was that uncertainty that made me pause, and when I looked at the man leaning on the side of my wagon, I knew the truth—that he was cheating me because I was a woman, and he knew I wouldn't protest, and the fact was, he was right. I couldn't protest because I wasn't sure, because I didn't know how to talk to a man like him, how to argue. I had no idea how to bargain, or how to convince him that he was wrong, and so I shut my mouth and watched as he and another man unloaded those cherries, and then I took the money he gave me and felt a despair so deep that I could barely speak as Will drove the empty wagon away from that tent and back toward home.

As we headed back over the prairie, through the sage-covered hills, turning gray now with the onset of evening, I felt Eli's letter burning through my pocket into my side, and my uneasiness was so heavy that when Will said, "He was wrong, wasn't he? Those cherries were fine." I shook my head and motioned for him to be quiet, afraid that if I started to speak I would cry, afraid of everything I was feeling, and of what I would have to tell my husband.

But mostly, I was afraid of what he had to tell me.

When we finally got back to the farm, the sun had set and the farm buildings were just shadows in darkness. Will let me off at the house before he drove the wagon back to the barn, and I stood at the window and watched his lamplight pressing against the night, and imagined him doing all the things Eli usually did, unharnessing and settling Pete into his stall, milking the cow, who was bawling at the door. Then I left the window. I took the bill from Mason out of my pocket and tucked it carefully into this year's ledger, and then I pulled out the letters. I looked at Eli's for a long time, rubbing my fingers over the paper, feeling his touch as though his fingers had come through the pages to linger on mine. I thought of my failure today, and I imagined his disappointment, the bitter end of his hopes. I knew him so well. Which was why, when I turned the letter over, meaning to open it, something made me pause as my fingernail eased beneath the flap.

Instead, I put it aside and took out my mother's letter to read. But her words went in and out of my head—something about Ellen's new beau and some piece of farm equipment my father had just bought—I hardly remembered anything she'd said when I was done.

Finally, I laid it there on the table and picked up Eli's letter again. I took it upstairs with me, leaning it against the lamp on the night table as I readied for sleep, thinking I would read it lying there in the bed we'd shared. But instead that envelope stayed propped there, untouched, a pale white shadow in the darkness, deep into the night.

7

I didn't read that letter the next morning, either. I glanced at it there on the nightstand and told myself I had to get breakfast ready for Will. I would read it later. Perhaps this afternoon, if I could find an extra hour or so.

I went downstairs, and as I stoked the stove, I saw Will through the window. He was sitting on the porch, the way he did every morning, cleaning a pair of boots, and I found myself hungering for his company—or if not his, someone's, I didn't care who. Yesterday was still sitting in my head, nagging at me, and the worry of Eli's letter only kept it burning there. The disappointment of the cherries, Mason Albright's bill . . . I wanted the hours until I read my husband's letter to be forgetful ones, and I figured Will Bennett could help me do that. I opened the door, and he put aside his boots.

"Breakfast ready?" he asked.

"Not yet. But you can do that inside, if you want."

If I surprised him, he didn't show it. He was the most composed soul I'd ever known. He glanced down at the boots and shook his head. "They're pretty dirty, Lora."

I stood back from the door and motioned him in. Will hesitated, and then he gave me a strange look before he went past me to the kitchen table. I ignored that look, and how it made me feel transparent, and turned away to pour coffee beans into the hopper fastened to the wall. When I ground them the noise was so loud we couldn't talk, and that was fine with me. I wanted a presence more than I wanted conversation, someone to fill the emptiness Eli had left.

The minute the coffee was ground, Will said, "I've been thinking about those cherries yesterday."

I felt it as if I were standing on that street again; I smelled the fruit and the dust and my own anxiety. I saw that Beaman's buyer with his mean little eyes, and I wished I'd left Will out on the porch. I'd forgotten who he was, his discomfiting questions, how he liked stirring things up.

"We should go back there and get what's due you. It isn't right, what he did."

I didn't know what to say to him. Justice was not something I expected from life. Certainly not something I would demand. "There's no point."

"Those cherries were fine."

"I don't know that for a fact, and neither do you."

"You don't believe that."

"It doesn't matter what I believe. What's done is done. I've got thirty-two dollars. I guess it'll have to do."

"But Lora—"

"I'm not going back there."

"Eli would have got a fair price."

"Maybe," I said quietly, though we both knew he was right.

He leaned across the table, his eyes burning like a preacher's focused on damnation. "I'll go back for you."

His innocence was like an ache that kept hurting no matter what you did to assuage it. I brought the butter to the table and looked into his eyes, tempering my voice so it was soft and kind. "What do you think'll happen if you go back there, Will? You're not Eli, either. They won't deal any more fairly with a boy than a woman. And you're just a hired hand. There's no reason for them to want to make you happy."

He stared at me for a long moment, and I could see that I'd hurt his feelings.

I squeezed his hand before I went back to the stove. "It's all right. I appreciate your trying to help."

He was quiet for long enough that I thought he'd put it aside. I cracked some eggs into a skillet, and when the coffee was ready, I poured him a cup.

He curled his fingers around the handle. "I don't understand people like that."

His voice was steady, but I heard his genuine puzzlement. It made me wonder where he'd been all these years, how he'd managed to escape people like that Beaman's buyer before now. There were plenty of them in this world. I could not believe he'd never met a one.

"It's all right," I said again.

He looked at me as if I were another mystery he couldn't solve. "It's not all right. Don't you understand, Lora? The only world worth living in is one where everyone does what's right. Cheating you just because he thinks he can get away with it isn't right. Making things harder for you just because he can . . . Don't you see? It doesn't make sense. He's only hurting himself."

"Hurting himself? He just saved Beaman's money."

Will clucked his tongue at me sadly. "Whatever good there is in the world benefits everyone, Lora. The bad hurts us all."

The eggs were crackling in the pan. I was glad of an excuse to turn away from him. I couldn't make myself understand, and that failure left me uneasy, as if there were some scarcity in my soul, some lack, that kept me from it. I suppose my soul *was* meager. Even God had lost His footing there, and normally I accepted the hard truth of that, but Will Bennett had a way of making me regret it, and I was still angry enough at God to want to stay angry.

There were things I didn't want to think about, but with Will around, talking all the time about things I didn't understand or believe, it was becoming harder to find some thought that was safe, that didn't bring some memory, some hurt. When I set the plate before Will, he looked up at me expectantly, waiting for me to take breakfast with him, and I waved him away, impatiently. "Go ahead. I'm not hungry this morning."

He had stolen my appetite. As much as I had wanted him there, I now wanted him out of my house. But when he had finished breakfast and left me there alone again, staring at the dirty plate I'd insisted he leave behind, I felt my solitude like a deep wound in my soul. I found myself thinking of how strange Will was, of the answers I didn't have for him. Eli would have known what to say. Eli was good at making things right.

That wasn't quite true, of course. He hadn't been able to make things right between us. But there in the loneliness of that house, it was easier to remember things the way I wanted them to be, easier to think of how good things could be when Eli wasn't there to remind me of how they were bad.

It was that, I suppose—my own illusions—that brought the image of Eli's letter into my mind. I wanted to hear his voice, and I wanted not to feel as helpless as I felt without him. Will had reminded me of all the things I could not do without my husband, all the ways I could stumble.

Not reading Eli's letter was only one more, I knew, and in that moment I wanted just one good thing to say to him. I wanted to be able to pretend I'd opened his letter the minute it was in my hands. I went upstairs and took it from the night table. I stared at his handwriting and felt the tension knot me up inside again, but I tore open the flap before I could change my mind, and unfolded it. His words were thin and blotchy, racing down the page, cramping up at the margins as if he needed to save space because there was so much to say. My legs were suddenly shaky; I had to sit down on the bed. The little attic room was sweltering, and my hands were sweating so much that when I smoothed out the paper, my fingers smudged the heavy blotches of ink at the edges

of the paper. I drew them back and held the letter as
gingerly as I held my old memories of Eli.

July 1 1885
Longins Camp
Wishkah River

Dear Lora,
    Arived here at Longins Camp last Wednesday and
have been working so hard I have not found an hour
to write to you until now It took me ten days to get
here—the ferries on the Snake werent much good—had
to wait longer than I planned But Im here now They
took me on right away at Longins and this is the hardst
work Ive had to do in a long time 10 hrs a day but
pays 12¢/hr I expect it will pay well enough if I can
hold on without wearing out.
    The camp is not much if you can imagin this: the
bunkhouse full of about 50 men at a time sleeping in
double bunks runing on evry wall with 1 window at
the end and a big stove in the middle with a bench all
around Its dark enough to need a lamp to read at
noon but I dont have much time for reading Im
writing to you now by bending over a lamp while the
others sleep They are teling me to put it out Most of
them dont have wives they are single men hoboing
from camp to camp so they laugh at me for having a
wife to write to Many have worked evry camp in this
part of the country and they have no ties to anywhere.
    I know things have ben bad between us but I
would rather have you to write to than not This is no
life for a man, Lora I miss you Nothing but bad

*cooking and worse sleeping here and men so coars and
loud it makes you long for a woman and a quiet voice.*

*But its pretty here to Lots of water to look at and
trees the green of your eyes The forests are so big you
would not believ it—I saw one tree fifty feet acros it
took ten of us to fell it They took a picture of it I will
send it sometime Seems it takes forever to get a single
tree down but ther are alredy many cut and big
barren spots all over with nothing but dirt and stumps
left to show where forest was Makes me think of home
These forests are prety but I like seeing my way acros
without things to block the view.*

*I wonder how things are ther Guess the cherries are
picked and sold by now How many lbs did we end up
with? Did you get a good price and how did Will work
out I keep thinking ther were things I forgot to tell you
but I guess I will here from you soon and you can let
me know I know things are hard Lora but this is the
best thing for now Send any letters to the addres abov
and they will get to me Write soon and take care of
yourself*

> *Yr husband,*
> *Elijah*

Letters are like strangers' voices. The words you
know, the sentences are familiar, but there's nothing
else there for you to grab hold of, no gestures you recognize, no guideposts to tell you, *Yes, this is what I
mean.*

These were Eli's words, and yet not his. There were
so many things left unsaid, words falling between the
lines, no emotions to read too easily in his eyes. The

force of his voice faded in stiff and distant sentences. What had he been thinking about? He said he missed me, but I knew it wasn't quite that. It was another life he missed. He did not want to come home to the house and the marriage he'd left, but to the woman whose green eyes he dreamt of when he looked at the trees, the woman who ran into his arms or rubbed his shoulders after a long day.

I felt lonelier than ever when I finished. Even as far away as he was, I heard the yearning in his questions; I knew how disappointed he would be when I answered him.

I could see how, sitting in that dark bunkhouse, Eli would imagine the trees heavy with cherries, how he would be yearning for good news, for surprise, even as he told himself not to expect it. Distance has a way of creating hope, the way the heat wavering against the parched ground makes you believe in water until you ride a little closer to find only clay and a bone-dry gully. I imagined his face when he finally read my letter, when he saw that not only had his hopes vanished, but I had not even been able to get a fair price.

I put the letter aside and tried to get the vision of his face out of my mind, but it stayed with me as I left our bedroom and went outside into a sun so bright the glare hurt my eyes.

My garden waited for me patiently, not giving up on me though it had every right to, but I set out the culled cherries on sacks to dry in the sun before I went over to it. Then I fell to my knees in the dirt and grabbed my trowel, taking vicious satisfaction in digging up the weeds, jerking them from the ground, turning up their dirt-crusted roots to wither in the sun. With each one I felt a little strength return.

I worked for a long time, until I was sweating and my eyes burned from staring at the brightness of parched earth. I had forgotten what time it was, and my mind was empty of everything but the garden. Pea pods and little yellow pear tomatoes and nothing else, and it was a relief; it was what I yearned for. Seeing nothing but cabbages in my head—there were days when I thought it was what heaven must be.

I could have worked longer, into the night perhaps, without knowing even that it was dark, but then a shadow slanted across the ground before me, blocking the sun so I had to blink to see.

"You look about ready to give out, Lora."

I shoved hair out of my face and twisted to look over my shoulder at him. "I'm fine."

His head tilted, and he smiled when he held out his hand to me. "Come on. It's past suppertime."

I glanced back at my garden, at the clean order of the plants now, the ground swept of weeds. At the sight of it I felt peace again, a sense of victory. In my battle against this land, I'd bought one more day.

That was how satisfaction came in a place like this. Moment by moment. I set down the trowel and wiped my hands on my apron, and then I took Will's hand and let him pull me to my feet. He was strong for a boy; he pulled me up without any effort at all.

"I'll get supper on," I told him. "I'm sorry. You must be starving."

He smiled at me again. "Why don't you let me make you some supper tonight?"

I'd never heard a man make such an offer to a woman. I hardly knew what to make of it.

Will didn't wait for my answer. He turned back to the house and left me to follow. It was a minute before I could rouse myself to hurry after him, and it wasn't until we reached the stairs and I saw he was serious about making supper that I managed to say a word.

"There's no need. Will, you've been working all day. I can do it."

"You've been working all day, too," he pointed out. That smile of his was endearing enough to steal protests. "And I can cook, Lora."

He went inside the house. I rushed after. "Will—"

He stopped just inside the door. I saw his gaze settle on Eli's letter, still lying where I'd left it, unfolded on the table. Will glanced back at me, and though I saw the question in his eyes, he didn't ask it. He went to the stove and opened it up to feed the coals that I'd banked that morning.

"Eli's fine," I found myself telling him. "He's working at a camp over on the Wishkah. A place called Longins."

"That's good."

"He says they felled a tree fifty feet across the other day."

"Fifty feet? I would surely like to see that. What else does Eli have to say?"

"Nothing much. He's doing fine." I picked up the letter and scanned it again before I tucked it into the pocket of my apron.

Will gestured toward the door. "Why don't you go

sit on the porch while I get supper ready? You could write Eli back."

Will's kindness made me think of an evening—it was fuzzy in my memory now. Eli had come up behind me while I was doing the dishes; he'd swept me off my feet and settled me onto the porch. He'd brought me my embroidery hoop and my sewing basket, and we sat on the bench together and watched the sun set behind the snowy sentries of Mt. Rainier and Mt. Adams. The only sounds were our breathing and the sound of my needle swishing through the fabric and the *grrrrng whoosh* of a grouse rising in a flurry from the alfalfa in the field. We'd sat there until it was so late I could no longer see the patterns I was sewing. We left the dishes sitting in the washtub until morning.

It was that kind of peace I felt now, the sense that something had turned out right, and I didn't want to spoil it. Those feelings came so rarely. It was as if Will had known I wouldn't sit out there with nothing to do, and he'd presented me with a chore I could not object to. Writing to Eli was something that felt right just then, and I felt that maybe tonight I would find the words to tell him the things I regretted having to say.

I grabbed a piece of paper and pen and ink from the shelf over the kitchen table, and one of the ledger books to serve as a desk. Then I went outside. I sat in that old rocker and bit the end of the pen and wondered how to start, what to say. The sun had gone behind the ridge, leaving the mountains dark and the long, straight clouds at the horizon pink and gold in an otherwise colorless sky. Gray was moving over the land, softening the sharp edges of it, smoothing out the colors, making it look gentler than it was. Dusk always made me believe all things were possible.

That was how I started the letter to Eli.

11 July 1885

Dear Eli,

I imagin it is evening to where you are I am watching the sunset on the prch while Will is making supper Yes I know it is strange He hs ben verry helpful to me while your gon I am glad now you left him with me.

It is hard fr me to imagin you in such a dark spot but I gues its better then here I gues your probly glad to be rid of me becase Im such a misry to you You will not lik hering this but I didnt do so well with the cheries We got 800 lbs 500 Royl Anns 250 Lamburts & 50 Bings & the man at Beemans said they were split & wold only give me 4c pr lb so ther is only 32 dolers for the whol year Im afrad it does no good for me to tak them in becase I am easy to cheet I am sory to tell you that Mason sent his bill to & ther is no good news He will wait til the end of the month but no longer I hav not done any thing yet so you cn tell me what to do I did sell butter to Ben for 4 dolers & he will take eggs to so we will bea fine that way.

Will hurt his hand so he cant dig for awhil but it is not to bad John & Boyd helped us pick I think he will be fine in time for apples but dont think the ditch will be don when you get home You sholdnt be mad bcase it is not his fault He is a good boy.

I think of you feling that tree—I wold surely lik to see a pictur of it but I want you to take care of yourself to & it wories me to think of you by 50 ft trees so ples be careful Ther are days when I cant imagin you coming back & it is not what I want even if you do.

The garden is good The apples are almost ready & the wether has been hot & dry.

> *yr wife,*
> *Lora*

8

After that day, Will came inside every morning to wait for his breakfast instead of staying on the porch. I would come down the stairs to see him sitting there, working on something—a leather strap or a rusty bolt or a hinge. His hand had begun to heal, and he'd taken off the splint days ago, in spite of my protest, and now wore only a thin wrap of bandages to keep it stiff. In those few days, he'd grown adept at managing things, holding them steady with his knees or the crook of his elbow while he worked. He was a clever boy. I wondered if his mother had thought him so, too, if she'd had any doubts sending him out on his own to discover the world, if she worried about him now. I thought about that a lot, almost every time I looked at him. I pictured her waiting for his letters the way I would have, and I wondered if any had ever come. Though Will was a considerate boy, I didn't really think he was the kind who thought much about the things he'd left behind. It made me sad to think it. When he left, I would worry after him, I would wonder. And I expected I would never hear from him again, and that too was a little nagging thing inside me, something else I didn't want to think about.

I'd grown used to seeing him sitting there at my table. I liked the way he took up time, how I could trim and fill a lamp for him every morning and think of him out there in the barn, reading that book I'd seen him with by clean wicks that didn't smoke and clear glass chimneys. He gave me a picture in my mind to work for, someone to think about while I cooked, someone whose preferences I had to know— though I had yet to find something he didn't like. He was the most appreciative eater. I expected he had spoiled me for anyone else.

Will Bennett made that hole inside me feel not so empty, not so *there*. He expected nothing from me, and that made me feel as if I could give him every- thing. I could mother him, and he only smiled at me and let me do it and never said a word about what he wanted back.

At least, he never did until that Saturday.

When I came downstairs and said good morning, he smiled and looked down as if he was hiding some- thing, and though I wondered about it, I let it go as I cooked breakfast. I was in the middle of frying up some salt pork when he said, "I have to go into town today."

I turned. "What for?"

"There're a few things I need." He didn't look at me. He was working with some piece of leather, and it was stiff and he was having trouble with it. "Nothing much."

I didn't think he had any money. I certainly hadn't paid him anything. But I didn't know how to ask it without seeming impolite, so I said, "Whatever it is, Eli probably has—"

"No. I've got to go into town for this. You want to go with me?"

"Oh, Will, I can't. There's so much to do—"

"I could use your help."

"For what?"

"I . . . I need your advice about something."

He looked strangely bashful, almost embarrassed. I'd never seen him look that way before. It put me in mind of a schoolboy crush; I wondered if there was some girl somewhere that he'd become attached to. Something he hadn't told me.

It was endearing to think he'd kept that secret, though it seemed unlike him. Will was somehow beyond those things; I'd imagined his quest for Freedom and Simplicity left him too occupied for the plain yearnings that troubled the rest of us. I was glad he wasn't—it made him more human, and I felt myself loosening, smiling. I couldn't help teasing him. "My advice? I can't imagine there's anything I can tell you that you don't know already."

"I'd appreciate it just the same."

"You'd know hinges and nails and things much better than me. Why, all I could help you with are ribbons and things like that. What use could you have for those?"

He hesitated for a minute, and I saw him weighing in his head whether to tell me. Finally, he looked up at me with a sheepish smile. "The truth is, I need a gift. For a lady. I thought you could help me pick something out."

"A gift for a lady? Anyone I know?"

"Just come with me, Lora."

There was a plea in Will's voice that made him seem so young, and I felt his need of me like a restorative. It took away my protest, and I heard myself saying, "Well, if you're sure you need me . . ."

His smile was a sudden, blinding thing. It ached in my heart like a bruise, a young, pretty smile so like another one I'd known. I gathered it into that hungry spot inside me.

"I'm sure I need you," he said. "Maybe you could wear a pretty dress, if you have one."

I thought of the invisible green in my closet. I shook my head. "No, I don't think I could."

"Something other than the black, then. What you have on is fine."

I glanced down at my dress, a faded indigo cotton with a tear in the skirt, worn to colorlessness at the edge of the hem. The thread at the seams was starting to wear through, darker than the fabric now after so many days of use, so many washings.

I did not want to go into town, and I had no desire to see my neighbors. There wasn't a woman in the valley who wanted to be seen on a Saturday in North Yakima in her working clothes, and I wasn't any different. I could already hear the gossip that would pass if they saw me come to town in this dress. They would believe I couldn't even afford a Sunday gown, and I was not going to let them think that.

I put Will's breakfast on the table and then I went

upstairs to change. I reached for the black silk, but when I pulled it out, the memories came with it—the morning Eli had shoved those cloth-covered buttons through their loops for me, how he'd looked with red-rimmed eyes and sleeplessness etched on his face—and then I thought of the last time I'd worn it, and the Beaman's buyer, and suddenly I did not want to put that dress on again. Maybe it was Will's plea, or maybe it was just that I wanted again to be the woman who could wear invisible green and laugh over pretty ribbons, but I hung the black back on its hook and lifted out the green.

The twilled surah was stiff, and its folds still held the scent of the lavender toilet water I'd worn the last time I had it on—it was a party at the Zimmermans'; it seemed a hundred years ago. But the music and the laughter seemed to whisper in the very pleats and ruffles of the gown, and as I slipped into it and buttoned it up, those memories caught me, and I forgot the reasons I didn't want to go into town. I forgot about everything but how nice it would be to do something as easy and thoughtless as choosing pretty ribbons.

When I came downstairs again, Will was standing at the washtub drying off his plate. When he turned to see me, I saw the quick light in his eyes, his sudden smile. "Well. Don't you look fine."

I won't say I didn't feel warmed by it, because I did. I felt a little rush of pleasure, and I was so glad I'd decided on the green. "I haven't worn it in a long time."

"You should wear it more often. It makes your eyes look greener."

I thought of Eli, and how much he loved this dress, the way he would lean close and whisper, "You have such beautiful eyes," every time I wore it. There was a melancholy in the memory, and I pushed it away and focused on Will's smile.

He put aside his plate and said, "You have anything you want to take into Ben today? Eggs, maybe?"

It seemed a waste to take that trip clear into North Yakima and not have anything to bring in, but Will had taken in a couple of trays of butter and some eggs for me earlier in the week, along with the letter to Eli to mail, and I hadn't expected to go in again until there was more butter to sell. Not for three or four more days at least. "No," I said. "We should go. I want to get home early enough to get to the garden."

He looked away from me and nodded, and again I had that feeling he was hiding something from me, and it had nothing to do with some girl he wanted to buy ribbons for. But he went out to the barn to harness up Pete, and I forgot all about it. Throughout the long ride to town, I didn't think of it at all. But when we came upon the long line of moving buildings migrating to North Yakima like birds escaping a harsh winter, Will didn't follow them. Instead, he turned the other direction. Away from the new town. Toward the old.

That disquieting feeling came back to me then. I thought maybe he'd forgotten which way to go—but then, how could he have? Those businesses were like bread crumbs tossed to leave a trail for anyone to follow. I looked at him, and he stared straight ahead as if he was trying to avoid my questions. I watched him for a moment, waiting for him to face me, but he never did, and a deadening feeling began to work its way over me, a little panic.

"We aren't going to town, are we?"

"No."

"You're not buying a gift for a lady. There's nothing you need my advice on."

"Afraid not."

I pressed my hands together, but he'd put a fear into me that even that motion could not soothe. "Take me home."

"You don't even know where you're going."

"I don't want to know. Take me home."

"Lora—"

"Take me home."

"I think you need—"

"You don't know what I need," I snapped. "It's none of your concern. You don't know—"

"Irma Peavy's having a tea party today," he reminded me quietly. "I thought you should go."

His quietness took the force from my fear. I felt words shrivel on my tongue and my panic harden into a tiny, cold ball that melted beneath the sadness in his blue eyes.

"We're almost there," he said. "I'll take you home if you like, but it seems a waste to come all this way for nothing."

He could not know how much I'd resented Irma's invitation, what it would be like for me to walk into that room, to see those prying eyes. I had not been to one of Irma's tea parties for a year, and now they would see me standing in that hallway with the finely carved coatrack and the gleaming Hepplewhite table with the silver card service, and they would assume I wanted their confidences again, that I was willing to share mine. Their sympathetic words of comfort would shred the wall I wanted between us.

Just the thought of it was cold on my bones. "I don't want to go. Take me home."

"It won't be that bad."

I turned away from him, staring out at the brown hills, the sage shivering in the wind. "Please, Will."

He pulled on the reins. The wagon stopped; a piece of old metal rolled around in the bed, cracking into the sideboard hard before it went silent, and there we were, sitting in the middle of the dusty prairie, a dot on the blight of the world. The valley was never quiet, and its sounds filled my head, the wind and the rustle of a nearby clump of bunch grass—even the clouds seemed to scrape across the white-blue sky. The shouts of the movers in the distance and the creak of rollers and settling planks echoed over the land, bouncing against ridges, so they sounded as close as Will beside me.

"I don't think Eli would want you to isolate yourself this way," he said quietly.

"I don't think Eli would care." I couldn't keep the bitterness from my voice.

"Well, then, me. *I* don't want you to isolate yourself this way."

The words warmed me, but they hurt, too. I thought of his mother, and how he'd walked away from her, and his leaving loomed in my mind. I wondered how long Eli had convinced him to stay, if there was a time limit in Will's mind, a date he'd set for himself to move on. "It's all right, Will, really. I'll be fine."

"You're not fine." His eyes clouded. Slowly, he reached out, and before I could move away, he brushed a spot below my collarbone, just over my heart, with the tips of his fingers. The touch was so gentle I barely felt it. "You're dying inside, Lora."

It made me think of the oak tree in our yard, slowly dying from the inside out, each spring another branch showing black and withered and budless. I understood too well what he was saying to me.

"You think a tea party is going to help?"

He shrugged. "Couldn't hurt. It might help to take your mind off things."

I stared into the distance at a tiny building, at a cloud of dust. "Sometimes I see my life all laid out across this valley—like a quilt, maybe, with the threads coming loose and these little squares just drifting apart. There's nothing between them but dust and heat. You ever feel like that, Will? As if your life is just a bunch of meaningless days, and all you're doing is just waiting?"

"No. I've never felt like that."

"I suppose you're too young yet."

"You know, Lora," he said slowly, "I left Massachusetts because I didn't want to die one day and discover that I hadn't lived. I mean, living . . . it's all we have, so I guess we've got no choice but to find what meaning we can in it. There's nothing else. You say you're just waiting, and I'm telling you there's nothing to wait for."

He paused, slapping the reins idly against the

palm of his hand. "Look, I'll take you home if that's really what you want. But I wish you'd go to this tea party. I wish you'd go for me."

I heard the discouragement in his words, but I was still seeing my life laid out on that parched ground, still seeing the way a little girl with a whole-face smile had touched each and every square until without her there was no point and no meaning. I knew Will would never understand how that felt, what it was like to have your spirit stretch out empty with a grief and a guilt you couldn't bear to think about.

Yet there was something in him that reminded me of that smile I'd worked so hard to forget, and his pensiveness weighed heavily on me. It made me think of everything I'd lost, everything I missed, and I didn't want something else to regret. I didn't want to disappoint him. I told myself I could bear a few hours of talk and sympathy. Those women would not press if I didn't let them. I could make their compassion disappear by smiling and pretending I no longer needed it.

"All right," I said. "I'll go."

I saw his smile from the corner of my eye. He slapped the reins against Pete's flanks and the wagon jerked to a start, and those things I told myself ground away in dust. In the end, my fear was not so easily banished. It just grew bigger and bigger the closer we got to Yakima City and that big white house. When Will pulled the wagon up in front, it seemed my insides were nothing but one big, shivery dread.

"Look at those flowers," Will said. There was awe in his voice, as if he'd never seen flowers like that before, and I understood it, because the first time I'd seen this place I'd thought the same thing. Irma Peavy's house was like an oasis in a desert. Since her husband was no farmer, they sprinkled that precious water from the irrigation ditch over the land simply for their own pleasure. The house sat in the middle of a big square of green at the edge of town, bordered on three sides by bunch grass and rolling brown prairie, and on the fourth by an empty lot that had once held the drugstore.

Flowers surrounded it; tiny pink roses climbed up the latticework and bloomed fragrant and sweet while yellow ones nodded at the steps and spicy red ones bordered a swing at the edge of the porch. The big fluffy yellow flowers that she was famous for filled a bed at the side. Those flowers must have been four inches across, and they had broad leafy bases and slender stems so the heads shivered in the breeze coming off the ridge. Their beauty reminded me of everything I'd wanted from this valley, everything I'd hoped for.

Will jumped down and came over to help me down. He held out his hand, and I finally managed the strength to grab it.

"I'll wait out here for you," he said. I'm sure he meant his smile to be reassuring, but it only took away my last chance to tell him to take me home. I turned away from him, and I left him there behind me as I walked up the steps to Irma Peavy's porch and stood at the door with the sun breaking in patterns through the latticed sides. From inside I heard voices, a rush of laughter that filled my ears like a foreign language. I felt out of place; suddenly I could not remember what it was I'd talked to these women about, what we'd had in common.

Before I could turn away, I heard footsteps in the hallway. Then Irma was behind the door, smiling as she pushed it open. "I thought I heard someone out here! Lora, I am so glad you decided to come!" She ushered me inside, taking me under an arm clad in yellow striped silk and rose water, hurrying me along the hallway so fast the fancy table and silver and coatrack were only a blur. "Look who's here!" she announced as we went into the parlor. "Lora Cameron!"

I saw those faces looking at me, and I felt myself go stiff waiting for the sympathy to come into their eyes. But I didn't see it. Not in a single face, and that disconcerted me; I felt even more out of place, as if the world had shifted on me. I was ill at ease as they smiled and murmured their greetings in warm, smiling voices.

I knew all of them but one. There was Ursula Anderson, the wife of the minister of the Methodist church, who was no doubt wondering why I hadn't set foot through that door in months; Minnie Reiting, whose husband owned the Feed and Seed; Pamela Porter, the spinster seamstress with a lazy eye that had kept her from a husband even though she was the kindest of souls. The other woman there I'd never met; she was pretty, with her brown hair all done up smoothly and her hands folded gently in her lap. She looked to be the peaceful sort. She looked at me curiously before that curiosity fell away again in calm acceptance.

"I think you know everyone," Irma said to me.

"Except maybe Elizabeth Carter. She's new to town. Just come in with her husband a few months ago. He's with the railroad." Irma looked at Elizabeth and said, "Lora's husband's gone to the Wishkah for a few months. It's what most of 'em should have done, you know. The cherry season's been hard for everyone. No use trying to survive on promises."

"Tom was talking about putting in some fruit for our future," Minnie said. "I told him I couldn't imagine anything less secure."

It seemed impossible to me that anyone could talk so easily of hardship, that these women didn't burst out with their hatred of this place every time they saw me, that I didn't remind them of everything they'd lost.

"It'll bring a good living if you're lucky. I just don't believe much in trusting Mother Nature to bring me luck." Ursula reached for her tea.

"God has a plan for everyone," Pamela said. She smiled at me and patted the chair beside her. "It's good to see you again, Lora. I know it's been hard out there on the bottom."

Ursula said, "We've missed you at church. You have so many friends there. Jane Reese was asking about you the other day. She said she's sent Marcus out at least twice to ask you and Eli to dinner. I told her Samuel and I had done the same."

"And I appreciate it," I murmured. "It's just that with the farm—it's such a busy time of year—"

"Of course. It's like that for everyone," Minnie said. "I've probably got five bushels of tomatoes waiting to can."

"Once winter starts, there'll be so much more time. We should plan something now, don't you think?" Irma asked.

The others nodded in agreement, and I was tense and uncomfortable, holding my breath, waiting for them to chide me for turning down their invitations of comfort and sympathy, to mention the things that kept me away, but no one said anything else about it, and in a way I felt cheated. As if not getting the sympathy I didn't want was unfair, somehow. I wanted allies in pain, and these women were so content the way they sipped their tea and nibbled on cakes made with fine white sugar and egg-salad sandwiches on bread baked of Calla Lily white flour. As if hardship was something to talk about but not to experience. As if the money that bought these fine things could water cherry trees or beat a killing winter. I was already dreading the end of harvest season, when visits were commonplace and long, wondering how I would keep them away.

I took my seat beside Pamela, but I felt a terrible resentment of this tea, and this fine room and the tables that glistened with beeswax and the unfrayed upholstery of the cushioned chairs. It was all an illusion. All the mahogany in the world could not disguise the brown hills rising outside those sparkling windows. You could pretend in a room like this, but you could not escape.

But then Pamela turned to me and smiled again. "Tom Robinson bought some of your butter at Ben's the other day. He said it was some of the finest he's tasted. And then, of course, he said it was a blessing

Ann Robbe's cow went dry, but I try not to encourage that kind of talk."

"Oh, good heavens, Ann Robbe's been making rancid butter for years," Minnie said. "If you ask me, it *is* a blessing."

"I hear she's been too busy to care much about butter." Irma paused, then lowered her voice to a dramatic whisper. "I don't want to be passing gossip, you understand, but I hear she's been encouraging the attentions of a certain blacksmith."

"Not Harvey Jenkins!"

"Now I'm not saying anything. That's just what I heard."

"Oh, my. Well, I suppose if anyone deserves good things, it's Ann Robbe. She's had some hard times herself since Andrew died. She told me last year that the nights were seeming pretty cold."

"Well, I don't imagine they're cold now."

"Irma!"

"The things you say!"

They laughed, and I couldn't help myself. I grinned. Pamela patted my hand. Her eyes were warm and bright. "There now, Lora, it's good to see you smile. Isn't this just what a body needs sometimes?"

I'm not sure how it happened. One moment, I was resenting the women in the room and their easy happiness, and the next, I was warming to Pamela's touch as if I'd just broken out of midwinter and was starving for the light. Their laughter and their talk grabbed me and held on, and before I knew it, I was eating sandwiches and drinking tea rich with cream and sugar, and leaning forward to catch every word.

We talked about the move to North Yakima and the hope that Yakima City would not die, and our husbands' kindnesses and failings and the new shipment of fabric at the mercantile, and with every word I found myself forgetting the world I hated, the memories that haunted me. I'd come into this room thinking I had lost the ability to care about such trivial things, but the mindlessness of talk and laughter was somehow soothing, and by the time two hours had passed, I felt strangely lighthearted. I was glad I had come.

"Come outside," Irma said finally, putting aside the teapot. "I want to show you all the new bed of flowers."

We all rose obediently and followed her. She took us around the house, past the huge bed of yellow flowers, to another, smaller bed that held the same. Elizabeth Carter was beside me. When I looked at Irma, who was explaining to Minnie something about using the flowers to make wine, I caught Elizabeth's glance. She looked out to Will, who was waiting on the wagon, and gave a little nod. "Irma said your husband was on the Wishkah, but that can't be your son."

I shook my head. "Our hired hand."

"It's good your husband left you with some help. I can't imagine what I would do if James went off and left me to fend for myself."

I didn't know what to say to that, so I was silent.

She went on, "I would have my Jimmy to keep me from being lonely, I suppose."

"Jimmy?"

"My son." She smiled tenderly. "He's just five now,

and I declare I love him more with every day. You have any children?"

"No." I looked toward Irma's flowers. The yellow seemed to blur before my eyes.

"Oh, that's too bad. How lonely it must be out there for you."

"It's not so bad," I managed. "I have Will."

"But I thought Irma said your husband—" Her voice went a little flat. "Oh. You must mean your hired hand."

"Yes."

"Hmmm."

There was something in her tone that bothered me, but all I could think about was her five-year-old Jimmy. I wondered if he looked like her, and what he loved, and how he slept. And then I wondered if there would ever be a time when I heard of other children and didn't hear a crying in my heart.

I felt myself foundering, my lightheartedness turning into this little desperation that had me searching for a glance of Will. He was right where I'd left him, in the shade of a huge maple at the edge of the yard, his foot balanced on the wagon brake as he read, and it was strange, but for a moment the whole scene blurred before my eyes, and I didn't see the hills beyond or the bleakness I hated, but just Will's hair shimmering where the sun slanted through the maple leaves. I felt that soft, familiar warmth again, like the touch of light on my skin, and I smelled the roses and the grass and the green scent of water.

Deep inside me, the crying hushed.

"You must take some of these." Irma was beside

me suddenly, pushing a huge armful of yellow flowers along with the leaves into my arms. "Boil those greens up. They're quite a restorative."

"I will."

"And Lora—" She bent close to whisper in my ear. "I am so glad you came. You will be sure to let me know if I can be any help at all?"

I nodded and walked back to the wagon. Will straightened as I came near, and when he saw those flowers in my arms, he smiled. His eyebrows rose in question. "Everything fine?"

"Yes." I buried my face in the flowers, pulling their sour smell deep into my lungs before I handed them over to him.

He held them loosely in his hand, and bent to smell then, and then he pulled up again quickly with a grimace. "They don't smell like much, do they?"

"I like it. And they'll be pretty in the house."

He reached out to help me into the seat. The flowers were like little suns staring back at me, so bright, and his blue eyes shone above them. I thought of how they would look on the table, stuck in an old jar, and how maybe a ribbon wrapped around it would be a pretty touch.

Later, when I thought back on Irma's tea party, it wasn't the talk I remembered, or the companionship, but the way I'd felt looking across the yard at Will, those few seconds when my heart seemed whole again, when I'd seen colors instead of the lifeless landscape of a faded tintype, bent and darkened at the edges.

9

July 25, 1885
Longins Camp

Dear Lora,
    It is late & I am tired but I hav no other time to write to you my dear Today was a hard day and I wish I was home agin I confes I am tired of the smell of pitch and the sawdust and splinters Somtimes my muscles ache so bad it is hard to sleep and my hands are sticky and black all the time but I am sur you dont want to here of my misery
    When I read your letter I wish I had not gon but there is nothing to do about it now. I am disapointed at the cherries I had thought we would get at least 6 cents to the lb and maybe 8 They were not split when I left— did you tell Beamans they were in good shape? I cant believ they are paying only 4 cents per lb so I asume they were cheating you and you must take care that they do not for the apples Be firm Lora They cant cheat you if you dont let them Tell them I will hold them responsible when I get back Dont forget to be firm.

I had counted on 6 cents per lb for the bills and we are sorely hurt by this but there is nothing for it now As for Mason send him a ten dollar payment the last day of the month if you can aford it Tell him I am making good money here and will pay him the rest when I get back Do not give him more and if he will take five and be hapy that is all you should give him.

I had thought to stay longer than we planned but now I am thinking I should come home I hate to give up such good money espes. since it looks like we will cut into the winter if the weather stays dry but with Will hurt I dont feel I can leave you there alone The ditch has to be done before spring or we will have another bad season which we cant aford I supose he wants to move on to and he cant wait forever for me to come back Also I dont want you to get lazy having him fix you supper all the time Im joking my dear I didnt know Will had so many skils but Im glad hes taking good care of you.

Maybe a few more months What do you think? We can use the money I dont plan to stay into the winter but maybe 'til October if things stay this good and you are alright there with Will You must tell me if you think youll be alright.

I think of you all the time and dream of you every nite I keep thinking of when I first saw you and you smiled all the time I miss that smile The other day I was remembring the day we got snowed in and we brought the blankets from the bed and lay around the stove and there was nothing to do but hold you in my arms and you wanted it to I always thought that was

the day . . . well you dont want to here it I guess tho I
want to say it.

But I think of that time and wish for it again and I
can't help wishing that you did to I wonder if things
will ever be that way again What do you think Lora?
Do you think of me to? Has this time apart changed
anythng between us?

I supose I should go to sleep now The days start
early here and the others are alredy asleep I hate to
close my eyes becase all I do is dream of you and when
I wake up theres nothing of you to touch Not much
difrent than at home is it?

I must go Take care of yourself and tell Will to
mend his hand and take care of you to I didnt bring
him out there just to laze thru the summer.

Elijah

2 August 1885

Dear Eli,

Do not wory about Wills hand It is geting beter all
the time but he still cant do much withot help Befor
long it will be good as new He is a help to me even if he
cant dig the ditch yet so I think you sholdnt wory

The weather has been fin & hot cloudless skies &
no rain yet The Pippins are redy & Will & I have
started to pick He is verry fast & a good helper Im
hoping for 500 lbs of those & Spitz. look good for fall.

Last week the fence broke & I had to help Will fix
it due to his hand The fence had rusted lose behind the
barn We fixed it w/some wire Bessie had a good walk

by herself She was nearly to the ridge when Will caugt her Her milk has tasted off for a few days I wonder what she ate out ther Couldnt make butter with it but now its fine.

I supose I shold tell you Will made me go to Irmas on Sat. for tea I didnt want to but he tricked me into it Irma & Minni Reting & Ursula A & Pamela Porter (her eye seems beter thes days) & a lady I didnt know whose name is Eliz. Carter Her husband is w/the railroad & she is nice enough She has a 5 yr old son I didn't want to go but I had a nice time & Irma sent hom some flowers for me They look prety on the table I put thm in a jar w/some blue riben around it Will says it makes him smile to see it & I think you wold like it to.

I hav ben thinking about your staying until Oct at the camp & tho I wold not like it much I think you shold We owe so much mony I havent talked to Will about it but I gues you hired him to stay as long as you were gon & he doesnt seem unhapy her I think he likes someone taking care of him.

I know you are unhapy w/me Eli & so I think its best if you work for awhile & make some mony You mite not beleave me when I say I wish things wer beter between us tho that is how I feel Maybe one day everything will work out I dont know I miss you but I know this is best The house seems empty without you but I gues Will is her to keep me compny.

I think of you all the time to.

Take care of yourself

> *yr wife*
> *Lora*

August 11, 1885
Longins Camp
Wishkah River

Dear Lora,
    It is just dinnertime here and alredy Im so tired I
can hardly think Ten hrs a day doesnt seem so long
until your out cutting trees and then it is forever Ther
is a man here who has worked all the camps and he
says Longins is one of the beter ones If so I would hate
to see worse They call the forman here the bull of the
woods and he is mean as a snake Last week he put a
rat in a mans cork boots becase he didnt like the way
he worked We could here the yelling clear into the
woods.
    Still the pay is to good to leave Im still deciding
what to do about staying to Oct or coming home
sooner but in any case this is between you and me only
Do not tell anyone else these plans in case they get to
woried about money If anyone asks tell them I will be
home to pick the Spitzenbergs That should set them at
ease.
    I am glad you went to Irmas party It seems its
been a long time since you did that I supose Will is
good medicine for you Lora but remember not to get to
close to him Remember you have a husband who loves
you.
    I do wish I could see those flowers I would like it if
when I cam home ther were pictures on the wall again
I always liked that flowered thing you sewd Do you
think you could do that for me? Sometimes when I
cant sleep I think of you bent over your sewing You

always seemd so peceful then I would like to see it again.

    Dinner is over and they are caling us back to work so I must go I will decide when to come home by the next time I write but remember its a matter between us only Remember what I said about Will to He likes the feel of dust under his feet.

Yr afectionate husband,
Elijah

10

Will and I were picking the Pippins when we heard hoofbeats pounding on the road. It was a Sunday, but there was no Sabbath to celebrate when there was picking to be done. Everyone was busy, and I wasn't expecting visitors. Even during the best of times, it was rare for anyone but John to make the journey out here, so when I heard the horse I stopped in surprise and turned to look at the road. Below my ladder, Will had done the same thing. Slowly, he straightened over the half-full apple barrel. Then he looked up at me, frowning. "It's not John."

It was a stranger, a man dressed all in black, a shadow on a horse. I thought for a moment he would keep on riding, but out here there was nowhere else to go. He turned into the yard.

Maybe it was the black, maybe it was just that he was a stranger, but I felt a creeping dread as I climbed down the ladder.

"It's probably just someone passing through," I said as I started toward the house—though I didn't believe it.

Will's hand came out to stop me. "Stay here. I'll go see."

His protectiveness raised my growing tenderness for him, but I didn't let him go ahead of me. I shook my head. "Stay out here. Keep picking. I'm sure it's nothing."

He stood back then and let me go. I thought he'd gone back to the ladder, but when I got to the house, I realized Will had followed me and stood in the shadows so that when the man on the horse looked at me, he had to see Will hovering only a few feet away.

The man was no one I'd seen before, and when I approached, he took off his narrow-brimmed hat and nodded politely. "Miz Cameron?"

"Yes."

"I'm here to talk to your husband, ma'am." He glanced behind me as if he were expecting Will to say something.

"My husband's not at home just now," I said. "Can I help you?"

"I was told to speak to Elijah Cameron."

"He's on the Wishkah. I don't expect him back for some time."

"Ah, well then." The man put his hat back on his head and dismounted. His booted feet thumped hollowly on the dusty ground of the yard. His gaze shot to Will again, then back to me, and he looked uncomfortable as he said, "Hate to bother you on a Sunday, ma'am, I truly do."

"What's the trouble?"

"Name's Earnest Smith, ma'am. I work for Prentiss and Field."

The name was familiar. I saw it scrawled in Eli's handwriting, falling across the ledger page as if it were running downhill. I saw the number behind it. *Prentiss & Field Lumber, $8.75*. Then again, *$6.40*. Then *$49.85*. Sixty-five dollars. More than we'd made off the cherry harvest. More than I thought to have in my hand until Eli came back from Longins Camp.

I nodded toward the porch. "You've come a long way, Mr. Smith. Can I get you a cup of coffee?"

He nodded a little nervously, took off his hat again to run his hand through his thinning hair. "I'd appreciate it, ma'am."

I turned back to Will. "You go on," I said. "I can take care of this."

Something went through his eyes, and his mouth tightened. He turned away, but he didn't go toward the orchard again. He disappeared around the corner of the barn, a closer distance. When he was gone I motioned for Mr. Smith to follow me into the house.

I had not had time to care for the house since Eli had left, and when I brought that stranger inside and saw the dirt on my floors and the bareness of the room, I bent my head to hide my embarrassment and shame. He sat in a chair Eli had fashioned from black birch with a seat woven of leather, and I went to the stove and poured him a cup of coffee from the pot that had been stewing there all morning. It was black and thick and bitter, but he didn't take cream or sweetening in it. I sat on the settee across from him, a hand-me-down from my parents, an old medallion-back with faded striped upholstery that was frayed at the edges. I had poured myself a cup of coffee, too, but mostly because I wanted something to hold on to, something to pause and look into to give myself time to think about what I suspected Mr. Smith had come here to say.

In that moment I wanted Eli there so much the yearning was a sharp taste in my mouth. I would have given anything, I think, to see him ride up.

But the yard was silent except for the chickens. In the distance I heard a steady *chop chop chop*. Will was cutting up sagebrush for the stove.

Mr. Smith took a sip of his coffee. Then he put it down on the table beside him and cleared his throat. "Miz Cameron, it pains me to have to discuss such delicate issues with a lady."

"You're here about the bill, I imagine."

He looked surprised. "Why, yes."

"My husband gave me an accounting of things before he left."

"So you're aware the amount is quite sizable."

"Sixty-five dollars."

He nodded somberly. "We've carried the debt on our books for some time, Miz Cameron. I'm sure you understand that we can no longer do so."

He waited for me to respond. When I didn't, he went on. "I've been sent out by Mr. Prentiss to either collect the amount or—" He bowed his head. "Or bring back something of equal value."

I laughed. "Equal value? Mr. Smith, look around you. Do you see sixty-five dollars anywhere on this land?"

"I did see a cow."

I went cold. I thought of the fence Will and I had mended only days ago, of Bessie wandering aimlessly out toward Ahtanum Ridge. In that moment, I wished she'd kept on going. "You can't have my cow."

"I'm sorry, Miz Cameron, but I've got a job to do."

"Mr. Prentiss seems like a kind man. I'm sure he wouldn't expect you to take my only way of making a living."

Mr. Smith looked uncomfortable. "I have my directions, ma'am."

"It's Sunday, Mr. Smith."

"And I feel badly about it, ma'am. I truly do."

He said the words, but I felt the steel beneath them, and suddenly I understood why Mr. Prentiss used this man to collect his bills. Smith was not leaving until he had something in his hand, and if that meant he had to take Bessie, he would do it.

I did not know what to do. Eli's direction to ask people to wait until his return seemed suddenly impossible—when we'd talked, it was about ghost people, friendly neighbors. It was easy to imagine them smiling and agreeing to wait. But now this man was real in front of me, and I could not imagine how Eli and I had been so naive as to believe people would be kind.

But I tried the words anyway. "My husband will be back at the end of the summer. We'll take care of everything then."

"It's already been much more than a year, Miz Cameron."

"I can't imagine it would hurt to wait a little longer."

"No offense, ma'am, but a business can't run on promises."

"I don't have sixty-five dollars."

"Then what do you have?"

He pushed, and I crumbled. It would be rude to tell him to leave, to order him off my land, and I was not strong enough to make him go. I had no defenses against him. He played my uncertainty and my desperation without sorrow or compunction, and under his steely gaze I found myself going to the ledger where I'd shoved the thirty-two dollars from the cherries and drawing out ten of it. I held it out to him with trembling fingers.

"This is all there is," I said in a whisper, and all I could think of was Mason Albright's bill in there, too, the ten dollars I'd already paid him. All I could think was that the money was nearly gone.

Mr. Smith turned those bills over in his hand and looked at me sorrowfully. "This isn't enough, Miz Cameron."

"We're picking apples now," I said quickly. "I can give you two barrels of apples in a few days."

I saw the calculation in his eyes. "Four barrels, Miz Cameron, and I think I can convince Mr. Prentiss to wait for the remainder until the fall."

Four barrels. It seemed a lot, more than I wanted to promise, but I wanted to be rid of him so badly I could hardly think. I wanted his stink and his clever eyes out of my house. "Four barrels," I agreed.

He stuffed the ten dollars into his pocket and lifted his hat from the table. When he put it on his head, he nodded and smiled, friendly now that he had reduced me to nothing, sweetness now when I wanted to be mean. "Thank you, ma'am. For the coffee and your understanding. I apologize again for the Sunday call."

I didn't show him to the door. I watched him leave and from the window I watched him ride off, and it occurred to me then that Prentiss & Field Lumber had sent him out on a Sunday on purpose. No one would expect him then. It was planned to be disconcerting. As I saw that stiff-backed man head back toward Yakima City, I realized how he had manipulated me, and I felt a quiet despair at the thought of telling Eli what I'd done. I was not good at this. He should never have left me here alone.

I turned away from the window. I had a sudden urge to run after Mr. Smith, to demand back my money and my pride, but I stood there alone in the kitchen until the urge passed and in its place came the hopelessness that I was beginning to grow used to. Its shadow moved over me like the cloud shadows racing across the ridge; I felt small and cold where it touched me.

I began to hear those voices in the room again, those whispered admonitions, and I jerked open the door and stood out on the porch where I could not hear them. At first, I thought they had followed me there, that they had become louder in my head, more real. But then I realized that I was hearing something else—music. Singing. A man's voice coming from the barn.

I had not heard a man sing in so long—forever, it seemed—and the sound of it now pulled at my heart.

Eli had a beautiful voice, deep and full. He had sung to me when we were courting, and later, I used to sit on the porch, embroidering and listening to his voice upstairs, the low, soft strains as he sang lullabies.

It was why I followed this voice now. It was a haunting sound, not quite beautiful, slightly off key. I went toward it quietly. I think I believed it would dash away like a butterfly if it felt me coming too near. The voice grew louder and louder, and when I peeked around the corner of the barn, it was there, in front of me, all around me.

It was Will, of course. I don't think he saw me, or even knew I was there. His back was to me as he stacked chopped sagebrush against the shelter Eli had erected next to the barn. He was sweating, there were wood splinters clinging to his shirt, a fluttering gap on the sleeve where barbed wire had torn it when we fixed the fence. He had on Eli's work gloves, and he was singing in rhythm with his stacking: "Rock-a my soul" *thump* "in the bosom of Abraham" *thump* "Oh, rock-a my soul" *thump*.

He finished the song and stood back, swiping his forearm across his face, turning to grab another piece. I'm not sure why, but I stepped back so he wouldn't see me, and when the chopping started again, and another song, I crept away, back into the yard, toward the house.

I was nearly there when I recognized the new song Will was singing, a sweet hymn that brought back a memory of darkness and campfires, of the lone howl of a coyote in the distance, the soft bubble and hiss of Soda Springs beyond, the cool of the night and a sky filled with stars and Eli's arm warm and strong around my shoulders, his breath against my ear. They tell me that no tears ever come again, in that lovely land of unclouded day. . . .

I stood there for a long time, hearing that voice, and it wasn't until I felt the chickens pecking and clucking around my feet that I realized it wasn't real, but only a memory.

Eli had not sung for a long, long time. I wondered how it had escaped me, how I had never seen that Eli had grown quiet and still these last months, that his joy had dried up with his voice. It made me sad that it took his absence for me to see that something had disappeared without my missing it.

And though I went to the house and started supper, the sadness didn't leave me. The memory of that night at Soda Springs with Eli stayed in my mind, the things I'd forgotten about him, and I wondered how those things had got lost, how I had let them fall away from me. Sometimes life made it so easy to forget the good things. What was hard was wanting to hold on to them so they didn't go missing again.

11

19 August 1885

Dear Eli,
*   I am afrade you will be sory you left me here alon this summer I have more bad news Prentis & Field sent out a colector last week on a Sunday (!) & I am afrade I had to pay him some mony He said he wold take Bessie if I didnt so I gave him 10 dolers & promised 4 barel of apples He said he wold wait for the rest when you got hom I know you will not be hapy for this but I could think of nothing els to do Now with 10 dolers gon for Mason we have only 12 dolers from the cheries I am sory Eli but what else could I do? I could not give him Bessie.*
*   I supose you must think what a poor wife I am & I dont blam you for it Im trying as best I can Eli you must beleave me I promis to get beter & you must not think of coming hom sooner becase of it I think you shold stay as long as you can After that bill colecter I dont think anyone has much patiense w/us anymor & we need the mony.*

We hav picked 7 barels of apples so far & hav
more trees to go It is just me & Will picking this time
becase John is to busy w/his own trees Boyd came out
to tel me he was sory they couldnt help Ther is not
really enough to need them.

The other day I cam upon Will singing whil he
choped wood & tho he isnt a good singer he mad me
think of you & how you used to sing I had forgoten
that Eli—the way you sang so Remembr when we
went to Soda Springs that time & you made me laugh
when you made up the words to "The Old Gray
Mare"? I remeber to that song "The Unclowded
Day."

I mis that Eli You used to sing to me when we
wer courting & I always loved it Tho if you dont
want to sing anymor I gues you have reson Maybe
you are singing in the trees now wher I cant here
you.

Take care of yourself.

> Yr loving wife,
> Lora

August 25, 1885
Longins Camp
Wiskah River

Dear Lora,

You must be more firm with these people I talked
to Prentiss & Field before I left and we had an
agrement to wait til I cam back so they were taking
advantage of you knowing I was gon They will be

lucky now to get the rest of it I will have a word with Jim Prentiss when I get back but for now do not giv them one more thing Jim wold sooner have money than apples I think so do not take them the 4 barrels you promised Sell them insted and I will take it up with Jim when I get back I dont know what prices are this year but they must be more or the same as last so do not sell those apples for less than 2 cents lb Take John Zimerman with you if you must to get a fair price.

We got paid last week so find in this letter ten dollars to keep for me until I get home Write to me befor you spend it so I can advice you and tell Will I want him to stand firm w/you against anymore bill colectors If he cant work becase of his hand he can at least do that.

I dont know now about staying thru October I dont like to think of you alon and at the mercy of bill colectors who should know better It wories me so I cant sleep and I spend my days tired enough alredy Some nights I am awake until the work bell rings in the morning You must know what Im thinking about I remember how you feel against me and how your hair looks in moonlight I remember Soda Springs to and how we stayed awak and your smile when we talked about our plans Maybe they didnt all work out Lora or maybe what hapened was Gods will but I think its wrong to giv up trying I dont think thats what is ment for us.

Yr Husband,
Elijah

2 September 1885

Dear Eli,

    Everything is fin We got 12 barels of apples John took them in to sell with his & we got 2¢ per lb We had 600 lbs so ther is 12 more dolers in the ledger now But the Spitzinbrgs are worse now they are not geting as big as they shold Just as big as last yr which you know was bad. Wether is hot & dry & no sign of storms so that is good news.

    Wills hand is much beter now.

Yr wife,

Lora

September 12, 1885
Longins Camp
Wishkah River

Dear Lora,

    Im glad about the apples Well hav to see about the Spitzes they might not be as bad as you think and no one is having a good yr so I dont think they will be wors than anyone else.

    Now that Wills hand is beter I hop hes working on the ditch again We must get as much dug before the winter as we can We cant go thru another bad spring or Ill be back here agin next yr.

    Lora it would be nice if you would write me some loving words I liked your letter about Soda Springs but your last one was cold and that is not what I need here so far away from you I supose you do not want to talk about the things I want to talk about and if you ask me not to I gues I will not mention them agan But befor I do that I have to say that I think of you all the time and I dream of Eva to I remember that first day she cam to us and how clos you held her and how you smiled I miss her Lora more than I can say but I think she was sent to us for a reson and taken away for one to She was to good to stay here with us I think you know that to Nothing makes it beter Lora but we could make it barable together.

That is all I will say about it now In your next leter plese send kind words to becase I miss you and it is lonly here.

Yr husband,
Elijah

It was late at night when I read Eli's letter, and when I saw Eva's name, for a moment, I felt her arms around my neck, warm and soft. I felt little hands sticky with berries and fallen green apples, small wet lips that puckered to kiss mine. I smelled her—milk and dirt, sunshine on skin—and my heart reached for that smell.

I sat there in the darkness, alone, my eyes so dry they burned, and then I folded the letter until it was a tight, tiny square, and tucked it away in the night table so I could not find it again. So I would not remember.

~ *part* 2

God answers deep and sudden some prayers,
And thrusts the thing we have prayed for in
   our face.
A gauntlet with a gift in 't—Every wish
Is like a prayer, with God.

—ELIZABETH BARRETT BROWNING

12

There are days that change your life forever. Sometimes, you know when they're coming, or at least, you
recognize the moment that changes everything.
Other times, those changing days sneak up on you.
It's not until long after the day fades, and the years
pass and blur together, that it stands out in your
memory so you can look back and say, *Yes, that was
when it happened, that was the time. . . .*

But usually, you don't get a warning. You wake up
in the morning, and you think you know the contours of the day stretching before you. You think you
know its shape. But a day is uncertain, and there's
never a sign to show you that in one hour or two,
there will be none of the old you left. All you get is
hindsight and the sense that you were a fool for not
seeing the obvious.

On the morning everything changed again, I
wasn't thinking much of anything. I was up early to
do the wash, and my head was full of soap and kettles
and sorting linens from ginghams.

The house was dark and quiet; even Will hadn't

stirred yet. It was still cool, though it wouldn't be for much longer, and I hurried to light the stove and draw water from the well. Laundry was something best started early, before it got too hot.

I didn't like doing wash. I'd never known anyone who did. But that morning, standing there in the soft pink dawn of my kitchen, filling kettles with water to boil, I wanted the way it would claim my hours for the next two days, the peace it would bring me at night—the blissful ache of muscles too tired to stay awake, the bone-tired silence of my mind. I wanted to think of nothing but piles of freshly folded laundry and perfectly ironed linens, to feel nothing but the roughened, cracked skin of my hands and the burn of harsh lye soap in my nostrils—a smell that lingered in my nose for hours after.

By the time I heard Will's footsteps on the stair, the kettles were starting to boil, and steam was clouding in the kitchen.

Will stopped as he came in.

"Wash day," I told him before he had a chance to ask. I'd pulled a pair of Eli's old ragged trousers and a shirt from the trunk at the foot of our bed. I pointed to where I'd laid them on the chair. "Put those on. Eli's taller, but they should fit all right until I can get your clothes washed."

"My clothes?" he asked. He shook his head. "I won't have you washing my clothes, Lora."

"I'm doing everything. Might as well do yours, too."

"They're clean enough."

I glanced over my shoulder at him. "You smell like the Ahtanum."

He hesitated, and I saw him weighing things in his head. His voice was quiet. "I don't want a servant. Not any man, but especially not you."

I sighed. "Some things don't ask to be sorted out like that, Will. I don't like people thinking that I can't keep you in clean clothes." He looked like he might protest again, and I was already hot and too irritable to argue with him. "*I* don't like you looking so grimy. Please."

He closed his mouth and took Eli's clothes, and then he left without another word. When he came back he was carrying a limp feed bag with a bulge in the bottom. He set it on the floor near the door. "Here they are. I wish you wouldn't, but . . . thank you."

"You can't go on washing your things in the river."

He shrugged. "It serves well enough."

"What happens when the fall comes? Do you know how cold that water gets? It could freeze up come winter, all along the bank. How would you wash your clothes then?"

He gave me a look, and I glanced away, not wanting to read it, not wanting him to say what I knew he was thinking, that he would not be around in the winter to care. And I suppose it was what made me say, "Eli's thinking of staying on into the fall."

I was not looking at him, but I felt Will's stiffening in the change of the air. His voice was expressionless when he said, "Into the fall?"

"Till October, maybe."

I waited for him to protest. I felt that waiting all up along my spine, and for a minute I closed my eyes, thinking that maybe if I pretended I hadn't said it, he wouldn't answer, wouldn't talk about his leaving.

"He must be making good money over there."

I tried to keep the relief from my voice. "He says he is."

Will didn't answer, and I told myself that was good. I told myself this was an unspoken agreement, that as long as he didn't say *I'm going*, it meant he would stay.

But I was still on edge waiting for him to leave. He was working on the ditch again, now that his hand was better, so I knew I wouldn't see him for most of the day. But I kept watching for him, and not seeing him made me nervous, as if he might just walk away without saying good-bye, leaving me with his clothes and nothing else while he took to the road, Eli's trousers cuffed in fat rolls at his ankles, flapping at the legs.

I tried not to think about it as I did the wash, but then I saw the rip from tending barbed wire in Will's shirt, and I wasn't sure which was worse: thinking of his leaving or thinking of how ragged he looked, and how Eli had gone to the Wishkah looking like a hobo—and how I should have done something about it.

By the time I'd finishing rubbing and rinsing and put the clothes in the tub to take around back, it was past noon. Behind the house some distance was a fire pit Eli had built so I wouldn't have to do the boiling in the house. The washtub was near the back door, an old, blackened thing made of iron and heavy as the world. I prodded it with the long wooden wash paddle leaning against the wall, making sure no rattler had decided to take up residence in the weeks since

I'd last done the laundry. It took nearly all my strength to drag it over to the fire pit, and when I pulled the washtub full of rinsed clothes over to it, I felt the ache all through my body. The sodden clothes were heavy and hot; I was sweating and my apron and the front of my dress were soaked through as I lifted them into the tub and drew more water to fill it. Then I scooped soap into it, built the fire, and stood back.

The clothes had to be boiled for thirty minutes, and it was my least favorite part of wash day. Except for stirring it now and then, there was nothing to do but wait. I couldn't walk away and do something else, because of the fire danger. The wood was full of sap that snapped and sparked; there were already black spots in the yard where I'd stamped out little fires from other wash days.

I was standing over that kettle, stirring it with the wooden paddle and trying to keep my dress tucked between my legs so my skirts didn't catch in the flames, when I first heard the horses and the creaking rattle of wagon wheels. The last visitor had been Mr. Smith from Prentiss & Field, and since he'd been out I'd been on edge waiting for someone else. In every cloud of dust in the distance I saw a horse and rider— even when the wind faded and the dust settled to nothing.

Now it seemed that all those panics gathered together in my chest, and they turned into an anger that I'm sure showed on my face when a man I didn't know rounded the corner of the house.

He stopped short when he saw me. He looked disconcerted for a moment, and then he raised his hat

and spoke quickly, as if he were afraid I would run
him off. "Miz Cameron? You are Miz Cameron?"

I thought of Eli's words, written in hard-pressured
pencil, underlined. *Be firm.* I lifted the paddle from the
washtub, but I didn't put it down. I held it like a
weapon. "Who wants to know?"

The man swept a nervous hand through his dark,
too-long hair. "Harry Wheeler. My name's Harry
Wheeler, and I—" He cleared his throat. "I—uh—got
your husband in the wagon out front. I'm afraid he
didn't take the trip too well."

I was sure I hadn't heard him right. "My husband?
You must have the wrong place. My husband's on the
Wishkah."

Harry Wheeler shook his head. "Not anymore, he
ain't."

His words were a jumble in my head first, and then
they lined themselves up, I heard them again. *I got
your husband in the wagon. I got your husband. . . .*

I dropped the paddle. I heard it thud with some
part of my mind, but I felt frozen there, and dread
and fear moved through me like the current in a river.

"They didn't send someone to tell you, then?"

His words snapped something inside me. "Tell me
what? What happened to him?" It sounded as if my
voice came from far away, and it was high and
shrieky. A wind came up, dust swirled up around his
legs, and the steam billowed before my eyes, so he
looked like a ghost standing there. I backed away,
stumbling over the rocks rimming the fire pit, hitting
the ground hard with one knee.

He was there beside me in a moment, helping me

up. I saw kindness in his brown eyes. "It's all right, ma'am. Truly, it is. He's passed out, is all. That ride ain't easy on anyone. I won't lie to you. He's in bad shape. But he ain't dead. Though I guess there'll be times he'll wish he was."

All I heard was *But he ain't dead,* and my breath just stopped. I was glad for the steadiness of his arm as he led me around the corner of the house to the buckboard I'd heard only a few moments ago, drawn by two sweaty and tired-looking mules, who were already taking water from the scum-covered trough in the yard. Eli's horse, Old Max, was tied to the back, looking resigned.

I'm not sure what I expected to see. It all felt unreal, somehow—this man I'd never met before, the brown-faced mules, a splintery gray wagon in the middle of my yard. I think there was a part of me that refused to think he had the right farm, that it wasn't Old Max standing there, that there was another Eli Cameron somewhere who was hurt, but not mine.

So when I let go of Harry Wheeler's arm and went to the side of the wagon to look in, I expected to be able to turn to him and say, *This is not my man.*

Instead, I saw Eli lying there.

I felt the blood leave my face. I couldn't take my eyes from him, and my first thought was that Harry Wheeler was wrong, that Eli had to be dead, because I had never seen him look this way, so still and cold and white. His eyes were closed, his lashes dark against his skin, his cheeks drawn in hollow and empty. It was a moment before I saw that he was breathing, little, shallow breaths that barely raised

his chest. A dirty blanket flecked with wood chips
and splinters and dust covered him from the waist
down.

"It's his legs," Harry Wheeler said from behind
me. "It was a widowmaker."

I glanced up, and that was when I saw Will beyond
him, coming from the orchard, pulling up when he
saw Harry Wheeler, then running as if he sensed
something wrong, Eli's trousers bouncing around his
ankles.

"What is it?" Will stopped, breathless. He looked
at me, and then at Harry Wheeler, and his eyes nar-
rowed. "What's going on?"

Harry shook his head. "It don't look good. I
thought it would be best if he was covered—"

Will glanced at me again, and then a look of fury
came over his face, something I'd never seen before.
"What the hell are you doing, letting her see this?" He
crossed to me in two steps and grabbed my shoulders, yanking me away. He pulled me into his arms
and pushed my face into his shoulder. He was shaking, and he pressed me into him so hard I felt the
dampness of his shirt against my lips, tasted the salt
of his sweat. "Lora," he said in my ear. "Lora, I'm
sorry. I'm so sorry."

I pushed my hands against his chest. Maybe it was
just his touch, but suddenly my shock was gone; I
could think of nothing but that I wanted to see my
husband's legs. I had to see them. I thought of my
father, jerking through the wheat fields, and I imagined Eli like that, and then I had a horrible vision of
his legs gone completely, of Eli's never needing

trousers again. Will held me as if he was reluctant to let me go, but then finally, he did.

I reached for the blanket covering my husband, and at my touch Eli stirred, he jerked a little.

Will jumped back. "Jesus! He's moving!" He looked at me in confusion. "But I thought he was . . . dead."

"Could have been," Harry Wheeler said. "Not many men live through a crush like that."

I heard the words in the back of my mind, but I was thinking of something else, of Eli striding into the yard, his legs tight and muscled, that easy smile on his face. I was afraid to look, but I couldn't stop myself from pulling down that blanket. And then . . . and then I felt as if everything inside me just stopped.

His legs were there, but they were bandaged and splinted so he couldn't move them, and the bandages were oozing blood in places, as if the wounds had been jarred open again during the hard journey. One leg was wrapped up to the hip; his long underwear had been cut to allow for it, and the edges were jagged and unraveling, tiny threads trailing across the dirty bandages. The other leg was wrapped only to mid-thigh. But the bloodiest bandages were on that leg, and as I pulled the blanket down I saw that his feet were wrapped, too, even his toes.

I pulled the blanket up again and looked up to see Will watching me closely. His gaze lingered on mine for a moment, and then he looked at Harry Wheeler. "What happened?"

"We'd best get him inside first," I said.

Eli mumbled and twitched as they moved him.

His skin was burning hot, his lips cracked and dry with fever, and when they grabbed his legs to lift him from the wagon, he croaked a scream, a low, horrible thing, and then he went limp.

Harry sighed. "Thank God."

I did not know how they would get him to the bed, and when they got him inside the house, I saw Harry glance at those close, narrow stairs. He was struggling with the burden of Eli's legs while Will held his shoulders.

"I don't know if we can get him up there," he said.

"There's no place for him down here." Will jerked his head to the settee. "Just that."

The settee was hardly long enough for Eli to lie down. There was no other choice than the loft, and I was glad Eli was unconscious as they tried to bring him up there, because I did not think I could stand to hear that scream again. I hurried upstairs after them, watching them struggle with him, hovering over my husband, and everything else fell from my mind, all our troubles, the reasons I'd wanted him to stay away—everything except how to keep him alive. Things listed themselves in my head: I needed laudanum, and there was comfrey out by the back stoop to pick and boil down for poultices. I had to find more pillows, and the doctor would have to come out. . . .

I thought of those things instead of the fear that he would die. I wouldn't let myself think of it. I pulled back the covers on the bed and Will and Harry almost dropped him into it. I knelt at his side, pushing back the damp hair from his sweaty forehead. "Will, get some pillows," I ordered. "Take them off the settee—

and there's an extra blanket in the trunk." Harry stood back while I did my best to make Eli comfortable, and he never lost that sorry, hopeless expression that filled me with dread. I had to stop looking at him. I put the pillows under Eli's legs when Will brought them and tucked the blankets around. Even though it was hot in the room, Eli was shaking with fever.

I left Harry and Will there to watch Eli, and I hurried downstairs and picked comfrey leaves from the plant behind the back door, and boiled them up into a poultice. When I took it upstairs, and went to undo the bandages, Harry stepped forward and put out his hand to stop me. "I don't think you'd better do that, Miz Cameron. It ain't a pretty sight."

I looked up at him. "He's my husband," I said, and then Harry stepped back and Will went still in the corner of the room. Neither of them said anything more as I began to unwrap Eli's legs.

I don't know what I expected, but it wasn't what I saw. I had never seen anything like it. Eli's right leg was a purple so deep it looked almost black, and though the bones had been set, there were big gashes where they'd torn through the skin, and those were oozing deep red and sticky. It shook me, and I grabbed the edge of the bed and swallowed, trying to calm myself, focusing instead on the other leg, the one Harry had said was not so bad. There, the bruising was dotted across pale skin, a big purple mark at his thigh and another sliding over his calf, not black again until the ankle. They were both so swollen they didn't even look like legs, and his feet were terrible, mangled and misshapen, swollen so they were archless, formless. When I saw them, I wanted to cry, but I made myself go on.

Eli didn't even flinch when I applied the poultices, and I was thankful for that, because I could not imagine how painful my touch must be. I focused on packing the warm herbs tight around his legs, and making sure the splints were straight when I rebandaged him, tying the pillows around him with cloth strips. I tried not to think that this was my husband lying there, I tried to see those bruised and swollen legs as someone else's, but when everything had been done, the image of them kept coming into my head, and with it came a worry that wouldn't let me leave his side.

Will brought up some coffee and handed a cup to Harry Wheeler, who sagged into the chair that had always held Eli's clothes at night. Then Will offered some to me. I took it, but I couldn't drink it. I kept thinking: *Is there something else I could do? Something I've forgotten?*

But then Will said to Harry, "Why don't you tell us what happened?" and I found myself straining to listen, needing to hear.

"He was lucky," Harry said. "You might not think so, but I seen men killed with less. Me and him were anchored into a big one this time. Maybe twenty feet across, branches big around as I am. We had it maybe half cut. It was starting to creak, you know. Just about the time to cut loose and let her fall. Then one of them branches snapped off. By the time I heard it, it was already on him. Snapped his springboard right in half, trapped him underneath. If it'd fallen a few feet to the left, it would've killed him. A few feet to the right and he'd be in the bunkhouse today boasting about a close call."

Harry took another sip of coffee. The story lingered, words I barely understood, things I couldn't picture. My lungs hurt; I could hardly breathe thinking of that branch falling, trapping Eli, wondering how much pain he'd felt, if he'd thought he was going to die, what he'd said.

"What did the doctor say?" I whispered. "Is he . . ." I couldn't bring myself to say the words. I couldn't even think them.

Harry gave me a sympathetic look. "The truth is, I don't know, ma'am. Doctor wanted to amputate his right leg at first, but then he decided to wait. You saw it, Miz Cameron, so I won't lie to you. It got crushed pretty bad. They said every bone's been broken from the knee down. Some twice. His left leg's broken in two places, up here"—he touched his thigh—"and down under the knee. That foot's in bad shape, though. I'll be honest with you, ma'am. You should get your own doctor out here right away. That fever keeps on, or blood sickness sets in . . . Well, it's possible, they said, that they may have to take off one or the other. Maybe both. I don't like to tell you this, ma'am, but . . . the doctors at camp said maybe he won't walk again."

I didn't know what to say. The words seemed so unreal. Just as Eli felt unreal, how still he was, how quiet. Not the man who'd written from the Wishkah with pitch on his hands, missing me in darkness.

"Thanks for bringing him home," Will said.

"Yes, thank you," I said.

"I was leaving there anyway. Time to move on."

"You should stay the night. Let me thank you by resting up your animals, feeding you some supper. It's the least I could do."

"I'd surely appreciate that," Harry said. "It's been a long way. He wasn't . . . well, it was hard work getting him here. I could use a rest."

Will nodded. "Let's get your animals taken care of, then. I'll show you where you can put your things."

Harry rose. "Oh, I almost forgot." He reached into his pocket and pulled out a stained and crumpled piece of paper. "His final pay," he said, handing it to me. "It ain't much. The doctor took most of it."

I took it and smoothed it out. Thirteen dollars. A summer's worth of work, and all there was to show for it was this and the ten dollars Eli had sent me earlier, and my husband lying crippled on the bed beside me. I almost cried then. I nodded at Harry and pushed the draft into my pocket. My voice hardly came out at all. "Thank you."

Harry sighed. He had a slumped look about him, as if now that he'd brought Eli home, his reason for being was gone. He was just a hobo logger like the others Eli had written me about. Men who had nothing and no one. Men who yelled at him to turn out the light as he was writing to his wife.

They went out the door, and I heard their footsteps and their voices fading as they headed across the yard. I sat on the edge of the bed, listening until there was nothing left to listen for, only the sound of the wind and the birds, and then I looked at Eli. I could almost think of him as sleeping, if not for the sickroom smell of comfrey and the image of those legs lingering in my head. It was like a long-ago dream: his dark head against the threadbare white pillowcase, the dirty gray of his underwear. I had never seen Eli so still. Even sleeping, he'd always tossed and turned restlessly, as if he read lists in his dreams of things that had to be done, things he could not delay. This still man was a man I didn't know, and I wondered if these two months away had changed him, if this life away from me had turned him into someone I wouldn't recognize.

He didn't move as I came closer, or when I pulled his empty chair to the side of the bed and sat down. After a while, I reached out, and it had been so long since I touched him that it felt wrong now to do it when he wasn't awake to see—an intimacy he wouldn't welcome, one I didn't want him to discover.

His skin was damp, hot, but I didn't take my hand away, and it surprised me to have the memory of him come so strongly back to my hand. I knew the feel of his muscles and his bones. There was a scar on his shoulder, and unerringly my fingers remembered it, traced the ridge of it beneath cotton like a river on a map.

I couldn't take my hand away—I felt him living beneath my palm, his breath, his pulse, and I tried to take hope in that, to not let myself think about how he might die. I sat there that way for a long time. I didn't move even when I heard yelling outside, Will's shouts for Harry to come quick, there was smoke in the back.

The wash had boiled dry.

13

Eli spent the night tossing and turning while I watched from the chair and tried to keep his fever down. I had Will chip some ice from what was left in the icehouse, so I had cool water to sponge Eli with, but by the time even an hour had passed, the water was lukewarm again. The nights were cool now, but the loft held the heat close. Our bedroom was always hot in the summer and cold in the winter, and well before dawn I went downstairs to sleep as best I could on the settee, because I was afraid I'd hurt Eli just by being near him.

But the settee was hard and uncomfortable, and I couldn't sleep anyway, worrying over him, over those bloodied and broken legs. The thought that I might lose him haunted me the rest of the night. All I could think was, *Not him. Please God, not him too.* Three times I went back upstairs to make sure he was still alive, and his breathing was so shallow and light that I had to bend close and hold my own breath to hear him. Even then all I heard was the pounding of my heart in my ears, and finally I had to put my hand on his chest to measure its rise and fall. By the time morning came, I could not believe I'd ever let him cut trees on the Wishkah.

I heard Will ride for the doctor before sunup, when the faint light was just beginning at the horizon. He didn't come in for breakfast or to see how things were, he just rode off. I heard Pete's hooves pounding, and they were gone in a cloud of dust. Soon after I heard Harry Wheeler make his slow way out of the yard. He didn't even stop in to say good-bye or ask for breakfast, and that was fine with me. I didn't have time for that.

There was nothing important now but Eli. When I wiped his brow with the cloth, he stirred a little beneath my hand, and then he groaned again, that horrible dry scream deep in his throat. When it was over, I left him, but that sound banged around in my head as I milked the cow and stoked the stove. I made a thin mush that I knew he would not wake up to eat, and I brewed coffee so strong the bitterness burned my tongue when I drank it. Then I went back upstairs and watched the ridge from the bedroom window, and waited and worked to keep my panic from making me any more afraid.

When Will and the doctor finally did ride up, I was so relieved I ran downstairs. But Dr. Lockwood looked grave even before he dismounted and climbed the steps to the porch.

"Has he woke up yet?" he asked me.

I shook my head, bristling at his gruffness. I'd always thought John Lockwood was too tired and old to be a good doctor. There was no compassion left in him, as if the weight of the land and the dying had simply pressed it into a place so far inside him that he could no longer find it. He'd been a circuit doctor when Yakima City had been nothing but two or three houses bundled together in the midst of a vast and treeless desert, and now he had a little office next to the livery that he didn't like to leave. But in that moment, I would have welcomed anyone.

Lockwood reached into his coat pocket and took out a handkerchief, patting it over his face, lifting his wire spectacles to mop up what looked like a river of sweat coursing from his temples. He glanced through the open door and grabbed the bag Will handed him. "Where is he?"

"Upstairs," I told him. I stood back to let him inside, and made to follow him. Will's voice stopped me.

"Lora, are you all right?"

He was frowning, and there were tired smudges beneath his eyes, as if he hadn't slept either for worrying, and it was the one comfort I took from the morning—that Will cared enough to worry, even though the mother in me did not want him bearing that burden. I tried to smile reassuringly. "Everything will be fine," I said, though I didn't know myself if I believed it. Then I followed the doctor upstairs.

Dr. Lockwood was about fifty, and he was a big man. He puffed as he climbed those steep, narrow stairs, the heavy leather bag he carried banging against the wall every second or third step. When he got to the top, he paused. "Whew." He pulled at the collar that looked too tight for his neck. The handkerchief made its rounds again. "Hot up here."

"I tried to keep him cool," I said. I gestured feebly to the open window and to the basin of water beside the bed.

"Good." It was little more than a harrumph. I had to listen to hear the word in it. I stood back, grinding my hands in my apron and waiting for him to speak the words I was terrified I would hear, that there was no hope for Eli, that he would not survive this. But Lockwood only pulled back the blankets to look at Eli's bandaged legs. His sigh was heavy, world-weary. It was not the kind of sound meant to give hope or bolster faith.

"Can you help me here, Lora?" he asked. He glanced at me over the top of those too-frail spectacles. The bottom half of his eyes seemed huge—like fish eyes. It was disconcerting enough that I had to look away. "I'm going to cut these bandages off so I can take a look. I'll need you to hold him if he starts to thrash around. Can you do that?"

"Yes." My voice was a whisper.

"It won't be pretty. If you're planning on swooning, I'd just as soon have that boy up here instead."

"I've seen them already. I'll be fine." I wasn't sure of that—I didn't know if I could stand to look at those legs again—but it was my duty to help my husband, and I was not going to add the shame of swooning to everything else.

Dr. Lockwood fumbled around in his bag and took out a pair of shears. I could not take my eyes from them as he cut the bandages down the length of Eli's leg. Those blades were rusty-looking, flecked with dark spots that it occurred to me must be blood from some other patient. Eli didn't move. When the doctor was done, he set the shears aside and began to peel away the bandages.

"Comfrey," he said, taking away the poultices and letting them fall with a plop to the floor. "Better than nothing, I guess." But then he started muttering to himself, and I caught the words *bad* and *hopeless*. He prodded and poked, testing here, feeling there, twisting . . . Eli jerked in the bed, screaming out before he fell back again, blissfully unconscious, and it was so quick I didn't have time to grab for him, to hold him still. I was afraid to look at Dr. Lockwood then, but I felt his displeasure, and I heard his muttered "Women . . . where's that boy?"

Finally, he looked at me and shook his head long and slow. "There's a lot gone wrong here, Lora. I think the left leg'll end up all right. Maybe a bit of a limp. Won't know that 'til we see how that foot heals. If it does. The other one . . ." He shrugged, and his gaze was straightforward and blunt as his words. "Might be better just to take it off. But we'll see. There's no rotting set in yet. You'll have to keep it dry and clean. I suppose comfrey can't hurt."

I felt tears start at the corners of my eyes, and I looked down so he wouldn't see.

"You'll have to keep his fever down. Just keep the water as cool as you can. I know it's hard in this god-forsaken heat. And—" He fumbled in his bag, pulling out a thick brown bottle with a flourish. "Give him laudanum for the pain. It won't take it away, but it'll help some."

I took the bottle and slid it into my apron pocket,

where it banged against my thigh, a reassuring heaviness. As Dr. Lockwood put laudanum-soaked rags on Eli's legs and rebandaged them, I listened to his other instructions carefully, drawing hope from each word, feeling more relieved every second. Eli was not going to die. The doctor had said nothing about dying.

But then, just as he was leaving, Dr. Lockwood looked back at me from the doorstep. "Eli have any other family?"

"No. I mean, he hasn't heard from them in years. They're back in Ohio."

"You might want to get in touch with them. Just in case."

The threat of it was there again, that terrible ghost nodding over the doctor's shoulder, waiting, and I had a sudden vision of another coffin in the ground—*ashes to ashes, dust to dust*—this land welcoming us the only way it knew how.

"I'll send the bill out," the doctor went on, "and I'll try to be back in a day or two. But rot can get into that leg so fast Eli could be gone before I can get out here again. If that happens, you send that hired hand of yours to town to let me know. Don't want to make the trip all the way out here for nothing."

I suppose I watched Dr. Lockwood go, but I can't remember it. I stood gripping the porch rail and hearing those terrible final sacraments in my head, echoing into the wind, so that when Will came hurrying around the corner I barely heard or saw him. I felt grim and desperate, and it must have showed on my face, because Will skidded to a stop when he saw me and nearly ran up the porch stairs to grab my shoulders. My hands would not let go of the rail; gently Will peeled them loose and forced me down onto the bench. He sat close beside me, and he was so warm. So wonderfully warm.

"What is it? What did he say?"

My voice, when it came, sounded numb and dead. "He doesn't know if Eli will walk again. They might have to take his leg—if he doesn't die from it first."

Will was quiet for a moment. I expected the usual things: sympathy, words meant to console that only made the pain cut sharper. I was used to such consolation. It did not seem so very long ago that it had filled every day.

"Eli's got a strong will. You think he'll object to living, even if he's got only one leg?" he said, and then pulled me into his shoulder. I could feel the smooth thickness of his hair against my cheek.

I didn't know how to answer. The last year had changed Eli and me. I didn't know what we were anymore, or what he held inside him. The only true thing I knew was what I said. "I shouldn't have let him go. We should have found another way."

"There's no point in thinking that. Maybe there's a reason for all this, Lora."

Will's voice was weightless and soft, like a spiderweb spread across a pathway, but it stayed with me, the way a web sticks to your skin in that moment before you brush it away and go on. *We make our own world.* It was what Will had said that day we were picking cherries, the day he hurt his hand. It reminded me of Eli's letter, of words given presence and weight by his pinched handwriting: *I think she was sent to us for a reson and taken away for one to.*

I didn't believe in those things. I couldn't bear what believing would tell me about myself. But there was nothing else to believe in, either, and in that moment the burden of Eli's accident seemed too much, unbearable. I could not think that fate, or God, or destiny would demand so much of me.

I pulled away from Will, and his arm fell limply to his side. I remembered then that he would be leaving soon. Now that Eli was back, Will would have to go out into the world he loved, and I would have to let him go the way all mothers release their children.

He squeezed my hand and said, "What can I do, Lora?"

"Don't leave," I whispered.

He gave me a little smile. "I'm not going anywhere."

"That's fine," I said, though my relief was so big those two words could not contain it. "That's . . . it's . . . thank you."

Courage comes in small doses. Sometimes, there's only enough of it to get on to the next moment, and Will's answer gave me that.

I drew back my hand and rose. Will made to get up with me, and I shook my head. "You go on back to work. I'll call if I need you."

Then I went back into the house and up those stairs, back to the close, hot room. I'd drawn back the curtains from the little window and opened it, but still the room was dark and airless. Eli was nothing more than a mounded shadow on the shadow of the

bed. The smell of comfrey and laudanum and sickness was so heavy it was already sinking into the
walls.

He was too quiet. I hurried over to him and bent
to feel the rise and fall of his chest.

"Lora."

The sound came from deep in his lungs, a slow,
wheezing breath. I jerked back, startled, and in the
dimness I saw the glint of light on his eyes. They were
open. Eli was awake.

"Either . . . I'm still . . . alive," he said, "or you're an
angel."

"You're alive. It's me. You're home. Harry brought
you home."

"Harry. Good . . . man."

"How do you feel?"

"Thought . . . I was . . . dead. But then . . . it
hurts . . . damn bad . . . figured I must be . . . alive."

I reached into my pocket and brought out the bottle of laudanum. My hands were trembling as I
unstoppered it. "Take some of this. Dr. Lockwood
left it—"

"Lockwood?" Eli jerked, and then gasped in pain.
But his hands groped the sheets, patted, checked.
"My legs . . . they're still . . . are they still there?"

"Yes. They're there."

He sagged back again, and his breathing was
ragged and harsh with little rasping sobs, the quiet
finish of a cry. "Christ, Lora . . . ah . . . it hurts. . . ."

I gripped the laudanum so tight the bottleneck
bit into my fingers as I knelt next to the bed. Eli
grabbed for the bottle, and I held it firm and slipped

my arm beneath his head to help him up enough to drink. Even that motion must have hurt, because he groaned, and his strength when he pulled the bottle to his mouth was hard to fight. He guzzled at the bottle, one gulp, then two, and I had to forcibly pull it away from him.

"No, Eli, that's enough. That's enough."

He cried out again, that hoarse and horrible sound, and my heart heard it and ached for him. The trembling of my hands turned to shaking as I stoppered up the bottle again and put it back into my apron pocket.

"Just give it a moment," I told him. "It will work in a moment," and then, as if he were a child, I stroked his forehead and felt the fever of his skin, the sweat wetting his hair. "It's all right. It's all right."

I don't know how many times I said those words. Fifty times, maybe, or a hundred, but gradually my own trembling stopped, and Eli relaxed beneath my touch, his breathing more even. He turned his cheek into my palm, and then he reached up and cupped my hand in his, holding it to his skin.

"I'm sorry, Lora," he whispered, and the words were slurred by laudanum and regret. "I'm so sorry."

He closed his eyes before I could answer, and I felt the slack in his body, in his hand, and knew he was asleep.

I waited a few moments, watching him the way I'd watched him so many times in sleep, the smudge of his lashes against his pale skin, the way his jaw disappeared in beard-shadow and darkness. I felt the fever heat of his skin and the pulse of his breath and his blood against my palm, and gently I drew away, and the hand that had held mine fell limp. Carefully, I laid it over his stomach, into a weak slant of sunlight. For the first time I saw the black pitch marking his knuckles, the dirty nails, the evidence of logging on his farmer's hands.

I went to the little window and lifted the sash as high as it would go, and it slid down again, loose, not catching until it had fallen another three inches. *Eli will have to fix that*, I thought out of habit, and then it struck me that it would be a long time before he could fix it, and I felt the tears then, blurring my vision, drying in the hot wind easing in through the window before they even left my eyes.

From this window, I could see the whole of the land before me, the cherry trees, the Spitzenbergs in the far corner of the orchard, the wilting leaves of my garden, the pea vines yellowed and browning now in the last days of summer, the tomatoes already canned or drying sweet in the cellar. And beyond all that, the irrigation canal, the shallow ditch of it already nearly dry, and the flash of sun against a white shirt. Will— far enough away to be only a speck of movement. I thought of his words again: *Maybe there's a reason for all this.*

I turned away from the window and looked again at Eli, calm now, laudanum-still. I thought of how we'd left each other, and how, just a few minutes before, he'd taken my hand and held it to his cheek, and how I hadn't thought it odd, how it hadn't started a tightening in me that made me tense against him even though we hadn't touched like that in a long, long time. And I thought, *Maybe it's better now. Maybe everything will be all right.*

The next morning I watched Eli's fevered sleep until I could not stand to anymore. With every labored breath he took, I felt him fading. The gauntness fell into his face, shadowing it until he looked like a corpse, and as the hours passed, so did my hope. Wishing was all I could do. Praying . . . I did not have enough faith left for prayer.

I was worried and afraid, and by midmorning, my worry was beating in the pulse of my fingertips, and I was afraid I would start screaming if I sat there much longer. I meant only to leave him for a moment, but once I was down the stairs, I kept going, onto the porch, down the steps, across the yard. My footsteps got faster and faster until I was running for the orchard, and before I knew it, I was deep in the Spitzenbergs, staring up at their fruit-heavy branches, at green leaves against the blue sky, breathing in their apple smell.

Those apples were our future now. The hope we'd had for the Wishkah was gone, leaving us forty-seven dollars in the ledger and Eli dying in a hot attic room. The rest of the year, the homestead, our lives, depended on the apples hanging full and round on these trees, these next few weeks growing and ripening with no sudden hail or windstorms or ice. Apples relying on the kindness of nature, hanging from stems that could break in an instant, that could be severed with a single snap—it seemed too fragile a thing to have hopes rest on.

The wind came up, and the trees shook. The apples rattled against each other. A small green one fell, and the sight of it shook me so that when I bent to pick it up, I felt as if I were trembling, though my hands were steady. I rolled it in my palm, too small, bright green, the flower end of it misformed. I stared at it and thought, *Why this one? Why should this one die and not another?* and somehow it got all tied up with Eli and me and my fear and guilt, and I squeezed that apple in my hand and looked at those trees and felt the breeze that made them sway moving through me.

I heard Eli's dreams rattling in the leaves. He was in every branch, in the deep center of these trees. I remembered how he'd cried that morning of the killing frost, how, after spending most of the night in the bitter cold building fires to warm the trees, he'd sat in our bedroom with tears in his eyes, covered with soot, listening to the crack and the pop, little explosions like gunfire. He'd been angry and frustrated that the cherries were gone. But his tears . . . his tears were for the apples.

I saw his life hanging alongside them, dangling from a slender, strong stem, and I promised myself that he wouldn't die, that the apples wouldn't die. As long as nothing happened to the apples, Eli would get better.

So many things could go wrong now. It was gaining on fall, and with the autumn came the storms that could ruin this harvest, too. Two weeks or so to wait; it was too long a time, far too uncertain. I clutched that little apple in my hand and stood paralyzed in those trees until I heard footsteps coming up behind me. I knew without looking who it was, and I turned toward him. He looked at me, and then at the apples, as if he was trying to understand, as if he saw something in my face that worried him. "I saw you standing out here. You seemed . . . Is Eli all right? Are you all right?"

I had no answer for him. His questions were so simple, but to answer was much harder. What could I tell him? That these trees suddenly meant everything? That I was so afraid of Eli's dying that I spent the nights bent over his chest, trying to hear him breathe? How could I say that I was haunted by the past and my failures and the times I woke deep in the night to the sound of a child crying? That sometimes I was clear to the corner where the trundle bed had been before I realized it was only the wind I heard?

For once, Will was quiet. I smelled him on the hot breeze—drying canal mud, musty water—a smell that carried tears into my chest and cradled them there. I looked past him to the trees, and a picture came into my head then, of Eli lifting an apple in the palm of his hand, twisting it off with one quick, deft motion, handing it down to a wobbly little girl who grinned and bit into it with tiny baby teeth, holding it tight in two hands while Eli smiled and grabbed my hand. *These trees will always be the best of us, Lora.*

"He's dying, Will."

"You're doing everything you can."

"Am I? I don't know what to do. I don't know how to make him well. I don't even know how to take the pain away. Last night I thought . . . I think he was reliving when that tree fell on him. He was screaming. . . ." I let the thought lie, seeing it in my mind, the way he'd arched on the bed, the scream caught in his throat that sent the tendons of his neck into sharp relief. "Everything about Eli is in these trees. Sometimes I used to tease him that he loved them more than me. I wish I knew how to make them my dream, too. Maybe it would help."

"Maybe. Or maybe it's better just to let them go. I mean . . . you're not Eli, Lora. Maybe it's time to dream of something else."

He said it as if there were something else, and I didn't know how to tell him that there wasn't, not anymore. The only dream I'd ever had was of Eli. From the first day he'd come striding up to my father's porch with that rolling, easy walk, Eli had been the only thing I wanted. He had come up to me and my little sister, Ellen, where we sat, and looked straight at me with eyes so blue they seemed to pull the color from the sky. "Excuse me, miss, would you happen to know where the boss is?" I'd stared up at him so tongue-tied and flustered that all I could do was point in my father's direction.

"You've got pretty eyes," he'd said as he turned away. It was days before he said anything else to me, but Eli Cameron burned inside me until I hungered for the sight of him, for the sound of his voice. I was starving for someone like him, and when God gave him to me, I could not believe my good fortune. To hear Eli tell it, he'd spent weeks trying to get my attention, worrying over whether or not I would welcome his courtship. But the truth was I'd loved him the moment he said "You've got pretty eyes."

I thought of him now, sweating upstairs, twisting with pain only partly dulled by laudanum. Dying up there. Only me and the apples to stop him. "It's Eli's dreams that are important now."

Will's look was thoughtful and sad. "I guess so."

"You don't understand. The apples are something I can believe for him. It's a way I can . . . make up for not . . . for not missing him enough—"

"But you did miss him," Will said, and there was a confusion on his face that made me pause, that made me stare at him. Because it suddenly occurred to me that to anyone else it might have seemed that I *had* missed Eli. I'd thought of him every day. I talked about him. Only I knew that I didn't miss the man who had gone to the Wishkah, but someone else altogether—someone who had been lost to me long before he left.

14

As if the God I'd lost faith in wasn't ready to abandon me just yet, the minister from the Methodist church in Yakima City appeared in my yard the next morning like some lost soul searching for salvation.

I was coming from the icehouse with a pail of cream for butter when I saw his wagon—a rusting, rickety thing that was just as bad, if not worse, than every other farmer's in these parts. He was wearing a battered wide-brimmed hat that shadowed his face, and I wouldn't have recognized him if it hadn't been for Ursula sitting on that seat beside him. Though her face was covered, too, with a dusty scarf, the hat she wore was the same one I'd seen at the tea party—so long ago now it could have been forever.

I couldn't remember the last time I'd been in church, and it had been a year since Samuel Anderson had set foot on this property. I remembered his last visit far too well, and though I knew he'd come out now because of Eli, for a moment I just stared, unable to think of anything but those days last year when I'd first turned in bitterness from a preacher's words, when I'd stopped listening.

I saw Ursula's uncertainty as she looked up and saw me standing there. She lifted her hand to wave, and then faltered before she waved again. In that movement, I found myself again, and I went to the porch steps and set down the pail of cream before I went to greet them.

Samuel came toward me, his hands outstretched, worry and concern etched on features that already looked worn from the strain of preaching the gospel in a town that faced too often the fickle will of God. "Lora, Lora," he said, reaching for me, clasping my fingers. I felt the soft weakness of his scholar's hands. "We've heard of Eli's accident. My dear, you have truly faced the worst of God's tests this year."

I tried to smile, but I couldn't. Gently, I pulled my hands away. "Thank you for coming out. And you too, Ursula."

"How could we not?" Ursula asked, coming up beside her husband. Her face was drawn with sympathy. "How is Eli?"

"Not good."

"Dr. Lockwood's been here?"

I made a bitter sound. "Oh, yes."

Ursula winced a little. Samuel said, "You've been in our prayers since we heard, Lora. You and Eli both. I have faith that God will lead you through this crisis."

I wished I had the same faith, and when I looked at Samuel, I wondered how he could be so strong in his conviction. I wanted to demand of him an explanation, proof that God measured out any kindness at all. Instead, I stepped back and gestured toward the house. "Please, come in. Can I get you something? Some buttermilk? Water? You must be thirsty. It's a long way from Yakima City."

They followed me to the porch. Samuel sat heavily, mopping his thin face with his handkerchief, while Ursula fanned herself with her gloved hand. I went inside to get some buttermilk, and when I came onto the porch again, I saw Will trudging up from the ditch, carrying the mud-crusted shovel over his shoulder. He looked up and paused, and when he came over to the porch there was a wary greeting in his expression.

"Here's Will," I told the Andersons. "He's our hired hand. Will, this is Samuel and Ursula Anderson. He's the minister at the Methodist church."

"Will. Of course," Ursula said. "You brought Lora to Irma's."

Will smiled then, and held out his hand to shake Samuel's. "Pleased to meet you both."

"He's been a big help to me," I said.

"Then we should all be thankful for your presence," Samuel said to Will. "And to the Lord for sending you here to this farm."

"Whatever you say, sir," Will said, and though the words were polite, and his smile equally so, there was something in his voice I heard, some little scorn. I tensed, thinking he would say something about freedom and simplicity and God's place in it, something to embarrass me and the preacher, but he didn't. He only looked down at his feet as if he was trying to hide his smile.

Still, I think Samuel heard it, too, because he

frowned a little, and when he turned back to me, he seemed disconcerted, so it took him a minute to find his words. "Now, Lora, I know it's been a goodly while since you set foot in church. I am at a loss to know why you would deny such comfort in your time of need. God is waiting to see you back again, as am I. This is a time to open your heart to the Lord, not to turn away."

I couldn't look at him. Will was watching me, and I couldn't look at him, either, because of that faint mockery I'd heard, and because, though I didn't share the minister's belief, suddenly I wished I could. I wished I could take comfort from his words, and from the community he offered me. I wanted to be a part of it the way I once had been, the way I'd worshiped in ignorance and habit before the world had been taken from me.

"I know," I said softly. "Thank you for your kindness."

"I would like to pray for you and for Eli. Would you pray with us, Lora? And you, young Will?"

Will stepped back. He hefted the shovel again. "I'll be with you in spirit, Mr. Anderson," he said. "But I'd best get back to work."

"Of course." Samuel turned to me, and there was such compassion in his eyes, such strength and force, that I nodded meekly and sat down beside them, saying nothing when he took one of my hands and Ursula took the other, so we were joined in a circle.

"Dear Lord, we thank Thee for watching over this house in the Camerons' time of need, and we ask that You continue to watch over our brother Eli, and comfort him, and heal him. We ask that You give Your blessing to our sister Lora, who is sorely afflicted in her heart and her mind, and that You ease her sadness and her trials and show her again the true forgiving and generous light of Your presence. We ask that You bring these two back into the bosom of their friends, that we might ease their burdens and show them the path of righteousness and hope. In Christ's name, we pray. Amen."

He spoke the Lord's Prayer then, the words I knew by heart, that I had known since I was a small child, and as Samuel Anderson said those words, and as I listened to them and felt the warm softness of his hand and Ursula's smooth fingers, I felt strangely comforted. Habit, I told myself, but I knew it was more than that. It was the fact that they had come, that I wasn't alone even though I often felt it. That I had friends who cared about me if only I chose to seek them out.

When the prayer was over, Samuel and Ursula stayed an hour or so longer. He went upstairs to pray over a sleeping Eli, and Ursula and I talked about little things, like the tea party and Irma's flowers, and how it looked like the weather might hold until harvest. I couldn't get my mind away from Eli, and though I appreciated the Andersons' kindness, I wanted them to leave so that I could get back to my worrying. But when they got into their wagon and drove out of the yard, I found myself wishing they'd stayed a little longer, because my troubles seemed so big again, my loneliness as unendurable as company had been only a few short hours before.

I was grateful when Will came around the corner of the house, though he didn't say anything as he stood there at the edge of the porch, watching with me as the dust from the Andersons' wagon rose into the air and faded away.

"The whole town must be talking about Eli," Will said finally.

"I imagine so."

"A pity they didn't bring out a new doctor. That's something we could use."

I laughed a little. "No, they brought out God. I guess they think He's better than a new doctor."

"That's the problem with the world. Too many people thinking God has all the answers."

"But not you."

"You think there's really some higher power to put all your faith in, Lora?"

"I don't know."

He was quiet for a minute, then he said, "You know what I think? I think those weeds over there have as much power over God as we do. They have as much right to Him. You want to put your faith in that, you go ahead. I think you'll be disappointed every time. The only person anyone should depend on is himself."

I didn't answer him. I didn't know what to say. Maybe Will was right; but it made me uncomfortable to think it. I guess that deep inside, I couldn't believe in the things he said. As angry as I was at God, the belief I thought I'd abandoned was still there, lingering on—weaker, maybe, but not gone. Perhaps I had not turned from Him as completely as I'd thought, because I couldn't deny the comfort I'd taken from the Andersons' visit—or my sudden realization that I truly missed the consolation of the things I'd once believed.

It seemed that the minister didn't have as much influence with God as I'd hoped. Eli didn't seem to get any better. Laudanum was his savior. When he was awake, which wasn't often, his eyes were glazed and his breathing labored. He was feverish and sometimes delirious, and sometimes he looked right through me. The laudanum let him sleep, which I imagined was the only painless place he knew, though I worried about giving him so much. When Dr. Lockwood came out again the following week, he brushed away my worries with a quick shake of his head.

"If it gives him peace, let him have it. He won't need it before long."

By that he meant not that Eli would get better, but that he expected him to die. Lockwood wouldn't have come back at all if I hadn't sent Will in for him a second time, and I saw the surprise in the doctor's eyes when he went upstairs to find Eli hadn't worsened.

"He's got a strong will," he'd said, but nothing else. No hope that Eli's will would somehow pull him through, nothing to hold on to.

But the laudanum he left was a blessing, and so I didn't complain. I sent Dr. Lockwood back to town with a squawking chicken, a dozen eggs, and three pounds of butter, and hoped that would take care of his bill, and then I went back to ministering to my husband, mixing a strong dose of laudanum into ham broth and spooning it between his lips whenever he was half awake. When he was drugged and asleep, I changed his bandages and hoped he wouldn't wake from the pain of it. Though the bleeding had stopped, his legs were still swollen and black with bruising, and there were times when I had to turn away because I could not stand to see how terrible it was. In those moments, it seemed hopeless all over again, his fever growing until the sheets were wet from sweat, his delirium increasing, the screams of pain. He was dying, I knew, but I could not face that. I told myself that tomorrow he would be better. *Tomorrow.* The days stretched into an endless string of tomorrows.

But I had to believe in it. I could not do everything; even with Will there to help, the farm that held Eli's dreams was failing. Caring for Eli took up so much of my time, and it seemed that everything else was dying as he was: the potatoes were getting eaten up by jackrabbits because I didn't have time to dig them, the corn was set on by raccoons one night, the broad beans were dry and ready to store. I hadn't made butter to take into town since Eli had come home, as much as we needed the money, and the cream was souring, the eggs left to rot in their hiding places all over the yard.

But the apples were all that mattered. I checked them constantly, as if my vigilance somehow guaranteed they wouldn't fail. I went out to that far field about a dozen times a day, until even Will commented on it: "They'll be fine, Lora. Worrying won't help anything."

Those apples were the only promise I allowed myself to have, and I did worry. I watched them the way I watched Eli, until the two of them were inseparable in my mind, and so when I woke up one morning a week after Eli had been home, and felt the change in the air, I panicked.

It wasn't a change I could even describe, but I felt it—a heaviness, and in that heaviness a charge that danced across my skin. When I looked out the window, the day was no different from any other in late summer, the sky clear to the ridge, blue and hot. But the wind was blowing hard enough to turn the oak leaves inside out, and I stared at the little dust storms fighting across the yard and felt a warning that gave me goose bumps.

It was late September, moving into October, into fall, with its storms that swept down the mountainsides to flash-flood the valley, and hail that turned the ground white. This was the time of year Eli watched the skies and cursed beneath his breath and paced. The fruit on the trees was swelling with juice and sweetness, and it was vulnerable now, no longer rocklike, but newly ripe, its red-speckled skin thin and easily bruised. Just as a single rainstorm could destroy an entire cherry crop if it hit just before harvest, a hailstorm or ice storm now could ruin the apples and split trees whose branches were already bowed and heavy with fruit. The price we could get for the apples depended on their quality, on perfect days and cold nights until they were ready to pick. We needed perfect days now. We needed them more than we ever had.

I told myself I was being ridiculous, that my worry over Eli's illness left me too inclined to see tragedy everywhere I looked. The sky was clear; there was no evidence of a storm. But I couldn't ignore the leaves spinning on that old, tired oak, or the expectation I felt in the air. There was a way the whole valley seemed to stretch for rain, as if the plants and dirt sensed it, heard the whisper racing over the arid land with the wind. *Water's coming.*

I glanced back at Eli, who was murmuring restlessly now. I imagined that he felt the storm the way I did, that he was pacing in his dreams, and I wished so hard that he were at the window instead of me, looking out over the farm and worrying, deciding what to do, if there was anything *to* do. I remembered when the apple trees were very young, about four years ago. There had been an ice storm then, too, about this same time, and together, Eli and I draped every feed bag and flour sack we could find over those frail trees, covering them as best we could, hoping it would help protect them.

But the trees were much bigger now, and there were more of them. Even with Will's help, I could not possibly cover them all.

It seemed that all I'd felt these last months was desperation, and now I tried hard to ignore it, but I heard Eli's tossing behind me and I knew that storm would come; I could hear it in his dreams.

I suppose I was a little crazy as I raced from the bedroom and down the stairs. Will was at the kitchen table, drinking coffee, and he looked up at me in surprise that turned to quick fear.

"What? What's wrong? Is it Eli?"

"A storm's coming."

He frowned. "A storm? But—"

I rushed past him and threw open the door. The wind swept in, dust and dry leaves, burning my eyes and my lungs so I blinked and choked. "It's going to hail," I said again. I stepped out onto the porch and stared hard beyond the ridge, toward Mt. Adams, trying to see it coming.

"There're no clouds for miles," Will said from behind me.

"It'll come up fast."

"From where?"

I didn't bother to answer him. I started for the barn, not looking back or waiting as he followed me.

"Lora, what are you doing? Lora—"

Bessie was chewing her cud in the fenced yard, and though she looked up at me as if I were foolish, I noticed she hadn't left the shelter of the barn wall. The chickens were huddling together and fluffing out their feathers. I glanced up again at the sky, and then I dodged through the barn door.

The bags were piled in the far corner of the barn, a solid shadow in the dusty, dim light. There were plenty of them, a year or more's worth of grain and seed. But the field of apple trees stretched out so far in my mind, impossible to cover. When Will came up beside me and looked at me in confusion, I motioned helplessly toward them.

"The bags . . . we need to cover the trees."

I expected him to tell me there weren't enough, or that it would never work, or any of the protests that

were in my own mind, but he didn't. He only hesitated for a minute, and then nodded, and the next
thing I knew he had the wheelbarrow, and he was filling it with armfuls of canvas and burlap and carting
it out again.

I followed him past the cherry trees and the bare
summer-apple trees. The Spitzenbergs hung round
and rosy, their inward sides pale, waiting for the cold
nights to start them on their full turn toward white-
speckled red. The trees were heavy with them, gnarled
branches dipping beneath the weight of fruit. When I
looked at them, I had the sudden vision of Eli standing there, staring up at them with that light in his
eyes.

"What do I do?" Will asked.

"Cover them as best we can."

Will eyed me doubtfully. "This will work?"

"It has to."

He stared at me as if he'd suddenly heard or seen
something to make him pause, and his eyes went
dark with concern. I saw the question he wasn't asking, the quick thought that I wasn't making sense,
that something was wrong, but before I could say
anything, the wind blew up again all around us, raising dust and rattling those branches so hard the
apples bounced. And suddenly, just beyond the ridge,
I saw the first clouds.

I grabbed bags and went to the first tree. My skirts
whipped around my legs, making me clumsy, and my
hair straggled into my face. I'd left the ladder there
the morning before, and now I climbed it and tried to
lay the bags over the branches, but the wind fought

me. The bags curled up and twisted and caught before they went heavily limp. Just as I grabbed them again, the wind swung them away from me. The first bag tumbled down the branch, out of reach, falling and rolling until it dropped onto the ground at my feet.

Will handed it up to me again, and then grabbed a handful of bags himself. "Keep trying."

But it was hopeless, and I knew it. I knew it as I struggled with those bags and my skirts, and the apples bounced and loosened from my efforts, dropping one by one to the ground. The wind came up harder, until I couldn't see for the wind and the dust blowing in my face, and the rocking branches scraped my arms, tearing at my already ragged sleeves, scratching my cheeks.

The minutes raced away, chased by dark clouds that sped across the sky so fast it seemed only seconds passed before they were on us. They came rumbling in, thunder first, lightning you could only hear but couldn't see.

I jumped from the ladder and grabbed another armful of bags. Will was struggling in the trees beyond. I saw the canvas bags peeling off those trees in the wind, sailing to the ground like big brown leaves in autumn, tumbling across the dirt. And all I could think of was these trees bending and cracking beneath the hail, Eli's heart breaking with them. Once the trees were gone, he would leave me, too.

I swallowed my terror and fought on, but it was useless from the start. There were too many trees; they were too big. The thunder came louder, making me jump. The sky darkened so it was like dusk, though it was only midmorning, and the dirt-filled wind took on the chill of winter where it touched my skin, where it blew into my eyes. When I felt the first few drops of rain, I thought they were my tears.

A gash of lightning split the sky, opening it up, and the air felt charged and alive in that moment before the hail came. It was fast and hard, as if God had just turned a bucket over the world. It was like snow, white in its fury, but it wasn't soft, and there was no silence in it. It was hard, and the crashing sound of it filled my ears, every little pellet stinging where it hit. I sat down on the top rung of the ladder and put my face in my hands and let it hurt.

I had not thought it would come so fast, the sound of ruin, but it did. The apples were heavy, the young branches thin and fragile, and the sound of their cracking and splitting, the thud of apples hitting the earth, was louder than the thunder and hail. When I took my hands away to stare at ground, the ice was already gathering, piles of hail heavy and gray, rough stones the size of peas. I saw an apple falling, rolling and thudding to a stop against the ridge of a crumpled canvas bag covered with ice.

It went on for so long it seemed like forever, so long that when I first felt it ease, I didn't believe it. I didn't believe it until I felt the rain that came after. Soft rain. Too late. I tilted my head up to it, feeling the wet against my cheeks, the water warming where it hit my skin until I could not tell where the rain ended and my tears began.

"Lora, come on down."

Will was shouting. I glanced down to where he stood at the foot of my ladder. His shirt was wet at the shoulders, his hair growing dark with rain. He held up his hand to me. "Come down."

I shook my head at him. "This will kill him," I said, and I couldn't make my voice loud enough for him to hear; I could not put strength behind my despair. "This will break his heart."

He could not have heard me. But he paused as if he had, and he looked so sad in that moment before he stretched his hand out to me again. "You're getting wet. Come out of the rain."

Because I could not think of a reason to stay, I took his hand. I crawled down from the ladder, my skirts growing sodden, flapping heavily against my legs. His fingers wrapped around mine, and it wasn't until I felt how warm they were that I realized how cold mine had been.

He put his arm around my shoulders and hugged me tight into his side, and numbly, I let him take me to the house. In spots, the hail was already melting in the rain, muddying the dust. As we went past my garden, I didn't turn to see the damage. Everything had lessened in importance to those apples smashing to the ground, to my own dull knowledge that the Yakima Valley had not finished with me, my fear that this time I would survive it alone.

I don't know what it was Will thought, or what he felt, as he walked with me back to the house. I don't know if he knew how hard those steps were for me, if he knew how I dreaded each one, or what I expected to find when we got there. But he was quiet. His presence was a comfort, his arm around my shoulders a reminder that I was still alive—that if it was possible to die of guilt and loss, I had not done so yet.

When we got to the porch, he sat on the bench and pulled me down beside him, and I sat there with him and watched the cold, hard rain and thought of how the hours in my life shifted with the weather. Even when I was a girl, it had ruled each minute. A too-wet spring in Walla Walla, and the wheat would be crippled with mildew. Not enough rain, and the wheat would be worth nothing, brittle and withering, heads shrunken to small, rattling kernels. A storm could bring an entire field to ruin in minutes. My father's moods changed with the rain—when it came, when it didn't . . . The rhythm of my life beat with his sullen silences and my mother's tears.

"My parents wanted me to be a teacher," I said, and I suppose the words were meant to be a reminder that once, someone had wanted something else for me. To Will, they must have seemed odd, coming from nowhere—or maybe they made perfect sense now. Maybe to him they sounded like the simple prayers murmured in the flush of failure. *Oh, Lord, what I could have been.*

And in a way, that's what they were, though I had hated the idea of studying, and speaking in front of people had always left me tongue-tied and stumbling. Being a teacher was not my idea, but I did as my parents asked because I had no other idea of my own. I finished eighth grade and meant to study for my certification, and dreaded every moment of my future. And then Eli walked into my life, and my course was set. I was a farmer's wife, and all I'd ever wanted was a family and children with Eli's dark hair. I had never imagined that wanting those things would hurt so much, and now it was easy to think that some other life would bring less pain, some life away from apple trees and dust and weather that set the tone of the hours.

Will sighed. Then he rose, and the sound of his movement was heavy and loud. He went to the railing and leaned over it, out into the rain. I started to call him back, the instinctive, age-old caution, *You'll catch your death of cold that way,* and then I realized how he looked, the way he lifted his face to the rain and let it wash over him, the way he seemed to breathe it in, and I was silent. Such simple pleasure seemed beyond me now, and I found myself wondering how it felt, what the rain meant to him, that he could see it not as an enemy or as salvation, but just as a sensation to wash over his face, to taste.

He turned to face me. He was soaking wet, his thin shirt plastered to his skin, his hair only brown now, not gold at all, and there was a gauntness to his face that I noticed for the first time. But his eyes were lit up, his voice on fire. "Do you know there are places where they eat alligator? There are lakes so big they look like oceans, and country the Indians filled up with burial mounds. There are places. . . ." He shook his head, as if he couldn't find the words, and then he reached into his pocket and took something out. An ugly gray rock, it looked like, and I wondered why he carried such a thing in his pocket until he turned it over and I saw the crystals in it like ice. He held it out to me. "There are places where even the rocks hold rainbows. Look at this, Lora. Rainbows. And you're . . . you're *here*."

He motioned around him, a wildly flailing arm, and I followed the gesture that took in rain and dirty hail piled in little mounds against the porch, and I won't say I felt a yearning for the things he talked about, because I didn't. I didn't want those things. But this . . . I didn't want this, either.

I looked away from him. "It'll be fine."

He leaned down so close I could feel the warmth of his breath. That rock sparkled in his hands, violets and deep blues in the crystals. "What if it's not? What will you do then?"

I didn't want to tell him what I feared: that things were already not fine, that it was the apple orchard keeping Eli alive, and without it now, my husband would be gone. I felt the certainty of it hurting so deep in my chest I knew I would never be able to touch that pain. I shook my head, and Will whispered, "You could be a teacher if you wanted. I could show you so much, Lora. Places that are beautiful, where life isn't so hard."

I looked up at him. He was so young. His eyes fairly burned with the things he wanted, and I knew I'd never looked like that. I didn't even know what it felt like. I tried to smile at him. "You've got your whole life ahead of you. You wouldn't want me along, telling you to put on your coat when it gets cold."

Something flickered through his eyes. He straightened, and his fingers curled around the rock, hiding the crystals so it was just ugly and gray again. He shoved it back into his pocket and turned once more to look at the rain. "You make me sad, Lora."

For some reason his words made me think of what he'd said to me on the way to Irma's tea party. The way he'd stopped the wagon in the middle of the prairie and touched my heart.

I got up from the bench. Without a word, I left him there and walked into the house and stood in the doorway, dripping puddles onto the floor, and the bareness of my walls struck me hard, the emptiness of the whatnot shelf. *I always liked that flowerd thing you sewd.*

The lump in my chest hurt when I breathed. I looked toward the stairs and wanted Eli so much. I wanted his surety, and his faith, and the innocence to believe in him again, to love him the way I once had. I wanted to believe what Will said, that you could make your own world, and I was afraid of that, too, of what my world now said about me.

My mother had always told me that I loved too much, but it seemed to me that I didn't love enough, that I didn't know how to hold on to things, that in my selfishness I let them slip away. Like Eli upstairs. I could not take him in my arms and hold him close and beg him not to leave me, and I believed the God who had laid out my life would hold me accountable for that. I believed He would take my husband from me because I couldn't make Eli's dreams my own.

As I climbed those stairs to our bedroom, the rain was a roar in my head. My sodden clothes smelled of mud and grief, and I could not think of anything at all as I walked over to my husband and sank into the chair by his bedside. In the dim light, he looked pale, and when I touched his hand it was cold, and it was then, with my fingers curled around his, that I felt the pain of his passing as a heavy press in my chest, a terrible ache.

"Oh, Eli," I whispered, and my jaw was so tight it was hard to say the words. "I tried. I tried so hard. I truly did."

The rain was pounding hard and loud on the roof, filling my ears with its noise and with the sound of cracking branches. I felt the rainwater dripping from my dress to patter on my boots, and I began to shake so hard I had to drop Eli's hand—it seemed indecent to hold it.

And suddenly I was remembering that day last year, how I'd dried her hair and wrapped her in a blanket because all I could think of was that she must be cold. It had been a hot summer day, but I could not get the thought out of my head. She had to be cold, because I was freezing clear into my bones; I could not feel my hands or my skin.

I felt that way now, too, so cold I couldn't think. I needed warm clothes. Dry clothes. My teeth were chattering, and my hands shook when I rose from the chair and smoothed down my skirt. There were a hundred things to do: I had to call Will, he would have to help me lay Eli out, and there was the funeral to plan. . . . While I was thinking this, I was tearing at my clothes, unbuttoning my bodice, unhooking the lining, peeling off gingham that clung wetly to my skin. I could not control my fingers; they were rough and clumsy, tearing right through the weak muslin of my chemise. I dragged off my petticoat and my drawers, and when the warm air hit my skin it felt like winter, and I was covered in gooseflesh and blind with cold as I stepped out of the pile of wet things and went to the trunk at the foot of the bed.

When I opened it, I smelled him. Lye soap and the outdoors, the scent of his skin. I hugged myself with one arm and dug for another chemise with the other. It was scorched, too, from the day I'd let the laundry burn dry, worse than the one I'd had on, and when I slipped it over my head, my elbow rent the fabric, so it tore along the fine lace edging at the neck.

Lora.

At first I thought it was my imagination, the way I still heard Eva sometimes in the still of the morning. Eli's voice was quiet in my head, and it hurt to hear it, the final reminder of how soft he could be, how kind. I wished I'd heard him say it one more time.

"Lora."

He moved in the bed. The blanket shifted, his head lifted. I froze in horror, startled, frightened. It was a moment before I realized his eyes were open, that he was staring at me, and that it wasn't the stare of a dead man. I saw him say something, but my heart was pounding so hard I couldn't hear. It was a moment before it finally hushed, before I heard him whisper, "My God, you're beautiful."

15

My hands were trembling as I lit the lamp on the bedside table only a few minutes later. The rain was steady now, but soft, and the sound of it was rhythmic and serene on the roof above our heads. The world outside was gray, and the little bedroom was dim even with the lamp.

Eli's hair was a dark shadow against the pillow, and he was staring out the window as if he could see something other than the leaden sky. His fingers flexed against the coverlet, whether from impatience or pain, I didn't know. Probably both. But I was so relieved; he was alive. It was such a miracle I could scarcely believe it, and I kept staring at him, half afraid he would disappear if I looked away, certain this could not last, that this was one of God's jokes.

"I'm afraid to know," Eli said, and just the sound of his voice, unslurred by fever or laudanum, sent a shiver through me. "But you'd better tell me. Is it bad?"

"Pretty bad," I admitted. He closed his eyes, and I leaned forward, suddenly anxious again. "Do you need something? Some laudanum—"

"In a minute," he said, clenching his jaw. He let out his breath in a long, slow sigh.

I talked to distract him. "I won't know until I go out to see for sure. Maybe . . . A few of those trees are strong."

"Yeah," he said quietly. "A few."

"We . . . Will and I tried, Eli. We really did. But the bags didn't work this time. The trees are so much bigger, and the wind just blew them right off again."

He turned his head on the pillow to look at me. "I know you tried, honey."

The same word that only a few months earlier had made me tense softened into comfort now. I could breathe easier after he said it, even though it was so intimate I was suddenly aware of how I was sitting there still in my chemise. I looked away, embarrassed.

"We'll get by." His voice was low. I saw the way his fingers clenched.

"I know we will."

He nodded and looked toward the window again, staring at it as if he were watching stories in the clouds. "I promised you so much, Lora."

"Oh, Eli. We'll be all right. You'll be well in no time, and we've still got the money you sent home. That'll last awhile. And Will's promised to stay on longer."

"He has?"

"He's a good worker, Eli."

"That's what you said in your letter."

"His hand's better now. He's been a big help to me. He cares about the farm so much you'd think he was our son."

Eli was quiet, but I felt his discomfort and his tension in the silence, and I was uncomfortable and strangely nervous. "He's not our son, Lora."

"Oh, I know, but—"

"He's not . . ." He took a rasping breath.

"Don't talk. You should sleep. I'll get the laudanum."

I reached for the bottle, and he stopped me with his hand. "Not yet."

"Eli, you can barely breathe—"

"It hurts, but . . ." He turned his head to me, and in the dimness his eyes were dark shadows; the light glimmered on them like tears. "It's been . . . so long. I just . . . I just want to look at you . . . awhile."

I crossed my arms over my chest, hugging myself tight, hiding myself from him. I did it before I thought, and then wished I hadn't when I saw how he sighed, his sad little smile.

It was my chance to make amends, the way I'd promised myself I would. It was my chance to show God how glad I was that He'd spared Eli's life, that my husband was still alive. Deliberately, I brought my arms down. But Eli sighed again and turned away, and his voice was dull when he spoke. "I'll take the laudanum now."

"Eli—"

"Please."

I was so disappointed in myself I could hardly bear to reach for that bottle. I poured the sweet liquid into a spoon and gave it to Eli. The heady, mediciney scent wafted to my nose, lingered there as I took the spoon away and recorked the bottle, and Eli and I said nothing else to each other as I sat there and watched until he fell into a deep, even sleep. Even then I didn't move. I sat there for a long time, thinking of how I'd believed he was dead, and how much it had hurt, and what I would have had left of him if he had died. A few letters, some clothes. Too many regrets. And though I'd tried to forget it, the words in his last letter came back to me, the memory of the best day of my life. The picture came into my head of the way she'd squirmed in my arms, the soft down of her hair, and I closed my eyes and felt the memories there in my mind, the weight of them held tight and dark—like rainbows in a rock.

The storm blew over, and the rain stopped. The sky was deep blue and swept with clouds—as if the day had just started out summer and stayed that way. But I felt the wind now; it had a bite in it. The storm had gone, but in its wake came the first coolness of fall.

I stepped onto the porch. The dampness in the air was a cold kiss against my cheek. Before me, chickens scratched and pecked in the mud, bobbing and weaving, clucking with delight at the worms the rain had brought to the surface. They were splattered with mud, their skinny legs black clear up into the feathers. There were mounds of hail here and there, dirty and partly melted now from the rain, formless bits of ice, and little rivers ran slowly through the yard, the thirsty land lapping them up before they had a chance to go very far. Everywhere were broken branches, twigs, the ravages of the storm. The hop vine at the corner of the porch had blown down. The old oak had lost one of its diseased limbs—it lay in a heap of shattered black wood at the base of the trunk, while the other pointed straight up into the sky like a finger at the heavens. Leaves torn from its branches littered the yard.

I was afraid to look toward the orchard. It wasn't until I heard the sucking footsteps coming from that direction that I turned to face it.

Will was coming from the trees. He carried a branch in one hand that he'd stripped to use as a walking stick. His wet shirt was clinging to his arms and shoulders, and leaves and a bit of twig stuck to a rip tearing out from the big scorched spot on his shirt. His trousers were muddy to his shins. When he saw me standing there he gave me a reassuring smile. "It's not as bad as you'd think. The cherry trees took a little beating, but not too many broke."

"What about the apples?"

He hesitated. Then he met my gaze evenly. "I thought it would be worse."

I didn't know how to take that, except to think the damage was worse than Will said. He didn't know about orchards; he had no idea what a hailstorm could do, or just how dependent we were on those apples in the far field. I didn't trust his ability to look at the trees and know how hurt they were. I wasn't even sure I would know. I could tell if a tree was split, or how many apples were gone, of course, but I didn't know by looking at it if a split tree would survive, or if the stress had killed it. I needed Eli for that.

It was strange, how quickly the joy of a miracle faded. How it only opened the door for more worries, more things to wish for. Eli would live, but he might never get up from that bed again, and that meant the farm was still mine. His dreams were still mine.

Carefully I stepped down from the porch. My boots settled into mud up to my ankles. I felt the pull of it as I lifted my skirts and made my way out to Will. "I guess I'd better go see."

It was hard work getting there. The wind whipped my skirts loose from my hand so they kept falling in the mud for me to get tangled in and trip over. Finally, Will put his hand on my elbow, and it was easier after that. With every step there were more branches and twigs, more leaves—cherry and apple drowning in the mud—and I grew more and more certain that we were facing disaster.

I wanted to see the apple trees first, and so we went around the side of the orchard and down to the far field. The closer we got, the more branches were on the ground, cracking beneath my boots. I stepped over fallen apples in little piles gathered by eddies that had drained away. I would collect those later, for applesauce or vinegar, but for now I let them lie. When we came near enough, I pulled away from Will, and I took those last steps on my own, until I was deep into the Spitzenbergs. Branches grabbed at my hair and scraped my shoulders, and sudden showers sprinkled my face whenever I brushed against the trees. Finally I stopped in the middle of the row and looked down. The ground was covered with apples and leaves and branches. I saw three trees rent clear into their hearts, splintered to show bright new wood that gleamed in the sun, and the smell of it was sharp and heavy on the air. Those wouldn't live, but there were fewer than I'd expected. Branches still carrying their heavy weights of apples had broken off and lay at impossible angles, caught in other branches, leaning crookedly against the trees. I did not know how to measure this. I hardly knew where to begin.

Will came up behind me. "Tell me what to do."

There was plenty to do, but just now I wanted to walk among the apples and look them over. I wanted distraction to make me laugh and take my worries away. I bent down and picked up an apple, turning it over in my hands, staring at the new blush just starting from the stem. It was heavy in my hand—it would have been a good weight.

I sighed and began to move, and Will walked beside me down the rows, counting trees, moving aside branches, surveying the damage. We moved slowly, as if we were taking a leisurely walk over rain-damp fields. As if the smell of apples and new wood and rain were things to savor. When I came to another broken tree, I said, "Tell me about this place where they eat alligators."

He went past me, picking up a branch that had fallen across our way, tossing it to the edge of the field. "It's hot there. Even in the winter, it's hot. It rains all the time, and that rain just fills up the swamps and stays there. You can hear those alligators roar if you get close enough, and I guess they're dangerous to hunt. They'll eat a man given half a chance. But it doesn't stop anyone. They're good eating, I guess. Down there, they smother 'em in gravy and call it some fancy name I can't pronounce."

"It sounds like a terrible place."

"No. No, it's not terrible. It's pretty there, actually. I think you'd like it. There are lots of flowers."

"I planted dahlias once. But they never grew. I always meant to try again, but I . . . I just gave up."

"In New Orleans there are so many flowers it smells like perfume all the time."

I could not imagine it. The smell of flowers instead of the grassy wind that filled my nose, the scents of fruit mixing with dry land and manure so that it was never a smell I wanted to breathe in deep. I picked up another apple—a redder one this time. "How nice."

"You should go there."

"Tell me about someplace else."

Will hesitated, and I tensed, thinking he was going to say something that I didn't want to hear, something about this farm, and me, and the things I wanted. But he only looked away again and pulled on a branch that was nearly cracked through, so it gave way completely. "You know those Indian mounds I told you about? There are caves nearby, and there are bowls worn into the rocks where they used to grind their corn. I slept there once, and I dreamed I was an Indian that night. I was making arrowheads—you know, chiseling at them with a rock. When I woke up, there was an arrowhead beside me. I carried it around for a while until it tore through the pocket of my coat. I think I lost it in Kansas somewhere."

"There are Indian paintings up near Selah Gap. You should go see them sometime."

"Indian paintings? Of what?"

I had begun to gather apples in the folds of my

apron, mindlessly, turning each over in my hands as if I could somehow make it ripe before I let it fall with the others. I felt the weight of them against my hips, settling into my pelvis, and the feeling was reassuring somehow, meaningful, though I couldn't say why. "No one knows. They look like . . . like faces, with these little eyes peering at you and hair standing straight up in little spikes." I smiled. "Eli said once that they reminded him of—" Her name stuck in my throat, along with the memory of how she'd knelt in her cradle, peering at us over the edge, her little fingers curled around as she tried to pull herself up, her hair tousled and spiked from sleep. Eli's laughter echoed in my head. *Look at her, Lora. She looks like those paintings up by the Gap, doesn't she?*

I swallowed and looked down at those apples in my apron. "Of a child." I didn't mean to let go of my apron. I don't remember thinking about it at all. But those apples fell in a cascade to the ground, tumbling one after another, until they were in a pile at my feet. I stared at them, and they blurred together in front of my eyes. It was all I could do to look up at Will again, to try smile. I meant to say, *Where else have you been?* to try to distract him and myself, but the *where* came out as *what*, and the rest followed as if the words had just been waiting there on my tongue. "What am I going to tell Eli?"

And then I could not bear to look at the concern in Will's eyes. I felt as if I was failing him, too, that I could not be brave and strong, that I could not reassure and comfort him the way I should. I turned away, leaving those apples there, walking away from the orchard toward the house. Except I didn't leave the trees. I walked through the orchard, and I realized halfway there that I wasn't going to the house. I was going to my garden. When I came near to it, my heart just stopped. For a minute, I thought I wouldn't be able to look at it. It would be flattened, ravaged, useless. My neglect would mean a scarce winter, and I was sorry for that now, disappointed with myself.

But it wasn't ruined. It was beautiful.

The storm had had an effect on it, of course. The bean vines were lying on the ground, along with the dying peas, and the potato plants had been flattened. But the hail hadn't beaten it. The greens were greener somehow; the leaves of the cabbages held droplets of water that glistened in the dying sunlight. The smell of warm earth and squash vines was heavy in my nose. The little edges of flowers that had already begun to turn into pumpkins and sweetmeats were tattered, but the hail had rolled off the baby squashes to pool and melt beneath them, and the potato leaves were stretching to grab the last bit of moisture from the air.

It was funny, how easily I'd neglected it once Eli came home. I'd left my canning and drying right in the middle of it and put all my strength and hope into his apples. The things I cared about had fallen away; my preoccupation with the garden had faded. I would have expected it to show my indifference. I had seen it already, in yellowed and dying greens and tangled vines, in everything I'd lost to the jackrabbits and sage rats.

But the garden had survived despite me. I had not managed to kill it. Even a storm strong enough to split apple trees had not managed to kill it. The outer leaves of those cabbages were spotted with worm holes, but the tight, round heads were green and wet, and I stared at them in surprise and stopped short, so when Will came up behind me he said, "What? Lora, what is it?"

"Look at it," I told him, motioning to the garden.

He frowned as he looked. "It's not so bad, Lora. All you have to do is pick up those beans again—"

"It's not ruined."

I felt his surprise, but he didn't say anything else, and I stood there looking at my garden and feeling something inside me swell and break away, so that I wanted to cry. I had not realized until then the things I had missed, the images Eli's illness had taken from me: jars boiling in a water bath, the kitchen ripe with the smell of cooking beans, the spice of pickles. There would be cabbages to put away in a ditch lined with hay and sand, and my cellar would be full of squash and pumpkins, the barrels heavy with potatoes and onions. The trees might be gone, but my garden had lived.

I wasn't sure even how to put it into words, what it meant to see those plants drinking up water, how they seemed to be reborn. But it filled my soul with faith, and faith was something I hadn't had in a long time. I looked over that devastated orchard, and the scene seemed to change before my eyes. Suddenly the wind rattling the cherry trees so they sprayed raindrops into the wind had a peaceful sound, and the wetness on my face felt good in the fading warmth of the sun.

Sometimes God gives you just enough so that you can go on. Every day on this farm had been a series of just enoughs, and I was growing used to having them fill me up as if they were bonanzas instead. *Only three cabbages ruined by worms! Only half the cherries cracked by rain! Prentiss & Hall taking ten dollars instead of the cow!* And suddenly I remembered something Eli had said that day we'd run out together to throw burlap and canvas over the apple trees, how, after the storm was over, his eyes had been wise and sad even as he'd smiled at me and gathered fallen apples into a bag. "Rain makes applesauce," he'd said, and when I stared at him in bewilderment, he'd taken my hand and led me to the house and told me stories to make me laugh and take my worries away.

That night, we'd eaten supper by lamplight and talked about the storm and the orchard, and how the apples he'd picked up were just sweet enough, and how it was one of the best things about the hail, that we were eating new applesauce for supper.

Except for the wet feel of the air and the damage it left behind, by the time sunset came there was nothing to show that the hail had been there at all. The mountains looked crisp-edged and beautiful. The clouds cleared out, and the sky lit up with purples and reds and a clear, pure gold, and it put its haze over everything, so the gray land looked made of impossible colors.

It was so pretty I wanted to wake Eli to show him, but I let him sleep, and I just watched it myself from the bedroom window and thought about how strange a day could be: one moment the stinging, fatal white of hail, the next a sky so clear you could see the stars powdering it like fine dust. I heard the coyotes howling in the distance, that long, lonely cry that sent shivers over my skin, but it was peaceful, too, and the exhaustion of the storm and everything else made my body so sore that when I finally went downstairs and curled up on the hard settee, I fell asleep in minutes.

I was dreaming about hail and apples and Eli's pain, when suddenly someone was shaking me awake. I opened my eyes, disconcerted, squinting into the darkness, and it was a minute before Will's face came into focus, close to mine.

"Lora, wake up," he whispered urgently. "Come on, wake up."

I heard it in his voice—something had happened to Eli. I jerked up so hard Will had to lurch back to get out of my way. "Eli . . . I'll be right there. Tell him I'll be right there—"

"Ssshhhh, it's not Eli. He's still asleep."

"It's not Eli? Then . . . what?"

"Ssshhhh. Come with me. Wrap the blanket around you. It's cold tonight."

He grabbed my hand, pulling me up so I had no choice but to go. I clutched the corner of the blanket at the last minute and dragged it after me. The room was cold, the frosty air bit my bare shoulders and cut through the thinness of my nightgown. Will stopped just as we reached the door.

"Put it on," he said, lifting the blanket and tucking it around me. Then, barefoot, I followed him out the door.

He went to the edge of the porch and pointed up at the sky. "Look. Shooting stars. There must be dozens of them out here tonight."

Shooting stars. He'd awakened me for stars. I blinked into the darkness, groggy and cold, and my feet were freezing on porch steps that still held the cold wetness of the storm. I pulled the blanket closer around me and turned back to the house. "That's nice."

He grabbed me before I could reach the door. "No. Look, Lora. Look at them."

I was too tired to protest. The sky was dark, dark blue, almost black, and the stars were so bright they seemed to glow on his face. For a minute I saw nothing, and then . . . and then I saw one. A star falling through the sky.

When I was a child, it had always seemed impossible to me that a star could fall that way, as if it just let go of the sky and trusted that God, or fate, would take it where it was supposed to go. Like a miracle, somehow. Back then, I'd made wishes on every one I'd seen, and each seemed just as strange and remarkable as the last. I'd forgotten that, somehow, or maybe it was just that I never looked up at the sky that way anymore, but now I looked up and I found my breath caught by the impossibility all over again, and then there was another, and another, and another, until the sky seemed to be filled with them, all shooting this way and that—and the impossible thing wasn't the shooting stars, but being able to find a place where they didn't dance across the sky.

"That's one thing about this place. It's got the clearest skies I've ever seen." Will's breath frosted in the air. Then he laughed, and he was like a child, pointing, saying, "There!" and "Look there!" as if it was his job to show me every single one of them.

It was beautiful, and there was a preciousness in it that made me think of Eli lying upstairs. There had to have been so many nights like this, where the two of us had stayed out to watch the stars, but I didn't remember a one, and it was suddenly painful that I would have forgotten, that I hadn't held on tight to a memory like that.

"If only Eli could see this," I said.

Will glanced at me. "I wouldn't like to try carrying him down those stairs again. Not just yet."

He was right, of course, and Eli needed his rest. It would be unfair to wake him now. So I didn't go. I stood there with Will a bit longer, but I found myself missing the feel of my husband beside me, and I thought again of Soda Springs and how he'd sung. The stars began to feel sad to me, as if they were falling simply because they were too heavy to stay.

I made myself smile at Will. "I'd better get back inside. There's plenty to do tomorrow."

He nodded, but he kept looking up at the sky, and I felt somehow as if I'd disappointed him. I touched his arm; when he looked down at me, I said, "I didn't thank you yet for today. You did more than your best, and I know it. I appreciate it."

"You're welcome."

"Good night, Will."

His answer was slow in coming. I was at the door before he said in a soft voice, "Did you like them, Lora? Are you glad I woke you?"

"Yes," I told him, and it was true, and he must have heard that, because there was a smile in his "Good night," and his voice was gentle and sweet.

I went inside and closed the door, shutting out the night. I was going to the settee, and then I wasn't. I couldn't just lie there anymore, and sleep had abandoned me. Even though I'd just been with Will on the porch, and I knew he was still there, only the thickness of a wall away, I felt lonely, and suddenly I was going up the stairs to Eli.

After the night's brightness, that room was so dark I couldn't even see shadows. I made my way by memory to the window. I pulled aside the curtains, and through the thick, wavy glass, I could barely see the stars.

The window scraped along the sill as I opened it, and I thought of Will down there on the porch, hearing it and wondering, but I didn't call down to him, and I didn't think about him again after the window was open. I let the cold air ease in and I looked up at the stars, and in my head I felt Eli beside me, leaning close to look out the window, his breath warm on my cheek. *There, look there! And over there—two at once!* The voice was so loud in my ear I almost jumped at how real it was.

The strange thing was, it became a memory for me, something I held close and precious even though it didn't really happen. And though Eli was sleeping soundly behind me, I wanted to believe that he was with me, watching the shooting stars with his arm around my shoulders, making wishes, and when the stars and the vision finally dwindled away, there stayed a yearning in my heart that I didn't really understand, as if something was out there, just beyond my reach, fading away, falling with the stars.

16

"There were six sage rats down there yesterday," Will said. He leaned the mud-crusted shovel against the railing, and the rip in his shirt fluttered open with the movement, revealing pale skin. He grinned up at me. "I like to believe all living things have a right to be on this earth, but I'm starting to hate sage rats. D'you think it might be a weakness in my character?"

"If it is, there are men all over Yakima with the same fault." I sat on the bench and leaned back against the wall. The leaves left on the old oak were starting to color. This morning the wind was cooler; since the storm, fall had been pushing out summer bit by bit. I raised my face to let the breeze brush over my skin. "Feels good, doesn't it? Fall coming on."

"Yeah." Will put his elbow on the railing and leaned against it, and that tear in his shirt ripped wider, just that simple motion running it up nearly to the shoulder. He put his elbow down again and glanced ruefully at it.

"I'm sorry," I said. "I shouldn't have forgotten the wash. It's ruined your clothes."

"Yours too," he reminded me. "And you had reason. Don't worry about it. Shirts are easy to come by. I'll pick up another one next time I'm in town."

"With what?"

He shrugged. "I'm pretty handy. Maybe Ben will hire me on for an afternoon."

"No." I said it more sharply than I meant. "I'll get you another one of Eli's."

"I imagine he'll need them himself."

"Wait here." I got up and went upstairs. Eli was sleeping, the calm, deep sleep of laudanum. I was going to walk right past him, to get the shirt out of the trunk and not disturb his sleep, but he looked so still, and I went over to check on him because I couldn't help myself. I didn't yet trust my instinct that he would be all right. I sat quietly on the edge of the chair standing as sentry by the bed, not allowing it to squeak as I looked down at him, and suddenly I was thinking of a time when we'd first come to this place. Eli had taken me to the top of Ahtanum Ridge. It was a hot, dry day in early summer, and the hills were already brown and seared, but he'd told me about the wildflowers he'd seen there in the spring, how they'd covered the ridge. He'd named them, flowers I'd never guessed he knew: camas and lupine, buttercup, larkspur. I sat beside him with my feet planted firmly to keep from sliding down the slope, and the valley spread out before us in the soft morning light, textured and rolling. I saw clear to the corners of our claim that morning, as if lines had been laid out on the land below to show me the boundaries. "Look at it—it's ours," he'd said. "We'll find everything we want in this place, Lora."

It was the same morning light that played over his sleeping face now as I watched him, and like that day so long ago, I saw the contours of Eli's face like a landscape boundaried on all sides, land that belonged to me. The day we'd sat on the ridge, I'd tried to memorize the landmarks of our claim; I wanted to feel my ownership of it the way I felt ownership of my hand. I wanted to be able to look at a rock and know just where it belonged, where it had come from.

When I looked at Eli now, I felt that same way. I had almost lost him, and now I wanted to hold him to me as tight as I could, and I was afraid of that, too, because like this land, Eli demanded everything.

He stirred, his eyelashes fluttered, and then he was looking up at me sleepily, blinking. I leaned over him and pushed back his hair from his face. "How do you feel this morning?"

He licked his lips. "Thirsty."

There was a pitcher of water on the night table. I poured him a cup and put my arm beneath his head to prop him up enough to drink. He struggled away for a minute, shaking his head that he wanted to try it himself, but when he put his elbow down, he winced in pain, and his weight fell onto my arm again.

He trembled as he drank, water dribbling to wet the blankets over his chest, but he gulped fiercely, and when he was done I set the cup aside and took the corner of my apron to blot up the water.

"I'm sorry," he said, turning his head away from me.

"It's all right. It's just water. I'll dry—"

He shook his head. "Not about that. I . . . I never meant for this."

"I know that."

He was quiet for a minute. Then he said, "Tell me what Lockwood said."

"He's just a lazy old man, Eli, you know that. Sometimes I think he wouldn't know—"

"What did he say?"

The question called for honesty, so that's what I gave him. "He thought your left leg would be all right. That you might have a limp, but he . . . he wouldn't be able to tell until he saw how your foot healed."

"What about the other leg?"

"Eli—"

"I've . . . tried . . . to look at it." He took a deep breath, and his hands fisted on the covers. "But I can't. It . . . hurts to try. I know it's bad, Lora. What I don't know is . . . How bad is it?"

"Eli—"

"Just tell me."

"He thought . . . it would be better to take it off," I whispered.

"He doesn't think it will heal."

"He didn't think you would *live*, Eli. But look at you."

He looked down at his motionless legs. His gaze grew distant, as if he was seeing it all before him again. "I heard it, you know. I heard it first, this . . . crash. Harry yelled something, but . . . I never saw it. Even now, I don't know what it looked like, or how big it was. All I really remember is how much it hurt."

"Oh, Eli."

He came to himself again, shaking his head slightly as if to clear his mind of the memories. "It still hurts, Lora. It hurts so damn bad I can hardly stand it. But what hurts more is the thought that I've left you this way. I . . . I didn't mean to be a burden. This last year has been burden enough."

"It's all right. It's all right. Don't talk." I spoke quickly, trying to quiet him before he said something I couldn't bear, and his look was so wise. It made me ashamed, how easily he saw through me. I glanced away, unable to face it.

"I'm sorry," he said. "This isn't what you expected, I know. I'll make it up to you, Lora. I promise I will."

"There's nothing to make up for."

"Oh, yes, there is," he said, and his voice was a gentle kindness that hurt my heart. "There's the last four years."

"Eli—"

"I made promises to you. No, Lora, I remember them. If they weren't to you, then they were to myself. That first time I saw you, sitting on your pa's porch, you were so serious. I remember telling myself, *Now, there's a girl who needs to smile.* And then, that first time I saw you smile, I knew I was right. Your smiles were like . . . they were like jewels. I told myself then, *You keep her happy, Elijah. Make sure those smiles are always there ready to come out.*"

He looked at me, and there was such sadness in his look, such wistfulness. He reached out and touched the spot above my heart, a soft touch that was so familiar.

"Instead, I took them away, didn't I?"

I wanted to cry. "No, Eli, of course not."

"I know you hate this place."

I couldn't tell him no, though I wanted to. The lie just wouldn't come, not even for him.

"I would leave it for you, if I could. I would walk away. I wish I could. But—I don't know how to explain. It's as if the only way to make her death mean something is to make this land work."

I got up so quickly the chair scraped back. I could barely hear for the whooshing sound in my ears.

Eli grabbed for me; then he gasped in pain and fell back on the bed. "Don't . . . go."

I stood beside the bed and stared down at him, unable to move now that I'd risen. When he reached for me again, more slowly this time, I watched his hand come for mine, the inch-by-inch movement, his hand in all its detail, big-knuckled fingers still stained with pitch. I didn't move away as they curled around my own, and when he tugged gently, I followed his silent instruction and sat again in the chair beside him.

"Don't go," he whispered, and then he began to talk, until the words were a balm on my spirit. "Listen . . . listen. Last night, I dreamed about the night before I left for the Wishkah. Remember? But in my dream, we sat there on the porch, and we were holding hands and . . . and listening to the crickets, and I didn't want to go."

I heard pain in his hesitations, in the draw of his breath. I reached for the laudanum, and he watched me do it, watched me uncork it. I saw his need for it stretching in the tautness of his throat, in the way he licked his lips. But when I tried to let go of his hand to pour it, he squeezed my fingers tighter.

"Lora," he whispered. "I wish . . . I wish it had been that way. Don't you?"

He closed his eyes then, and passed out. Even before I could give him the laudanum. So he never saw me nod.

His talk brought back that yearning I'd felt the other night, watching the stars. I felt unbalanced and strange, and I gripped the edge of the chair seat until the feeling faded, and I could rise. But I was shaken. I tripped a little on the uneven floorboards, and I had to put my hand on the wall for balance when I reached the stairs. It wasn't until I began to step down that I remembered why I'd even come up. I needed to get a shirt for Will.

My head felt fuzzy, and so when I went to the trunk and fumbled around in the half darkness, looking for one of Eli's shirts, I thought nothing of how long it took for me to find one. The first one I brought out was one of his Sunday best, and so I set it aside and pushed past my own scorched and torn chemises and drawers to find another. There wasn't one. I stared into the clothes for a minute, trying to clear my head. There had to be another. There were so many of them. Finally I took out everything, thinking I'd mislaid a few when I put them away, but there was only the one. Eli had one shirt left.

It seemed impossible. Just two years ago, when he'd first brought home the sewing machine, I'd made him six. Five shirts cut from a bolt of rough unbleached cotton, another one—Sunday best—from yards of fabric as shining white as snow. They could not all be gone. What could have happened to them?

Then I thought back to the day Eli had left for the Wishkah, how ragged he'd looked, with a torn shirt and trousers rent and unpatched. I thought of the rag bag I'd torn Will's bandages from. Full to bursting. Full of shirts made of unbleached cotton, torn from fencing or digging or picking. Shirts I had not been able to bring myself to mend.

I knelt there in the dimness of our bedroom and stared at the single shirt folded on my lap. It was soft, and the fabric was fine, though it wasn't white any longer. It was grayed, worn from many washings, and the collar was frayed, the button loose and dangling from only a few threads.

I felt the rent in my own chemise gaping with my movements, the roughness of scorched fabric against my skin, and I knew that each one in that trunk looked the same, some worse than others. Frayed, threadbare, old and needing buttons or edging sewn back on. All deserved to be in the rag bag.

Carefully I put Eli's shirt back into the trunk. I laid everything else in and shut the lid so it wouldn't bang and wake him. Then I got to my feet and went down the stairs. I felt unsteady, and I pressed my hand against the wall for balance. It seemed as if something was buzzing in my head, and I didn't want to think about it or look at it. I just wanted it to go away. When I went back onto the porch and saw Will still standing there, waiting patiently, I said, "I'm sorry it took so long. Eli woke up."

"That's what I figured."

"But . . . he's only got one shirt left. It looks like . . . I'll have to make some more." My voice seemed not my own. It was distant, as if it came from some dream, or someone else.

Will frowned. "Not on my account, Lora."

"It's . . . it's fine. I just need to go into town, get some cotton. And I guess some muslin, too. We need all kinds of things. It's just . . . it's been a while since I . . . sewed."

He looked at me strangely. "Are you all right?"

"Yes. Yes, of course. I'm fine."

But I didn't feel fine. I was imagining the thump of the pedal beneath my foot; my ears were full of the whirring of the machine, the soft *sshhusshh* of fabric moving across the table. Sounds so loud Eli used to curse when he came in the house: "I've been calling you, Lora." And then, "My God, Lora. My God, didn't you hear?"

I shook the sounds away and blinked to clear my head. I tried to smile at Will. "We'll have to go into town . . . sometime."

Some words have a power beyond their meaning. That single one—*sometime*—was something I clung to. I'd said I would buy fabric, that I would make clothes, but it didn't have to be today. Or tomorrow. Just . . . sometime.

Will opened his mouth to say something, but then we both heard the sound of hoofbeats on the road. I looked up to see John Zimmerman coming into the yard at full speed. He checked his horse just before he reached the porch, and the mare stopped in a flurry of dust. John's face was haggard, his expression dark with worry.

"I heard about Eli," he said. "You should have sent the boy to get me, Lora. I'd've been here right away."

The boy. As if Will weren't right there in front of him. It offended me, and made me forget the sewing machine and making clothes. "*Will* and I did just fine by ourselves."

John glanced at Will, and then he slid off his horse and nodded shortly. He reached into his saddlebags and pulled out a lumpy bag. "Well, I'm here now. Lizzie 'n' me'll do whatever we can to help. I would've come over after the storm, but . . . well, you know how it is. Lizzie's sent over a cheese, and there's some mutton in there for you, too. It makes a good strong broth. Lizzie swears by it." He handed the bag to Will. "How is he? I ran into the doctor in town. He said Eli's bad."

"He's doing better now."

"Good Lord, Lora. I can't tell you how sorry I am. I wish I'd known."

"There was nothing you could've done, John. It was bad there for a while, but . . . he's alive."

John's gaze was frank. "What about his legs?"

"I don't know," I said quietly.

John nodded. "Well. You'll need some help with the Spitzes, I imagine. How'd you fare in the storm?"

"We lost a few trees."

"You've had a run of bad luck lately."

"I guess so."

"Boyd 'n' me'll be over to help pick what's left if . . . well, if Eli can't do it."

"I doubt he'll be out of bed anytime soon. It was bad, John."

That old face of his sobered so he looked even older. "Lockwood told me."

"We're doing all right."

"Whatever we can do—"

"There's nothing."

"There is one thing," Will put in.

I looked at him in surprise, and John seemed as startled as if Will had turned into a nest of rattlesnakes right before his eyes.

Will pulled at the tear on his shirt. "Lora needs to go into town. I'd be happy to take her, but we can't leave Eli alone."

The sewing machine started its whir in my head again. I think I said something—"Oh, no," maybe—or maybe I didn't, because the two of them kept on talking as if they hadn't heard a thing.

"I'm going into town next week," John said to me. "I'll be happy to drop on by and give you a ride."

"Eli doesn't know me too well," Will protested. "It might be better if someone else watched over him."

John eyed Will with a thoughtful look that was a little disturbing, but I didn't know why I thought that. Then he nodded slowly. "You might be right. I'll tell you what. I'll see if Lizzie can come on over to watch—"

"Not Lizzie," I said quickly. I couldn't help it. Elizabeth Zimmerman hadn't set foot in my house for a year, and I didn't want to think of what she would notice. Bare walls, empty whatnot. A rag bag stuffed full of old shirts. It made me cold to think of it, to think of what I would see in her eyes.

John didn't protest. Maybe he knew how I felt. There was nothing in his expression to tell me. He only sighed and said, "Then Polly. I'll send Polly over." Polly was his oldest daughter. I guessed she was about thirteen now. I hadn't seen her in quite a while.

Will glanced at me. When I said nothing, he nodded. "That'd be fine."

"I'm sure Lizzie can do without her for a day. Tomorrow, then."

"Oh, not tomorrow," I said. "I've still got butter to make, and the eggs. As long as we're going in, I might as well take some things in to Ben. It might take a couple days. Maybe a—"

"The day after tomorrow," Will said calmly, without looking at me. He was talking to John, man to man, and I stared at him in surprise. It was strange, but he seemed so strong, standing straight that way, so earnest. Like a boy come into his own in a single moment. It frightened me, but I couldn't stop looking at him. I couldn't grasp the change, and I didn't want to. I wanted to protest, to say, *No, you're just my boy,* but then it came to me that I'd changed the rules the day I'd asked him not to leave. I'd given him the right to carry my burdens. I'd asked him to be a man.

So I couldn't argue with him as he made plans with John to get Polly over to our place, but I was confused and rattled. And after John said his good-byes and left with the assurance that he'd be back to check on us, all I said, when Will turned to me and asked, "Can you have all the butter made by the day after tomorrow?" was, "I think so."

17

The night before Will and I were to go into town, I was too restless to sit still. When I went up to be with Eli for a while, all I could think of were the things that had to be done: the floor needed sweeping, the curtains were stained from the constant dust and had to be washed, bandages and scissors and bottles and pans lay everywhere. I started to clean things up until Eli said, "Sit down, Lora, you're making me dizzy."

"You're awake."

"Who could sleep, the way you're racing around?"

I sat. "I'm sorry. Would you like me to read to you? The *Washington Farmer*'s been waiting the last couple weeks—"

"No. Not tonight."

"Oh. Well, I meant to tell you, John was here today. He said to tell you that he and Lizzie are praying for you."

Eli's smile was weak. "That's good. I suppose I . . . need it."

"He's sending Polly out tomorrow."

"What for?"

"Will and I are going into town. I . . . when you came home, I was in the middle of doing the wash, and it boiled dry. I ruined Will's shirts, and you've got none left to give him, so I thought . . . I thought I'd buy some material to make a few more."

I said it fast, hoping he wouldn't notice, but I had never been able to fool him. Eli looked at me for a minute, and his face grew quiet and thoughtful. "You're making new shirts."

He left those words out there as if he didn't expect an answer, but I felt his question, and I knew what he was thinking. "You say that as if it's a curiosity."

"You haven't sewed for a long time."

"I haven't needed to," I said, but I couldn't look at him, because that was such a terrible lie and we both knew it.

"What . . . what happened, Lora?" he whispered.

That whisper shook me, so I jerked to my feet too fast. I tried to cover it up by saying, "Nothing. We need things, that's all. Now I . . . I've got to mold the butter. We'll be leaving early, so Polly'll be here when you wake up." And then I left him before he could say the things we both remembered.

I didn't sleep well that night, and when morning came, I was still restless and bothered, though I didn't want to think about why. Polly Zimmerman was at the farm just when John said she'd be. Somehow I'd hoped to find in her an excuse to stay—she was too young and giddy to trust with Eli, perhaps—but at thirteen, she already looked worn and haggard, and she seemed to take to the idea of looking after Eli for a few hours. I guessed she probably welcomed the chance to get away from working at home for a while, and I didn't miss the way she looked at Will, either, her shy little smile.

Will had the wagon waiting even before I'd finished showing Polly what to do, and when I hesitated, he gave me a reassuring nod. "Eli'll be all right."

It wasn't what was bothering me, but I got silently onto the wagon seat, and I looked back at the house as we rolled away across the prairie, thinking of Eli waking up to find Polly bent over him instead of me.

It made me sad, and I forced myself to look away from the house and stare out at the passing prairie. The storm had left little gutters along the road, washouts that changed the familiar markers, eroding the landscape, shifting the way before me so the road was not quite the one I knew. It was disconcerting, and this trip was unsettling enough.

"Did you notice my hat?" Will asked.

I looked over at him and said, "Oh. It'll keep you from getting sunstroke," but I couldn't have told you a second later what it was I'd said. All I could see was how different that hat made Will seem. He was turning into a man before my eyes, changing when I didn't want him to change.

"I never get sunstroke, Lora. And I'll tell you, I miss the feel of the breeze. This is one hot hat." He tapped the brim. "I found it in the barn. I didn't figure it for Eli's. It looks too old."

"Probably some hired hand left it."

"We leave things wherever we go. I guess it's human nature not to want to be forgotten."

"I guess so."

He sighed and leaned back, resting his foot on the brake and holding the reins loosely in one hand. The seat jerked and settled beneath his weight. "One place I worked, someone had painted a portrait on the barn wall. Some harvester who thought he was an artist. It was supposed to be a picture of the wife, but she'd aged so much I couldn't see the likeness. It didn't matter, I guess. It served its purpose well enough."

"Its purpose?"

Will looked at me quietly. "She never looked at it without thinking of him. That was what he wanted. He was in love with her."

"Oh." I looked away, into the hills of sage. "How sad."

"Sad? Why?"

"Well, there she is, left with this picture he painted of her, and all these years to look at it and think of him. Don't you think it would have been better if he'd just left her nothing?"

"How is that better?"

I stared out at the passing prairie, a crow swooping down low to the ground. "Sometimes not remembering is better."

There was a pause between us, time for what I'd said to settle in and linger there. Then Will said, "My mother died two years ago."

I turned to him and found him gazing at me with that quiet, thoughtful look. I didn't know what to say, so I stammered the words I'd grown to hate, the ones that meant nothing. "I—I'm sorry."

"I wasn't there to see her. My father had no way to reach me. I didn't even know she was sick. I sent her a letter around Christmas time, and my father wrote right back. I got his letter just before I left New Orleans. She'd caught some fever and died within days." He jangled the reins in his hand, and his gaze was distant, as if he were talking about somebody else, not himself. "He sent me a pin she used to wear. The gift he'd given her when I was born. It opened up, and there was a picture inside of me when I was a baby. I don't know, Lora. I was gone, but I think it made her happy to look at that picture and remember me. And thinking of that . . . it makes me happy, too."

I looked down, watching the scrub grass crush beneath the wheels. "Remembering isn't always like that."

Will looked at me. "Whenever I smell sagebrush I'll think of riding into town with you."

His smile was bright and soft, and I had to look away. All I could think of was how simple things were for him, how his losses were only a shadow of mine. It would be difficult to lose a mother, but it was expected. Parents died before their children, and that was just the natural order of things, something you knew in your heart would happen eventually, something to prepare for. There were other losses more difficult to reconcile, grief you couldn't assuage no matter what you did. There were things it hurt to remember.

I did not know how to explain this to him, and there was a part of me that didn't want to, that wanted Will Bennett to remain innocent of such things. I tried to forget them as we drove into Yakima;

I tried to lose myself in the cramped, crowded town it had become, all these buildings and people shoved into these few acres in the middle of nothing. But I couldn't feel comfortable or awed—I felt like a stranger there, as if I'd left part of myself in Yakima City, with Irma and tea parties and a husband who took care of selling the fruit . . .

And a small plot of land tucked behind the Methodist church.

I didn't let myself think of it. When Will pulled up and tied the horses in front of Ben Schiller's, I followed him in and felt as if I weren't really there, but only watching through someone else's eyes. I saw Ben standing stoic and solemn behind the counter and Will setting the tray of butter and the basket of eggs there before he stood back to let me come forward.

"I'm sorry to hear about Eli," Ben said.

"I think he'll be fine."

That was all he said to me and all I could bring myself to say to him. He counted out the eggs and the butter and added up the figures while Will hovered off to the side. When Ben was done, he said, "Anything you need, Lora?"

I started to shake my head, but just then Will moved, and that rip in his shirt opened wider. I remembered then why I was there. The fabric. I needed to make shirts, chemises. We would be in rags if I didn't. The cold seemed to move into my fingertips.

"I need some material, Ben," I managed. "You think . . . d'you think there's enough there for a bolt of that unbleached cotton?"

Ben nodded. He took down the bolt of cloth and laid it on the counter before me. I stared at that fabric, and I smelled how it caught the dust and the sun. I knew its feel without touching it, the smoothness of one side, the light texture of the other. I knew how it sounded when I cut it, and how it would catch on my roughened hands when I pinned the pieces together and sewed the seam.

I couldn't make myself touch it. When Ben wrapped it up in paper, I motioned for Will to take it, and when he put it in the wagon, I had him push it under the seat so I couldn't see it, though I told him it was just to keep it protected on the way home. But when I started to climb up onto the seat, Will shook his head at me.

"Not yet," he said.

I stared at him in confusion.

He leaned over the sideboards, tipped his hat back on his head, and smiled. "You work too hard, Lora."

"Will, we need to get back. There's Eli."

"Polly's watching him. And there's cherry pie down the street."

"I'm not hungry."

"A cup of coffee, then, while I have some."

"Will, I really think—"

"Wait," he said. He looked down the sidewalk, and then he came around to where I stood. "Come on," he said, taking my hand.

"We should get back."

"This'll only take a minute."

"Will—"

He walked fast, pulling me after him down the

dusty street, until I saw where he was heading.

It was a tent alongside the boxcar serving as the railroad station. The flap that was its door lapped in the wind, and dust swirled about the stakes that held it in place. Out front was a sign that read, *Tintypes 15 cents. Cartes de viste 10 cents. Cheap to send to loved ones in all 39 states. Martin A. Grambush, Professor of Photography.*

Will stopped outside the door. "Let's get our picture taken, Lora. Please?"

He must have seen my hesitation, because that smile came into his face again, the alluring, cajoling one.

"Come on," he said in a low voice. "Something to remember me by."

I had too many remembrances. I could not bear the thought of another. But he was smiling, and when I looked at him I saw the man behind his eyes, and I missed the boy. I wanted him back. And I thought somehow the picture might find him again, that he would take off that hat and I would see his shining golden hair, and the naive smile in those blue eyes, and so . . . I said yes, and he pulled me into the tent where a big, lumbering man sat behind a desk that looked like a toy next to his bulk.

"Professor Grambush?" Will asked.

"That's me, son." The man got to his feet with a flourish. The fragile desk tottered at the suddenness of his movement. I thought it was going to fall, sending papers and bills flying. But it righted itself as he came around to shake Will's hand. "Professor Martin Grambush, at your service."

"We'd like a photograph."

The man smiled. His eyes swept me, and then went back to Will. "Ah, newlyweds. A nice wedding picture for the folks, eh?"

I thought for a moment he was talking about someone else.

"We're just friends, sir," Will said smoothly.

Professor Grambush frowned a little, but he said nothing more as he bustled to where a large curtain was drawn across the length of the tent. He drew it back to reveal a chair and a big, leggy contraption covered with a cloth. The last time I'd been in front of a camera came back to me in an ache that stole my breath. *She looks so peaceful . . . a little angel . . .*

I forced my gaze to Will. When Professor Grambush motioned me to the chair, I went and sat. When Will came up beside me and put his hand on my shoulder, it was all I could do not to grab it and hold on.

They talked, and I didn't hear anything. When the professor went behind the camera and disappeared beneath the cloth, I sat there stiffly, staring into the lens. I heard Professor Grambush say something, and I felt Will's fingers flex on my shoulder, and then the lights flashed and it was over, and Will and I were sitting in two uncomfortable camp chairs in the tent, waiting for the man to develop the picture.

I had fifteen cents in my pocket from the butter and eggs I'd sold that day, and without thinking, I handed it over when the professor told us what we owed. It was an extravagance, but that hardly occurred to me. When at last the man gave us the picture in a rough folding cardboard frame, Will and I went outside and stood on the sidewalk while he opened it to see.

It was a photograph of two strangers. The woman was straight-backed and unsmiling. Her skin was pale, her hair a pale shadow, and the gaze staring into the camera was a blank one. Beside her stood a man with hair that shone in the light, with deep-set eyes and full lips curving in a small smile. His hand on her shoulder was proprietary. They looked young, like newlyweds.

I closed the makeshift frame and handed it to him, then I hurried to the wagon. I was on the seat before Will could even get there to help me, and when he climbed aboard, he turned to me with a frown in his eyes. "Lora, are you—"

"We'd best get home."

I couldn't look at him, and I wanted to be alone so badly I could hardly stand to feel him beside me on the seat. Because I knew my boy was gone. Maybe he had never existed at all, except in my imagination. Eli's words came to me: *He's not our son.* And I realized I had made him that, and it was just an illusion. I'd made a son to take the place of my daughter, and without him, there was nothing, and I felt that barrenness so bleak and large and encompassing I could not see the end of it, so small it fit inside my chest, deep within my heart.

The drive back to the farm was long and lonely and silent. When we finally pulled up to the house, there was Polly waiting on the porch outside. I was out of the wagon before Will could say anything, and though I saw Polly's mouth move as I went past her, I heard no words, nothing but a buzzing in my head. I hardly thought. I just stumbled away. Will called out, "Lora—Lora, wait!" but I didn't stop for him. I had no idea where I was going, just that I was.

My dress caught in my legs, my hair whipped into my face. I went through the orchard, dodging branches, crushing rotting apples beneath my feet, and I was just going without knowing where or even why.

Until I was there.

The bank of the irrigation canal crumbled away beneath my feet. Little clods of dirt plopped into the muddy, fly-skimmed water below. It wasn't shallow now. The storm had fed the river, and the river fed the canal. There was an apple bobbing in it, a little green Spitzenberg floating lazily along in the currentless water, moving only when the wind sent ripples across the surface.

I sank onto the bank, drawing my knees to my chest, staring across to the other side. I heard the wind, the birds, a cricket, the hush of water. I saw the grass blow, and in my head the smell of strawberries came sweet and dusty, though there were no strawberries now.

I heard the sound of his footsteps behind me. I heard him stand there, I heard his breath. For a moment, he didn't move, and then he sat down beside me. He wasn't wearing the hat, and the wind blew his golden hair back from his face. He didn't look at me. He looked across the ditch, as if he could see what I was seeing. But, of course, he couldn't.

"Eighteen inches," I said quietly. "It's hardly even wide enough to be a rut in the ground."

His voice was soft, words swept by wind. "What happened here?"

They had told me my pain would fade in time. They had said it would get better. It wasn't true. I stared at that apple bobbing in the canal and thought of how my daughter had been motionless in four inches of water, her fine golden hair spreading around her head like river weeds, a blond halo. I had not seen that. Eli had. Eli had found her. The sewing machine was so loud I hadn't heard anything. It wasn't until I paused that I'd heard his shouting. I had been slow to come to him. I'd stepped onto the porch to hear him, and then the urgency in his voice caught me, and I'd gone running down to the canal to see him holding my limp little girl in his arms, her hair streaming over his hands, dripping from a face too pale and still to be real.

She had wanted strawberries, and I'd told her to wait for me because I was making a pinafore. But I couldn't get the ruffle right, and I kept working with it and working with it and she went to get them without me. The next time I saw her, she was already gone.

But I could not say those things to Will. Suddenly, he was a stranger, he was not the man I wanted beside me. I stumbled to my feet. "I . . . I have to go," I said.

He tried to reach for me. "Lora—"

I stepped away, and when he rose to follow me, I said, "No, please," and when he stepped back and let me go, I left him there looking bewildered and hurt, and I didn't care. I went back through the orchard, but until I was at the house, I didn't know what I'd been running for.

Polly was waiting on the porch, looking patient, or resigned, and when I came up the steps, she stared at me as if she knew something was wrong but wasn't sure if she should ask or what she should say. I went right past her. I went into the house and up the stairs, into the room where my husband lay, and it wasn't until I was there, in the darkness with him, that I could breathe again.

I thought he was asleep, but he moved when I came near, and I saw he was awake and that the lamp was lit. It was not dark in there after all—how had I not seen that? His eyes glittered in the lamplight, and he struggled to sit up and sighed with pain at the effort.

"How was town?"

"Fine. It was fine."

He was watching me with that steady look that made me think he saw everything. "It was."

"Yes."

I went to the window, looking down into the yard. Will was there now, standing by the wagon, talking to Polly and frowning as he took the bolt of fabric out of the bed.

"Lora," Eli said again. "You look . . . Come here. I think you should sit down."

I stared down at the yard. Will shifted the fabric in his arms. The sun reflected off the paper wrapped around the bolt; the cardboard frame of the photograph we'd posed for peeked from his shirt pocket.

"What's wrong? Lora, what is it?"

I tried to think of a way to answer him. "How did Polly do?"

"She was fine. What . . . what happened in town?"

"We had a photograph taken. Me . . . and Will. And I bought some cotton. A nice bolt of it. I can make you some shirts, and Will too. I didn't have enough to buy muslin, but my things can wait. My things . . ." The words caught in my throat, so I could not finish. I couldn't even think of what I'd been about to say. Behind me, Eli was quiet, and the silence between us was so loud it started that humming again in my ears, but when I heard his slow, whispered, "Lora," it quieted. He spoke my name, and nothing else, but I heard everything he meant in the word. I heard how much he loved me, and how sad he was, and I knew the memories in those syllables, the things he saw, everything he wanted, and I felt the tears come into my eyes, the words stumble out.

"I went to the canal."

He went very still. Then his breath came out in a long, hoarse sigh. "Lora."

"I . . . I don't know what to do anymore, Eli. I'm afraid. I can't . . . I can't make the fear go away. I've tried and I can't. I *can't*." I was crying again, and standing there, feeling myself collapse in front of him, that place inside of me so empty and dark. "Tell me how to make it go away."

My Eli, the man who had words for everything, said nothing. He held out his hand to me, and it was like a beacon, drawing me to him until I was kneeling beside the bed and his hand was against my cheek, tangled in my hair, the soft, warm strength of it, his familiar skin. "I can't stop remembering her," I cried into his palm. "I've tried so hard not to, but I just . . . can't."

He leaned close; I heard the hush of his breath, the pain of his movement, but he didn't draw back, and my nose and my skin were full of him. He whispered into my ear, "I heard this story once, an Indian story. They say that once there were two warriors who caught the spirits of the dead to bring them back to earth so the people could see them and remember. They put them in a box, but as they got closer to land, the spirits began to turn into men again. They grew so heavy the warriors could no longer carry them, and so one of them opened the box to see what was happening. When he did, the spirits flew out again, and they went rushing away, back to where they came from. One of the warriors wanted to go back to get them, but the other decided that they belonged in the land of the dead, that they were alive in our hearts, that our memories were . . . enough."

I started to back away from him, but he held me tight. "Don't you see what you're doing, Lora, don't you understand? When you try to forget her . . . it's like you're saying she wasn't here, that there was no reason for her to exist. But there was. There has to be."

I think she was sent to us for a reson, and taken away for one to. I closed my eyes. Eli's words wound round and round in my head.

"Oh, Lora," he breathed. "What has this last year been like for you? Trying not to remember?"

I didn't know how to answer him. I wasn't sure he even expected an answer. But I was shivering when I

opened my eyes and saw him looking so earnestly
into my face, as if sheer strength of will could make
me understand what I knew already.

"'Oh, will you wear green, Jenny dear, Jenny
dear . . .'"

His voice was low and hoarse. At first I didn't
understand, I couldn't tell what he was saying. Then
the words came louder, an effort, rough with tears.

"'Oh, will you wear green, Jenny Jenkins?'"

In my head I saw Eva laughing at him as she sat on
his knee. I heard her voice joining with his, high and
soft, stumbling over words in that singsong, untuned,
little-girl melody. *No, I won't wear green, it's the color of a
bean. . . .* I saw the tears on his cheeks lit by lamplight,
and the hard swallow of them in his throat, and I
cupped his hand against my cheek and held him tight,
afraid to let him go, afraid of myself. Because, in those
few moments, touching him, listening to the song, I
realized why I'd come to him now, what I'd wanted,
and that frightened me. I was afraid because the comfort I'd searched for, I'd found . . . in my husband's
arms.

⌒ part 3

You called me, and I came home to your
  heart,
The triumph was,—to reach and stay
  there . . .

—ROBERT BROWNING

'Tis not too late to seek a newer world.

—ALFRED, LORD TENNYSON

18

When I woke the next morning, it was early, the sky still dark, though the sun was starting to rise. Last night I'd fallen asleep kneeling by his bed, my head angled on the edge of the mattress, so there was a crick in my neck, and I had a headache before the day had even begun. Eli was still sleeping. I changed quietly and went downstairs, through the darkness of the house to the back door, and only the chickens were up to greet me as I went to the privy. When I washed my face at the well, the sight of the built-up frame brought me to tears again, remembering how Eli had made it because he'd been so afraid she would fall in. . . . I was raw and defenseless now, nothing but tears. After I washed them from my face, they only came again.

When I went back into the house, the sun was sending light through the windows. I saw the fabric lying there on the settee, pristine in its paper, untouched. New shirts, I remembered. Will was in rags. Eli had only one. I thought of the patterns I'd made of brown paper, folded and stacked neatly in a trunk in the attic, and the sewing machine silent beneath the eaves. I told myself I would go upstairs after breakfast and fetch them both. Today, I would make some new clothes.

The promise nagged at me as I went into the kitchen to start breakfast. The cotton was constantly there, a presence filling the edges of my vision as I ground coffee and sliced bread. It was unnerving, alive almost, something I could not escape. It disturbed me so much that when an egg slipped from my grasp to splatter on the puncheon floor, I just stared at it, yolk spreading, white dripping into the seams of the floorboards, the eggshell like shattered glass. I couldn't move, not until I heard the boots on the steps, the quick stride across the porch. Will.

Yesterday flashed into my mind, how I'd run from him at the irrigation ditch, and I grabbed a towel and dropped to my knees, ducking my head, mopping up that egg so I wouldn't have to see him when he came through the door, so I had time to compose myself, even though I felt composure was something I would never have again.

I saw the door open, the creaking scrape against the floor. I saw his boots.

"Good morning," he said.

"Good morning. I . . . I dropped an egg." The egg wouldn't mop up. It was on my fingers, dripping from the towel. "Breakfast will be ready in a minute—"

He was beside me before I knew it. "You're making a mess," he said gently as he took the towel from my hand. In a few short motions, he had the egg cleaned up, the towel gathered in a ball. I had no more reason to stay there on the floor as he got up and put the towel in the wash bucket, but it took me a minute to remember that. The only thing that got me to my feet was the thought that if I didn't, he would come over to help me.

I went to the stove and cracked the other eggs into the skillet, and I felt surrounded. The fabric on the settee seemed to glow, and Will was too close. When he reached past me to grab the pot of coffee, I ducked my head again, moved too abruptly out of his way, and I felt him pause. I felt his thoughtfulness as he poured a cup and set it back, his slow, methodical step as he went to the table and sat down.

"How are you this morning?" he asked.

"Fine. I'm fine."

"And Eli?"

"He's getting better all the time."

"I was thinking I should go up there. I could read the paper to him or something."

"I imagine he'd like that."

"Maybe later then, after I do some work on the ditch."

I nodded, staring at the eggs beginning to pop and brown in the pan. *The ditch.* I heard the question there. I didn't look at him when I said, "Will . . . about yesterday—"

"It's all right," he said quickly.

"No, it's . . . it's not. You asked me what happened at the ditch, and I . . . it was a fair question."

He didn't say anything. I felt his eyes on me. I felt his waiting.

"I had a daughter," I said. "A year ago, she drowned there. She was three years old."

I don't know what I expected him to say: maybe *I'm sorry,* or *My God, what a terrible thing.* I'd heard those words before, too many times. They raised a wall in my soul, and in a way I wanted that. I wanted to close up again, to be safe from my grief, to hide it away as I'd hidden it this last year, refusing to look at it, to feel.

But Will didn't say anything like that. He looked at me, those blue eyes sad with the knowledge I'd given him, and asked, "What was her name?"

What was her name?

"Eva," I whispered. "Her name was Eva."

I heard him move, and then he was behind me, putting his arms around me, resting his head on my shoulder so I felt the slick thickness of his hair against my cheek. "I'm sorry, Lora."

The words I'd waited for. In a way, it was good to know that Will was no different from any of the others, that death took his words as well. But it made me feel empty, too, and I found myself trying to hide it with bitter words. "Is that all? No wise words for me? No life lessons?"

He shook his head. "No. I understand now."

"Understand what?"

"What you've done to yourself. Why."

I pulled away. "What I've done to myself?"

He let me go, and then he looked at me with those eyes that seemed to see right into my soul. "It's like the picture on the barn, Lora, isn't it? It's why you said what you did about remembering."

Incredibly, I felt tears start at my eyes. There was no reason, but I could not seem to control them. I tried to pull away, but he held me fast, and then I think he was surprised to see I was crying, because the moment I lifted my face, he let me go.

"Lora. I'm sorry. I didn't mean to—"

I shook my head wordlessly. I tried to wipe away the tears with my fingers, but that only made things worse. The fabric shone on the settee, blurring and glaring in my eyes. "I'm . . . so sorry," I said, and I was laughing then, too, that terrible, sorrowful laughter, little short bursts of it. "I . . . I didn't mean to cry . . . like this." I took the hem of my apron to my face, but then he was pulling my hand away, handing me a handkerchief. It was soft and worn against my skin, and I felt swollen and too tender and so embarrassed I could not bear to meet his eyes.

"I keep . . . leaking," I said with a laugh as I wiped away the tears. "I'm sorry, I—"

"It's all right," he said quietly. "You don't have to be embarrassed, Lora. Not for today. Not for yesterday. Look, I just figured you need someone to talk to, and I'm here. I'll pretend I don't know, if it'll make it easier for you."

I looked up at him. He was watching me with such kindness that it brought an ache into my chest. I shook my head. "No, I don't want that. It's just that I . . . it's hard to remember her, though it seems like that's all I ever do. It helps to think that you know. It does. It's someone besides me . . . and Eli."

"Maybe talking about her would help."

"That's what Eli thinks. I . . . I've never been able to."

"Not before, maybe. But I'm here now. I'd be happy to listen."

I nodded. They were kind words, but I didn't think I'd take him up on it. I didn't think I could. "Well, thank you," I said. "Now I'd better get Eli his breakfast."

I felt him watching me for a moment, and then I heard him sit down and eat, the clanking of his fork on the enamelware plate, the soft thud of his coffee cup on the tabletop. I stared out the window, my back to him while I dried a cup, and found myself just staring at the orchard beyond, the rows of trees, the cherries, the Pippins, the Spitzenbergs, just wiping that cup over and over. I spoke before I thought. "They took a photograph of her when she died."

The sound of eating stopped. I felt Will's stillness, and the words spilled from me. Words I had not intended to say. I didn't know why I was telling him, why I wanted to, but I couldn't stop myself. The memory was alive in my head; I could see the lights the man set up and how they took up every inch of the room, along with the boxy camera. I saw the people—our neighbors—bustling and too silent. I could see myself, combing her hair through my fingers, making sure it was just right, spread across a lace pillow so in the light it looked like a halo.

"They said ... they said I would want it. To remember her. They insisted on it, really, and the man came out here to the house—I'd laid her out right there in the living room and lit candles all around. Eli and I sat there for three days, and I swear I never took my eyes off her. I waited to see her

breathe again. Every morning, I thought, *Today* . . .
today, she'll be alive. But when I saw that picture, I
knew she wouldn't be. She looked like an angel. So
pale and sweet, and the light in her hair . . . She had
this rag doll that she loved. We buried it with her, to
keep her company." I felt my voice break, and I put
aside the cup, hung up the towel. "I'd made it from
one of Eli's old socks, with string for hair, and she
named it Lucindy. She took it with her everywhere,
even though she had a beautiful china doll my parents had brought from Walla Walla. I always thought
that when she was older, I would ask her why she
liked Lucindy best." I turned to look at him. Will was
watching me with listening stillness, as if he heard
things in my words beyond what I'd said, and his gaze
was so intent. "Well. I suppose that's a wrong thing to
think, isn't it? To wait to say things. You never know."

"No, you don't." He looked so thoughtful, as if
there was something he wanted to say, but was somehow holding back. His voice was low and soft.
"Where's the picture now?"

"I put it away. I didn't want to remember her that
way. I didn't . . . want to remember her . . . at all."

He was quiet; I knew he was trying to think of
something to say, and I didn't want him to say anything. I motioned to the door. "It's getting late. You
should go out to the ditch."

He didn't protest; maybe he knew I wanted him to
go. I heard him go out the door and pick up the
shovel from the porch. I looked out the front window, and I saw the pale morning light touching him,
his slow stride as he headed out to the canal, and

wondered what it was in him that made me want to talk to him, to tell him things. Why had I told him that story?

It made me uncomfortable to think of it, and guilty, as if I'd betrayed Eli somehow. I thought of him upstairs in bed, waiting to see my face, waiting for me. These past months, I'd seen his yearning to talk about her in his eyes, I'd heard it in every word he said, and I had not been able even to say her name. And yet here was Will, a stranger for whom these memories meant nothing, and I had blurted out that story without even thinking.

My dried tears itched on my skin. I wiped at them with the corner of my apron, and then I saw again the bolt of cloth, gleaming now in the light streaming through the window.

As quickly as I could, I went and picked it up and slid it underneath the settee, where I could see nothing of it but the very edges of the paper it was wrapped in. I told myself it meant nothing, that I would still sew today. I'd simply had to move it for now. No one could sit on the settee while it was there. I didn't need to see it to remember the task I'd set for myself. But I felt relieved when it was gone. I heard the word in my head again: *Sometime, sometime,* and I went to finish breakfast.

It bothered me for the rest of the day: the things I'd told Will, the things I'd both revealed to and hidden from Eli. I went about my chores, peeling culled apples for drying, putting up the last green tomatoes in piccalilli, and it kept coming back to me, the way

Will had put his arms around me, and how comfort-
less those arms had been. And as the afternoon wore
on, I yearned for another pair of arms, for the ones
that had held me tight, for the smell of a skin that
had filled my nights for longer than I could remember. It was Eli whose arms I craved, and that made the
things I was afraid to say to him even more unforgiv-
able.

But I *was* afraid. I heard in my head the silly song
he'd sung the night before, and in the steam of the
jars I saw the ghost of his face, etched with pain and
simple joy. I felt the lean strength of him, and heard
the beat of his heart, and I felt vulnerable. I did not
know if I could look into his eyes now and see his
reaction to the intimacy we had shared. I did not
know if I could be what he expected.

But I was drawn to him just the same. During the
day, while he was sleeping, I must have gone upstairs
to check on him a hundred times, to touch those
strong fingers when they were relaxed in sleep and
remember how they'd felt threaded through my hair.

Still, my fears were stronger. It was easier to stay in
the kitchen and imagine his arms around me and hear
his voice in my ear saying, *It's all right, Lora. It's all right.*
So when I heard the creak of the bed upstairs and
knew he was awake, I took my time making him something to eat, and when I took the tray upstairs, I didn't
know whether it was the dread or the longing to see
him I felt more. In the end, it was the nervousness that
took over—it was so hard to learn again how to be with
Eli, and I was clumsy at it, shy and jittery, the way I'd
been those first months of our marriage, before the

day he'd taken me in his arms and whispered in my ear never to be ashamed of what was between us. I guess I needed to hear those words again.

I went into the room and laid the tray on the bedside table, and I couldn't look at him. "Here's your dinner," I said, and then I went to the window and opened the curtains so the light came in. "It's a beautiful day. You can feel the fall out there already. I'll be glad when the summer's over. This heat has been—"

"Lora," he whispered.

I turned around. He was looking at me with that deep blue gaze that seemed to touch me everywhere, inside and out. I felt it in a leap in my belly, the sudden rush of my breath. "You better eat your dinner. Before it gets cold."

"I will. Come on over here a minute."

I wanted to, but I couldn't move. Last night came into my head, my tears, the way I'd hardly been able to speak, the things I'd said. I made some useless, limp gesture toward the stairs. "I've got piccalilli cooking."

His gaze didn't leave me. "I've been waiting a year for you to say the things you said last night," he said, and the plain words shocked me and warmed me at the same time. "I guess I just can't let it go now. Don't . . . don't push me away again, honey."

The tears were in my eyes again, and he was nothing but a blurred shadow beyond them, light and dark. "I don't want to. I . . . I never wanted to."

"I know."

"Sometimes, Eli, it seems I've failed you in so many ways."

"Maybe we've failed each other."

I laughed a little through my tears. "You're kind to say that. But I'm . . . ashamed. All the things we talked about . . . that big family we wanted . . . and I couldn't . . . I just loved her so much, I thought my heart wouldn't have room for another, and now . . ."

He patted the bed. "Come here."

I went over to him then. I sat as gently as I could on the edge of the mattress, but the pain came into his eyes anyway. When I started to move away, he grabbed my hand and said, "No, stay here. It doesn't matter."

"I don't want to hurt you."

"I'd rather have you close." His fingers worked over mine, and he gave me the soft little smile I loved. "You know, I . . . I thought about what you said last night. About being afraid."

"Yes, I—"

He shook his head, silencing me. "I always thought, no matter what happened, I could keep my family safe. I thought I'd planned for everything: a railing on the porch, a guard around the well, staying only a call away. If Indians came by, I was there and I had a shotgun. I killed every rattler I saw and set fire to their dens and built this house far enough from the river that it's taken a mile of ditch to get water here. I did everything I could think of, and it wasn't enough. But I've been up here thinking, and it occurs to me that maybe I was wrong to try so hard. Maybe there's no way to be safe in this world, and it's better that way. Because I think . . . I think we've been working this last year to be safe from each other, and it's been the loneliest time of my life."

I swallowed hard.

"You think you can close yourself off from everything, Lora. But it doesn't work that way. This is only hurting. I'm tired of hurting. I want to think you are, too."

It surprised me that he would see that, that he would know what I hadn't said to anyone, what I couldn't bear to admit even to myself.

"I'm afraid. I don't want to love so hard ever again," I whispered to him.

"Oh, honey, I know. I know. I'm afraid, too."

His voice was soft, and he pulled me close so I was against him again, smelling him and feeling that warm skin. I felt his kiss against my temple, and the way he pressed his face into my hair, and for the first time since Eva's death, I found myself turning to the healing in my husband's eyes. For the first time, I began to believe the promises there.

19

It seems odd to say that when the man from Prentiss &
Field came out to the farm for the second time, I'd
been expecting him, but it was true. The moment John
Zimmerman told me that he'd heard from Dr. Lockwood that Eli was home, I'd known the news would
spread throughout Yakima. There wasn't much in
these parts that escaped anyone. Not for long, anyway.

So when I saw Mr. Smith riding into the yard in
his big black coat and hat pulled down low over his
eyes, I braced myself. He came in the afternoon, when
Eli was sleeping, and my first reaction was to run
upstairs and wake him. I wanted to leave it all in my
husband's hands. He could handle this so much better than I could.

But then I remembered the words in his letter
home. *Be firm.* How disappointed he had been in me
when he was gone, how angry with Prentiss & Field
for taking advantage. I knew what he would say now
if I woke him to tell him they were back, and it
seemed such a strain, something I didn't want him to
bear. A way I could take care of him.

Mostly, I suppose, it was simply about redeeming myself. In any case, I didn't go get Eli. I stood on the porch and didn't move as Mr. Smith dismounted and came slowly across the dusty yard. The chickens bawked and clucked at his feet so he had to almost kick them out of the way, and I didn't go out to shoosh them. I didn't make it easy for him to get to the stairs, and when he stopped there and took off his hat, I just stared at him as coldly as I could.

He kept his eyes respectfully lowered. "Good day, Miz Cameron. I'm here to see your husband."

"He can't see anyone just now."

"Ma'am, if you don't mind, I think if you told him I was here—"

"My guess is he'd haul you off our land if he could, Mr. Smith. But I don't intend to upset him. If you need to deal with someone, you can deal with me."

"Pardon my saying it, Miz Cameron, but this is a little more serious than the last time I was here."

I gave him my sharpest look, though I was shaking inside.

He looked at me consideringly, and then he reached into his coat pocket and took out a folded piece of paper. "It's a demand notice," he said, handing it to me. "Sorry to do this, Miz Cameron, but your husband promised us payment in full when he got back from the Wishkah. He's back now."

My fingers didn't tremble when I took that letter, though I expected them to. The paper was stiff and thick. I felt the mark of a pen indented in its grain. "I . . . I don't know if you heard, Mr. Smith, but it didn't work out the way he thought it would." I waited for him to say he knew, to offer his sympathy, but he just kept staring at me with those blank eyes, waiting for me to finish. I stumbled over the last words. "He's confined to bed just now. There was an accident."

"I'm sorry to hear that, ma'am, but I'm afraid—"

"If you could just give us a little while longer—"

"We've got his signature on a note, Miz Cameron, promising payment in full by the end of October. I'm afraid that unless we have it . . ."

I swallowed. Deliberately I thought, *Be firm.* It was hard enough facing Eli's disappointment in a letter. I did not think I could bear to see it in his eyes. "How much do we owe?"

There was a flash of surprise in Mr. Smith's expression, as if he'd expected me just to fold up on him and say *I understand* and watch Prentiss & Field swallow up the only things we had worth anything.

"There's still fifty-five dollars unpaid. You never did get us those apples."

"No. Eli told me you'd rather have the money."

"We don't have that, either."

"You will. I'll have it for you."

He sighed. "Miz Cameron. Perhaps it would be better just to admit—"

"I said I'll have it for you. I have until the end of October—isn't that what you said?"

"Well, yes, but—"

"I'll have it for you."

He looked at me consideringly. Then he nodded slowly and motioned to the letter still dangling from my hand. "You'd best have your husband read it, Miz

Cameron. Believe me when I say there's no point dragging things out this way. I . . . well, I hesitate to say it, but perhaps it would be better for everyone just to resolve this quietly."

He held no hope that I would have the money for him, I knew that. I saw it in his face, and I didn't blame him for it. I didn't hold much hope myself. I had forty-seven dollars in the ledger and what I could bring in from butter and eggs and the Spitzenbergs that were left hanging in the trees. I didn't imagine that all of those things together could bring in the money to pay off Prentiss & Field and all the other bill collectors waiting for us. Any day I expected to hear from Mason Albright. Even if I could pay them, there would be nothing left for the long winter ahead. And there would be no credit, either. We were already overextended at every store in Yakima.

"I'll talk to my husband," I said. "But I expect his answer will be the same."

Smith hesitated. He glanced toward the door as if he expected Eli to come walking out at any moment— and he probably wanted him to. I half thought he would demand to see Eli, and I was ready to dash to the door to block his way, but then Mr. Smith nodded and set his hat back on his head.

"I'm sure we'll be hearing from you soon, then. Good day, ma'am."

Well, at least I hadn't offered him coffee or water. It seemed no little thing, something to take pride in. But the moment he mounted up and headed out of the yard, I felt helpless again. I'd merely prolonged things. I would never find the money to pay them; I had only borrowed a few weeks, nothing more. I'd achieved exactly nothing. But I had been firm.

I watched him ride away in a cloud of dust, and then I stared out at the land that stretched to the ridge and wished I could let it go, that we could just walk away. How easy it would be just to give it up to Prentiss & Field and Mason Albright and everyone else who had some stake in us.

But Eli's words rang in my head. *The only way to make her death mean something is to make this land work.* I looked over the yard, the dying oak tree, my garden. I stared into the orchard and followed that line of trees clear to the irrigation ditch below, and anger came up in me so hard and fast I had to clench my fists on the porch rail to keep from waving them in the air and screaming, *Then work, damn you. Work for him, if you won't for me.*

The land just stared back at me. The wind kept blowing dust into my eyes. I glared back at it until my eyes teared up from burning—my own war of wills with this place, with this hateful dirt and the trees and the garden that took as much of my life as I wanted to give to it.

I turned to go into the house, and when I stepped inside I heard Eli upstairs, his soft call. I glanced back out the door, making sure Smith was gone. The chickens had massed in the front yard again, milling around as if he'd never been there. I hoped Eli hadn't heard him, but it seemed a vain hope, and I knew I would have to tell him anyway, though I didn't know how I would. His burdens were already so great.

Slowly I stepped up the stairs. Eli was sitting up in

bed, though the laudanum bottle and spoon were close by his side.

"Who's down there?" he asked.

I hesitated, but there was no point in lying to him. "Mr. Smith again, from Prentiss and Field."

Eli cursed beneath his breath. "Didn't they hear—"

"They heard. They just . . . he says he has a note you signed saying we'd pay them when you got back. Now you're . . . back."

He made to push aside the blankets. "Ahhh . . . dammit. Lora, help me get out of here. I'll talk to him."

I was at his side in an instant. "No, Eli, no. He's gone already."

"Gone?"

"I talked to him."

He sagged back against the pillows, but his hands were fists, and his voice was low and furious. "Damn. Damn! I'm so damned helpless!"

"Eli, no one expects—"

"*I* didn't expect this. Look at me, Lora! All I do is sit up here all day watching these legs rot away. What kind of a man lets his wife deal with bill collectors, for God's sake? I sit up here, and I listen to you and Will talking down below, and I can't hear a word. All I know is that he's talking to you and I'm up here, and . . ." He hit the mattress hard, and then gasped. "Christ! I can't—"

"Eli, it's all right, really. I—"

"It's not all right. It's not all right." He said each word sharply, one by one, emphasized. His eyes were hard when he looked at me. "I may not walk again,

Lora. Do you ever think about that? Do you know what that means?"

"We'd work things out."

"Would we? Would we? How long do you think you could stay married to an invalid? Am I a burden you want to have for the rest of your life?"

"There's no point in thinking that way."

"Well, why don't you try?" He looked away, staring at the window, and I realized that he couldn't see anything through it, that from his angle here on the bed, all he could see was sky. Just light, and nothing else. "Think about it for a while, Lora, and then tell me this is the life you wanted for yourself."

His words hurt, but I wasn't sure why, whether it was his lack of faith or the bleak future he presented. I had grown used to Eli's having dreams for both of us. "I married you for better or worse," I said softly.

"No one would blame you for leaving."

"*I* would."

He sighed, and then he reached for the laudanum bottle. He clutched it in his hand, turning it round and round, staring down at it without uncorking it. "I don't know what to do. I didn't plan for this. It's . . . I see the ledger numbers in my mind, and I go over and over them, and I just don't see a way out. If I could work, I could—" His voice broke in bitterness. "Ah, there's no use. All I've got is a hired hand working down there on land that isn't even his own."

"He would do whatever we asked of him."

Eli glanced up at me. The look in his eyes made me uncomfortable. "Would he?"

I swallowed. "He's like part of the family."

"But he's not family, is he, Lora? He's not our son."

I heard the yearning in those words and I turned away. I couldn't bear to look at him, thinking of the things he'd wanted from me before he'd left, the big family I'd denied him.

I could barely say the words. "We'll think of something."

"I can't . . . I won't lose this land."

I felt ashamed for having wished for it only moments before. "We won't lose it."

"I was thinking last night. I was staring up at the ceiling, trying to think the pain away. You were sleeping. I saw the moonlight on your hair, and your breathing was so quiet and soft, and I wished . . . I wished you were beside me here again, and it occurred to me that it might never happen. No woman wants to sleep next to a cripple."

"Eli—"

He shook his head slightly at me. "Things have changed so much. Maybe too much, I don't know. I was thinking of the day I brought the Royal Annes over. Do you remember? The nights were colder that year, so I was pulling them out of the wagon and building a fire for them every night on the way from The Dalles."

"You had soot all over your face when you got back," I remembered aloud.

He nodded. "They were beautiful trees, weren't they? Buds on them the size of a fingernail. And the way they took—d'you remember how they took? They just set their roots right into that wet soil and began to grow, and I thought, *This land is so rich.* It was like gold. I . . ." He let out his breath in a long, slow sigh. "After that first summer, I thought I'd found paradise. With you and those trees, and then Eva . . ." He gave me a quick look, as if he expected me to flinch, and when I didn't, he went on. "I expected that in twenty years, our name would be stamped all over these parts. Cameron River, Cameron Street, Cameron . . . I thought our life would be as fertile as this land was. But it didn't work out that way, did it, Lora? It didn't work out. Maybe I'm just a fool for hoping."

He looked so beaten, and the memory was so raw, so bright in my own head. The sight of those new trees waving back and forth in the wagon bed as Eli drove up. How he'd jumped down from the seat and shouted at me to come and see. Together, we'd planted them, Eli digging the hole and lugging them over, me holding their slender, smooth-skinned trunks steady while he settled them in, while he'd talked to them the whole time: "That's it, little one, drink up that water, that's the way." The two of us stamped down the earth at their bases, dancing around them as if they were maypoles, and Eli burst into "Ring Around the Rosy" and I'd laughed so hard when I fell into his arms. . . .

Those trees stood straight up from the earth, breaking the horizon, and I'd have loved them for that alone—for giving me something to look at besides the endless, treeless hills. I had watched them drink up the water the ditch brought from the Ahtanum and stretch to the sun, our happiness like wind in the lift of their branches. Paradise. For a while, it had seemed that.

I despaired thinking of those things now, and when I looked at Eli staring at the bottle in his hand, gripping it as if the pain was too much to bear, I had again that sense that Eli was tied to this land, that what happened to it happened to him, to both of us, that redemption was somehow in this soil that mocked me every day. This land and I were mixed up together, and I understood then what Eli had always told me, how our blood ran in these rivers, how the work we'd done gave it muscle and bone. And I had the strangest feeling, this desperate sense that somehow there were hopes out there still, lying fallow, waiting. There had to be.

All I needed to do was find them again.

20

Finding my hopes again was easier thought than done. The land was tireless, and with every hour that passed, there came something more to sap my strength and my will. I spent the next few days running between Eli and harvesting the last vegetables in the garden, putting up what I could, drying the broad beans, fighting the constant wind that blew up blinding dust storms in an instant. I dug the ditch to keep the cabbages without even being able to see the shovel through the dust, and at night I came inside shaking dirt from my clothes and my hair.

Every day I woke hoping that something would happen to save us. I looked to the sky as if God were up there waiting for me to give him the sign. I already knew what to expect from such a fancy—if God was up there, He wasn't inclined to help us, or He would have done it a year earlier, when I cried and railed at Him to bring my little girl back to us.

But no matter what else happens, no matter how much bad comes to take your will, you can't stop that little hope inside from burning, waiting. As I harvested, I told myself there would be enough vegetables left to sell. I put up the last of the green beans and counted how few jars there were and lied to myself—I could spare a half dozen or so to take into town, maybe a couple of cabbages, too, and a basket of potatoes. Expectations, again. I held out hope that with the vegetables and the apples, there would somehow be enough money for Prentiss & Field, though I knew in my heart there wouldn't be, and the truth was, there weren't enough beans to sell and I couldn't afford to give up even a single cabbage. But I didn't see any other way. The apples were turning a ripe, full red in the colder nights, and I told myself and Eli that there might be two hundred pounds left and knew there was maybe half that. They were too small. The biggest, heaviest apples had been the ones most affected by the storm.

But still, there was that hope. I watched the curled, stained calendar nailed to the kitchen wall with a growing sense of inevitability. Each sunrise, each sunset, was a reminder. I knew Eli was worrying himself into an early grave. He was hardly sleeping. When I came up with his breakfast in the morning, he was already awake, already staring out the window at the sky. I tried to reassure him, but I stumbled over my words—he knew as well as I that there would not be enough of an apple crop, and that my preserves would hardly bring enough to make going into town worthwhile. But we kept up the lies, neither of us wanting to worry the other.

Every day, I stood on the porch and stared out at the homestead, looking for something, some way to find money. What hay there was was stacked in the barn, sweet alfalfa, but there hadn't been much of that this year, either—what seed the sage rats hadn't got had blown away. We'd reseeded that ten acres three times before the alfalfa took. Eli had talked about growing wheat there next year, too, hedging our bets with twenty or thirty acres of it. But that was for the future; for now, the hay we had was enough to care for our animals this winter, with only a little to spare. Not enough even to try to sell to the cattlemen or sheepmen still lingering around these parts.

The treasure of this land was the dirt, and it was blowing away constantly, gathering in a fine layer over everything in the house, no matter how shut tight the doors and windows were. Only the sagebrush held it in place, and we could not grow sage or make money on it. I was growing desperate trying to think of something else we could do.

I was staring out at the horizon again one evening after dinner, my hands clenched on the porch rail, trying to find some hope in the mountains beyond, in the cone of Mt. Adams and the jagged top of Mt. Rainier pink-tinged by the sunset. I never looked at the mountains now without thinking of Eli on the other side of them, working in trees that I'd never seen. I had enough to hate about this side of those mountains, but it was the west side that had taken my husband's legs, and I couldn't forget that. I didn't know if Eli hated it, so I hated for him. I blamed the west side for all our hardship now—if not for the accident, Eli would be planning to come home about now, his pockets full of money to pay our creditors, the winter and next year assured.

"A penny for your thoughts."

I jumped at the voice and turned to see Will standing behind me.

"Sorry," he said with a little smile. "I didn't mean to scare you."

"You didn't. Not really." I turned back to the mountains. "I was just thinking that this is about the time Eli would have been coming home."

"Oh." Will sat down on the edge of the step and looked off into the sunset. He looked peaceful, but then, he always looked that way, as if the world's burdens were things that just passed him by. I envied him that. I wished I knew what it felt like. And it was that, the envying, the wish, that made me sit down beside him on the step, that made me confide in him the way I couldn't with Eli. I told myself it was because my husband needed to get well, and burdening him with worries was not good for him—he was already so burdened. But the truth was that I was afraid for Eli to see how little faith I had.

"I wish he were coming home now," I said in a low voice. "I wish none of this had happened. It just seems so unfair. He went to the Wishkah to help us out, and all that happened is that we're in worse shape."

Will picked up a curled oak leaf from the stair and twirled the stem of it in his fingers. "You're not looking at it the right way."

"The right way? I see what *is*. Prentiss and Field wants the money Eli promised them by the end of the month. And there's the cabinetmaker, and Ben Schiller, and the Feed and Seed—they were all waiting for this, Will. Every one of them. We could hold them off as long as we were promising to pay, but now . . ."

"The farm's a burden."

"It's been a bad year, is all."

He twirled that leaf again, and then he threw it down, kicking it away with his toe. He looked at me as if he was considering whether or not to say something, and then he stared again at the mountains in the distance. "Would it be so bad, leaving it behind?"

The words mirrored the thoughts I'd been having. I turned away, guilty suddenly, uncomfortable.

"This place, it's holding you prisoner," Will went on. "It owns you, and why? Why struggle this way? So a few acres of desert belong to you? So you can hand them down like some legacy? What's it worth, Lora? A few hundred dollars for a shack and a barn and acres that couldn't survive without that ditch out there? Who would want it? What kind of a legacy is that?"

He turned to me. "There's so much more to life than this, Lora. This *ownership* of things . . . wouldn't you be happier if you could own yourself?"

"You don't understand. This is Eli's dream."

"I know whose dream it is."

"He has such plans. . . ."

"Who's going to make them happen, Lora, if he never walks again, if he's confined to bed for the rest of his life?"

"I don't want to think about that."

Will leaned close. I could feel his breath against my cheek. "You owe it to yourself to think about it.

This is your life, too. What do you want from it?"

I stared out at the mountains, darkening now as the sun disappeared beneath the horizon. There was a sudden chill in the wind that made me shiver. Or perhaps it was Will's words, how uneasy they made me. They seemed to ask so much, to expect so much, and I didn't know what to tell him. I didn't know how to say that the world outside these boundaries held no appeal for me, because the world I lived in was the safest one I knew, and it had been dangerous enough to take my only child and I could no longer trust it. I could not imagine what horrors lay beyond it. I didn't want to know.

"I want for life not to be so hard."

"It doesn't have to be."

"I wish I could believe that."

"Thoreau says, 'In the long run, men hit only what they aim at. Therefore, they should aim at something high.' Maybe you're not wishing for enough."

I looked down at the dirt blowing into the cracks of the stairs, watching it disappear. "What should I be wishing for?"

"Whatever you want."

"I've wished for just about everything I could. This farm—"

"Not for the farm, Lora," Will said gently.

But the farm was everything I had. Once, it had been enough. Dreams could be built on such simple things. I didn't want a whole new world. I just wanted the one I had to be right. I wanted hope for myself again, the chance to believe again that life was possible here. I wanted back the woman I had been before

Eva died, the one who had held her child on her lap and breathed deep of fine blond hair and stared at the sunset and *loved.* That was what I wanted again. It seemed so little, and yet I knew how very much it was.

Will's voice was very soft. He was looking at me so carefully. "All I'm saying is that maybe it's time to move on."

I saw him then, so solidly. *Time to move on.* Will had been in a hundred places and moved on a hundred times, just as he would move on from our place. But moving on didn't take any effort. In the end, it was just going. Staying was what required courage.

It made me pity him, and it made me angry, too, because I wanted him to stay here. The son I'd loved, the boy I'd needed, was gone, though I felt a lingering tenderness for him, and what remained was a friend, someone who cared enough to show me a rock filled with rainbows during a storm. He wanted me to be happy, I knew, and he would think about me after he left and hope that I was content. But to stay to see me happy . . . no, that was not something he would do.

"Is that your answer to everything?" I asked him. "Moving on?"

He looked surprised. "My answer to everything?"

"It's easy to leave. What's hard is staying here, living through these killing winters, watching the ones you love . . . die. But to put your mark on something, isn't that worth dreaming of? Tell me, Will, wouldn't you like someday to come back here and see this land blooming and know you had something to do with it? In all your travels, have you ever stayed long enough to know that you made a difference?"

They were strong words, and I suppose I expected him to protest, to tell me I was wrong, that he understood commitment, and what it meant, that in this life it was the only thing that bought a future, the only thing that mattered.

But it was the flaw in him that he didn't, and I think I knew that even before his gaze moved over my face. Even before he said, "Then you won't leave."

My words had not even touched him.

I stared at him for a moment, and then I looked away. "No," I said with a sigh. "I won't leave."

I felt him nod.

"I want to stay. I can't tell you why, but I feel this place isn't done with me."

"No. It won't be done until it's sucked everything away." His voice was sad. When I glanced at him again, my heart wanted to break at how sad he looked.

"Just once more," I said. "I can't let it beat me yet."

He sighed. It was a long, drawn-out sound, and in it rang the song of the crickets and the call of a grouse in the field beyond. "Well, then," he said, and there was a smile on his face that made me want to smile soothingly back at him. "I told you to aim high. I guess that's high enough."

I went upstairs when it was just dark, after Will went out to the barn. I heard the gentle rise and fall of Eli's breath, and the lamp was out; the cool wind blew through the window so the curtains lapped against the sill. I tiptoed across the floor to close it, my boots skidding a little on the sand collected on the floor, and I saw Will's light out there, glowing from the cracks in the barn walls, and thought of all the times this summer I'd stared out the window at his light, taking comfort from it, feeling not so alone. I felt that way now, too, as if some of the burden had been lifted just by talking about it, by saying the truth I could not say to Eli. That I was frightened, that I wanted to win. That I was afraid we wouldn't.

I reached up to close it, keeping my hand on it so it thudded gently, not wanting to wake Eli. I started to draw the curtains closed.

"No," Eli said softly. "Leave them open so I can see you."

I let my hand drop back to my side. "I'm sorry. I didn't mean to wake you."

"You didn't."

I heard him stir, the rustle of the straw in the mattress, the creak of rope springs, his bitten-off curse.

"I was waiting for you," he said. "I . . . I heard you talking earlier. With Will."

My heart stopped. "You heard?"

"The window was open."

Of course. I looked at the window. We had been on the porch just below. He would have heard everything. I felt uneasy and guilty again, as if I'd betrayed him somehow, as if I should be ashamed, and it was a feeling I didn't understand. The things I'd said . . . I'd only needed to ease my worry, and I'd been so afraid to add to his . . .

"Oh," I said.

"You're close to that boy."

I spoke without thinking. "He's not a boy. He's nearly a man."

"Yeah." Eli's voice was a whisper. "He is, isn't he?"

It confused me. I wished I could see his face. But the room was so dark. "Eli, I was just . . . I didn't want to add to your worries."

"I know." He stirred again. I heard him groan. "Can you light the lamp?"

For no reason I could say, I was nervous. My eyes had become used to the shadows; I found the lamp on the night table easily. There was a box of lucifers in the drawer; the striking hiss seemed loud in the darkness, the tiny flame too bright. I lit the lamp and watched the glow catch and burn brighter until I could see my husband's face, the golden color of his skin in the lamplight, the darkness of his hair.

"I've been thinking about this all day," he said in a low, steady voice, "and I think I'm ready to try."

"Try what?"

"I want to see my legs."

Until the last few days, changing bandages had been too painful for him to bear. I'd never done it unless he was asleep, drugged by laudanum. His legs were ugly, still swollen, the bruising hardly fading, the crookedness of one foot growing more and more obvious. I still did not know if he would ever walk again, and Lockwood had not bothered to come out to check on his patient since that second time. Truthfully, I had not wanted him here.

"I'm not sure that's a good idea."

"Why not? What am I going to see?"

"It's nothing, just . . ."

"Is it going to tell me I'll never walk again?"

I couldn't look at him.

"Today, I listened to you talk to him down there and I hated myself. I don't want to be a burden to you, Lora. I . . . I want to know if there's hope, that's all. I want to see it for myself. If there's not . . . if there's not, I need to know that, too."

I saw the bleak honesty in his eyes, and I felt sick and troubled. But I nodded. I'd taken to keeping bandages and supplies in a bag under the bed, and I drew it out now. I took out a pair of scissors, and Eli pushed back the covers. Then carefully, I cut the knot and began unwinding the bandages.

I did it as carefully as I could, but still Eli gasped, and his fingers tightened on the bedstead—even in the lamplight, I could see his knuckles turn white from the strain. I moved the splints and unwrapped the second layer, and then I pushed the bandages aside so he could see.

His eyes were closed, his head thrown back. There was the sheen of sweat on his forehead. Then he took a deep, slow breath and looked at me again. His gaze went to his legs, and he went still and quiet.

They didn't look so stark in the lamplight, not so white, the bruises not so dark. The soft yellow glow evened out his skin, leaving the bruises as shadow. I saw his gaze move down his legs, taking in the healing cuts and the turn of one ankle, the feet still black from bruising, still swollen. Then he looked back at me.

"The foot," he said. "It's not right."

"No."

That was all he said. He sagged back on the pillows and motioned for me to bandage them up again, and I did, slowly and carefully, binding them tight.

"Tomorrow," he said, "I want to sit in a chair."

"Eli, you can't. You can barely sit up as it is."

"I can't leave you this way."

"You don't have a choice."

"I suppose if I went in to see Jim Prentiss—"

"Eli," I said softly. "You're not going anywhere. Not yet."

He closed his eyes. "No. I guess not."

I reached over and took his hand. I held it carefully; in the lamplight the veins and sinews stood out in shadowy relief, and I traced them gently with my thumb, caressed his hand with my own. He squeezed my fingers and whispered, "This is all more than you should have to do."

"Go to sleep," I whispered back. Then I leaned over and brushed his hair back from his forehead, lingering there to touch his skin, to feel his warmth. It seemed so natural then, just to kiss him. But when my lips touched his, I felt his little jerk of surprise, and I realized how long it had been since I'd done such a thing, and I sat back again. We had barely touched, but I felt the tingle of it in my skin and the heat of a flush on my cheeks.

Eli was staring at me. I looked away, pretending to busy myself with the rip of my apron pocket. "You'd better sleep. You need your rest."

That night, I had a dream.

I dreamt I was putting cabbages in the sand- and hay-filled ditch along the side of the house when Eli came running up from the irrigation canal. He was covered with mud, and he was yelling something about the sage rat burrows collapsing the side of the ditch. I ran after him as he went to saddle up Pete and get the plow, and my voice was high and shaky; I kept putting my hands to my mouth and saying, "Eli, you can walk! You can walk!" And he *was* walking, but it was with this strange, jerky limp like my father, and then suddenly, he was my father, and I was a little girl again, racing after him as he made his way to the canal. "Go back and tell your mother to get it ready," he yelled at me.

I ran back to the house to get my mother, and I kept telling her, "Get it ready, get it ready," though I had no idea what *it* was. And suddenly the wind blew up in a dust storm, and I heard my mother's gasp of fear and I felt it, too. Father wouldn't be able to handle the plow in this storm, and I needed to help him. I ran back out to the canal, fighting the dust and the wind, and when I got there I couldn't see my father anywhere. It wasn't until the wind died that I saw him, caught beneath the tipped-over plow, old Pete looking down at him with a long, sad look. My heart seized up, and I went running over there, but it wasn't Father caught beneath the plow, it was Eli. Eli, drowned in dust. I fell on my knees beside him and kissed his face, but his skin was cold. He was not my Eli, and it was too late for kissing. It was too late.

And then I knew what I had been asking Mother to get ready. A coffin to bury my husband in.

21

The dream left me with a worry I couldn't shake loose. In the morning, I hurried upstairs to make sure Eli was still alive. I raced up there so quickly I tripped on the hem of my dress. When I got there, he was staring at me as if I'd lost my reason, and I mumbled that I'd had a dream, that I'd thought he was dead, and his smile was so tender and sweet it made me think of how I'd kissed him, how warm he'd been beneath my lips. The coldness of his skin in the dream was still with me, and I felt this longing to touch him now, to kiss him again.

But I didn't know how to begin such an intimacy. It had been so long since I'd simply kissed him for no reason that I couldn't remember how to do it, and it seemed it would turn into something more if I did, something I would have to explain, because it was now so unlike me to do something like that.

So I only smiled and told him I'd bring his breakfast, and I left him there. But the dream, and Eli's despair of yesterday, kept me on edge. When Will brought the milk in, and I strained it through cotton into milk pans to set for the cream to rise, I was so distracted I poured the pans into a pot and set them on the back of the stove as if I were making smearcase. It was only Will's strange look that made me catch the mistake.

And then I had the idea. It came to me in Eli's words. *I'll go see Jim Prentiss.* I didn't know why I hadn't thought of it before. I'd been so rattled by Mr. Smith, it had never occurred to me to go straight to the man we owed. Jim Prentiss had come to this valley only a few years ago. Eli and I had seen him in church every Sunday before we'd stopped going. He was a Christian man. Surely he would listen to reason. He would understand.

I was seized with the idea—I was going today. Right this minute. I would not bear another day of this uncertainty, of this worry. And I would not allow Eli to bear it, either. I untied my apron and pulled it off, draping it over the chair. The eggs were still popping in the skillet, the bread still unsliced. Will was waiting for his breakfast.

"What are you doing?" he asked.

"Going into town."

He didn't even blink—as if I did such things every day. He started to rise. "I'll see if Polly can come out—"

"I don't have time for that. I'm going alone. I'll need you to stay here and look after Eli."

"Alone?" Will looked concerned. "But—"

"Would you mind hitching up the wagon for me? I'd ride Pete, but I think it'd shock him so much he'd refuse to go."

"I can't let you go alone, Lora. You know that. It's—"

"I'll walk if I have to."

I was ready to walk through him, and I guess he read my determination, because he finally turned and went out to the barn. I took the eggs off the stove and went upstairs to pull the black silk dress from the armoire.

"Will's going to bring your breakfast," I told Eli.

He eyed me as I changed, but his voice was steady, as if he were dealing with someone just short of deranged. "What are you doing, Lora?"

"I'm going into town."

"Not without Will, you're not."

"I need him to stay and look after you."

"No, you don't. I can take care of myself."

I buttoned the dress as far up as I could. "Don't be foolish, Eli. How would you even get the chamber pot by yourself?"

He looked hurt by the question; I suppose it had been cruel as well as indelicate, but I was burning to get out of there, to be gone. I didn't know what Jim Prentiss would do or say, but I was not going to give him a chance to ruin us without making him tell me to my face that he was going to do it. I heard the rattle of the wagon come up in the yard, and I hurried over to the bed, turning my back to Eli so he could finish buttoning me up, kneeling so he could reach.

"I don't like this," he said. "Why not send Will instead? What do you have to do that he can't?"

"Talk to Jim Prentiss," I said.

Eli's fingers froze on the buttons. "Lora, you can't do that. I told you I'd—"

"It was a good idea. But you can't go, and I can." I

twisted around to look at him. "I know what to say, Eli. I know what to do. One of us has to go. This time, it has to be me."

He looked so miserable I could hardly bear to look at him, but I was right, and he knew it. There wasn't much he could say. "He's not going to listen to a woman," he whispered.

"He won't slam a door on one, either."

Eli closed his eyes for a moment. When he opened them again, I saw his grim acceptance, and that made me feel stronger, as if he'd somehow joined his will with mine.

The wagon was waiting in the yard, but I went down into the cellar first, and pulled out six jars of beans and the two cabbages I'd left there. There were apples, too, the ones we'd picked up from the ground after the storm, culls, but good enough for vinegar, or applesauce if you sweetened it, and for drying, too. I asked Will to put a barrel in the wagon, along with ten pounds of butter, and a basket of eggs, and then I climbed onto the seat and took the reins in my hands.

"I'll be back before supper," I said.

Will eyed me steadily. "You sure you don't want me to go with you?"

"I'm sure. I'll be all right."

"If you're not back by four, I'll come looking for you."

I nodded. Then I said quietly, mindful of the window above, "Take good care of him, Will, won't you? He won't admit he needs it."

"Don't worry about us. You take care of yourself."

He stepped back, and I was off. It had been a long time since I'd handled the wagon myself, but I'd often helped my father when I was a girl, and those things come back to you. I suppose, too, I was driven by resolve, and I wasn't going to let something like a stubborn horse or a rickety, broken-down wagon stop me. It was a long ride, and it should have been lonely, but my mind was working too hard for me to care. I went over and over the things I would say to Jim Prentiss, the arguments I would make, and I hoped what was in the back of the wagon was worth enough to at least assuage him somewhat. Maybe he wouldn't take apples and cabbages in return for what we owed him, but I wasn't going to leave without trying.

The wind was blowing cool, but the sun was burning away in a clear sky, and I was sweating in the black silk when I finally pulled into North Yakima. I missed the old town; my failures in the new one were written on every stone. But I tried to ignore that, and at the edge of Naches Avenue I stopped and looked around, wondering where Prentiss & Field had moved to.

I didn't see it, and for a moment I was afraid—maybe they hadn't moved, and I'd come to the wrong Yakima. There were still businesses in the old town. I'd just assumed they were here, but maybe I was wrong, maybe . . . The certainty of it almost made me cry with frustration, and I was ready to turn the wagon around again and start to Yakima City when I saw the board at the corner. It pointed west, and written on it in fancy script was *Prentiss & Field Lumber Yard and Planing Mills: Repairing Done at Short Notice and at Low Figures.*

Seeing the name like that made me suddenly nervous. Somehow it was easier driving all this way thinking about coming face-to-face with Jim Prentiss than actually having to do it. But now that I was here ... I flicked Pete with the reins. By the time I pulled the wagon in front of the long, false-fronted building, my heart was pounding.

I walked inside and felt immediately out of place. There were men behind the front counter with pencils stuck in their shirt pockets and brown paper to write on. There were men standing there waiting and talking, men looking through folders of house plans and molding designs. Men everywhere. When I walked through the door, several of them turned to stare—I imagine women rarely set foot inside Prentiss & Field, if ever. Behind the counter, large doors opened out onto a yard filled with freshly planed lumber, window and door frames, stacks of shingles with signs reading *5M, 2M, 1M*. The sound of rattling wagons and men shouting came inside to fill the long, narrow room.

The idea that I could talk to the owner, that I could make him see anything, seemed suddenly so naive. Eli was right; I was a woman. Jim Prentiss wasn't going to listen to me. I couldn't even walk into the store without feeling out of place and unwelcome. I felt their eyes and their distaste, and I wanted to turn around and run out. I might have, too, if I hadn't seen just then a face I recognized behind that counter. Jonathon Hatch. He'd worked there for years; he'd helped Eli bring out the lumber to build the frame addition onto the house—and I'd fed him a dinner of chicken and dumplings and custard pie.

I was so relieved at seeing him that I smiled right at him. He looked confused for a minute, and then he put up his hand to tell the man in front of him to wait a minute, and leaned across the counter.

"Miz Cameron," he said. "Can I help you?"

I spoke in a rush of breath. "Yes. I'd like to see Jim Prentiss, if I could."

He frowned. "Jim?"

"There's something I need to discuss with him." I came up to the counter, and the men unwillingly parted to let me through.

"He's pretty busy these days. Why don't you let me—"

"I really need to see him, Mr. Hatch."

"But—"

"Please. If you could just tell him I'm here." It took all my fortitude to look into his face and be that firm. He hesitated for a minute, and then, reluctantly, he nodded.

"I'll see if I can find him."

He went out the big doors behind the counter. I heard his rapid walk down the narrow loading dock out back, and his call, "Where's Jim? Anyone seen him?" There was a call back I couldn't make out. Then Jonathon Hatch jumped down and disappeared.

I'd stopped being a sideshow; men went back to their business as if I weren't in the room, but I didn't budge from the counter. I gripped the edge of it until the fancy bevel hurt my fingers. It seemed I waited a long time, but finally Jonathon showed again, flushed and irritated.

He jerked his thumb toward a door at the narrow

end of the room. "Go on through there—it's his office. He'll be there in a minute."

I nodded my thanks. I heard my own steps, my sharp-heeled *click click,* and it sounded wrong in this place, too feminine. The doorknob slipped in my too-wet palm, and nervously I wished I'd thought to wear gloves. I wiped my hand on my skirt as privately as I could and went inside. Jim Prentiss wasn't there.

His office was small, and there was a door on the opposite wall that must have led to the lumberyard. His desk was covered with papers, and the lamp chimney was smoke-blackened, as if he needed a bright flame to work long hours, and kept turning it up higher to see through a glass that should have been cleaned long ago. His suit coat lay crumpled over one of two straight-backed chairs, and a coat-rack was loaded down with coats and pants and suspenders and at least five battered hats. Against one wall was a bookcase so heavy with ledgers and cases that it looked as if the addition of one more would send the whole thing crashing onto the floor. There wasn't a single window, and the room smelled of sweat and lamp smoke, sawdust and mud.

There was nowhere to sit, unless one of the chairs was cleared off, and so I stood and waited. The room seemed to grow smaller and smaller, and my nerves stretched tight. I waited a long time, until I began to wonder if I should go back out and ask for him again. Then, finally, I heard footsteps outside the far door, and it opened.

Jim Prentiss bent to come through the doorway. He was running his hands through his thinning dark hair and looking about as tired and sweaty as a body could look. The only thing on him that didn't look sloppy and ill-kept was a big, well-trimmed mustache glossy with wax. When he looked up and saw me standing there, he seemed surprised, as if he hadn't been expecting me, and I realized with sudden dismay that Jonathon Hatch had not found his boss, but had sent me in there to wait for Jim Prentiss just to get me out of the way. Prentiss had never said he would see me.

"Why, Mrs. Cameron," Prentiss said, looking as ill at ease as I suddenly felt. He pulled on his collar. It was horribly frayed in that spot, as if he did it often. "This is a . . . surprise. Did you—No one told me you were waiting."

"I'd asked Mr. Hatch to find you," I mumbled. My face was burning. But I remembered Eli's face the night before, and the thought of his worry gave me strength again. "I wanted to talk to you."

Prentiss pushed his hand through his hair again— no wonder it was thinning—and fumbled with some papers on his desk as if he were trying to find an excuse. "Well, I—"

"This won't take long," I said firmly.

He looked at me as if he'd expected me to meekly excuse myself. He hesitated, and then his expression was considering; I felt him taking my measure. "All right, then. Please, sit down. Or, eh—" He came around the desk quickly, pulling his suit coat off the nearest chair, though he didn't bother to shrug into it. I felt the little lack of courtesy like a sting, and I wondered a little meanly if he knew what he looked like—the coat would have only been an improvement over his grayed shirt. It was sweat-stained and frayed, too, and there was a little tear at the back seam of the sleeve. Jim Prentiss was one of the most successful men in this town, and yet he was running around in near rags. I couldn't remember if he was married or not. Certainly no wife would let her husband go around looking like that—

Then I remembered Eli leaving for the Wishkah, and the bolt of cloth hidden beneath the settee, and my own shame burst into heat on my skin.

He motioned for me to sit, and I did. I folded my hands in my lap. I felt shaky again; all the words I'd come up with on the wagon ride into town fell away from me, and I was left tongue-tied and silent.

He took the seat behind the desk, pushing papers to the side so that he could see me, and then he tugged at his collar again and said, "I don't have much time, Mrs. Cameron."

"I'm here to talk about our debt." My voice sounded scratchy and weak.

Prentiss looked startled and embarrassed. "Mrs. Cameron, not to put too fine a point on it, but such things are not meant for delicate discussion. Money is a crass subject better left to men. Perhaps your husband—"

"My husband can't be here today. I've come in his stead."

He squirmed. "I try not to concern myself too much with bill collecting. I would be happy to send Mr. Smith out. He could talk to Eli—"

"Eli's not well; he can't talk to anyone just now.

And begging your pardon, but I've already talked to Mr. Smith. Now I want to talk to you."

"I'm not familiar—"

"We owe fifty-five dollars," I said. "Your Mr. Smith was out a few days ago, threatening me. I don't appreciate it much."

Prentiss folded his hands and looked down into them. "I apologize for that. It's not how we like to do business. But perhaps you misunderstood him. I doubt you're accustomed to dealing much with these matters. If Eli—"

"Eli's bedridden," I said bluntly.

He didn't look surprised, and it only proved what I'd already known. The whole town knew of our hard luck. Prentiss knew, too. And he didn't care.

I felt helpless again. I would never be able to make this man listen to me. I was just a woman, and without my husband I was nobody. Maybe Eli could make a deal with him, but it was clear Prentiss wasn't going to bargain with me. "He can't *walk*, Mr. Prentiss. He's in bed, and I don't know if he'll ever get out of it. It wasn't what we planned on, but surely you must see that until he's better—"

"You've just told me he might not get better," Prentiss pointed out.

"That's not what I meant. I meant—"

"I appreciate your situation, Mrs. Cameron," he said, half rising. "But everyone else has had hard times, too."

"You must understand. We just need a little more time."

"I'm sorry. I can't—"

"I'm asking you, Mr. Prentiss. I'll beg if I have to. Isn't there some way I can convince you to wait? A few more months—"

He sighed, and then the blunt honesty came into his face, and I realized he'd known all this already. Of course he had. Eli had talked to him before he left for the Wishkah, and no doubt Mr. Smith reported everything to him. His talk about not knowing the bills had been just a lie to dissuade me.

"It's already been nearly two years. And Eli signed a note promising payment when he got back. I can't be responsible for everyone's misfortune, Mrs. Cameron; certainly you realize that. I'd be broke in a week. Now, I'm sorry you came all this way for nothing, but really, there's not a thing I can do."

He rose. He was ending the conversation. Desperately, I tried to keep him. "Mr. Prentiss . . . please, I— I've things to trade. Perhaps your wife would—"

"I'm not married."

"Oh. You're not. That's . . . too bad."

He tugged at his collar. "An unfortunate hazard of this business. I'm afraid a wife wouldn't take kindly to my work schedule."

"But the things you must miss. A man can't survive without a good meal now and then. And who mends your shirts? If you'll pardon me, Mr. Prentiss, you look like a man who needs someone to take care of him." The words burst from me; I could hardly believe I was saying them.

He was looking at me sharply now, as if he couldn't figure out what I was saying or where I was going. The truth was, I hardly knew myself. The more desperate I got to keep him from leaving, the more the words just kept coming.

"I've got a wagon out front. I've got six jars of beans and some butter and eggs. There's two cabbages I just picked and a barrel of apples."

He stopped. "Apples? What kind?"

"Spitzenbergs. They make a fine applesauce."

"Applesauce. Now, there's something I haven't had in a while."

"They're yours if you want them."

He laughed a little. "Mrs. Cameron, I can't make applesauce."

"I'll make it for you," I said quickly. "I'll turn the whole barrel into it if you like."

He hesitated. "I don't know. . . ." His hand went to his collar.

Later, I told Eli it was Providence, but the truth was that the collar had been ready to give for a long time, and it was just blind luck that I was sitting there when it finally did. He pulled, and I heard a rip, and the seam came undone. The button popped off and rolled onto the floor, spinning to a stop in a corner, and Jim Prentiss was standing there with a strip of torn collar in his hand. He looked at it as if he didn't believe it, and then he turned red as a beet.

"Mr. Prentiss," I said. "You need a new shirt."

He flushed even redder. He mumbled an apology, an excuse, something like, "I've been busy lately."

I saw that bolt of cloth in my head, shining there, flashing before my eyes, and all I could say to Jim Prentiss was, again, "You need a new shirt."

I think he heard me then. His flush faded a little;

he tilted his head and looked at me consideringly. "What exactly are you saying, Mrs. Cameron?"

I took a deep breath and held his gaze. I tried to make my voice strong. "You give me a shirt as a pattern, and I'll make you two and mend the one that's torn. I'll turn that whole barrel of apples into applesauce for you. Six jars of beans are yours, and two cabbages, and butter and eggs if you want them."

"And in return?"

"Cancel the debt and throw away the promissory note."

He looked at me, and then he looked down at that torn collar in his hand, and I saw the numbers go through his head, the bargain. "Fifty-five dollars, huh?"

I didn't say a word. I just stood there and held my breath, waiting.

He nodded, a quick, short nod, and then he held out his hand. "Mrs. Cameron, you've got yourself a deal."

It wasn't until I had Jim Prentiss's shirt in my hands and was heading back home with only a barrel of apples in the wagon bed that I realized what I'd done. I couldn't keep a foolish grin from my face, and I urged Pete to a faster trot and nearly ran over three people on my way out of North Yakima. All I could think of was that I could hardly wait to get home and tell Eli. I could hardly wait to see his smile.

22

At first, he didn't believe me. Eli looked at me in surprise and said, "You're sure? That's what he said? You're sure?"

It wasn't until I showed him the paper I'd had Jim Prentiss sign, agreeing to the deal, that Eli was satisfied. His fingers moved across the paper as if he were memorizing it with touch, and then he looked up at me with those blue eyes full of pride, and his smile was slow and easy. "You did good, Lora," he said. "You did real good."

I flushed with pleasure at his words, and when he reached out to take my hand, I felt almost giddy with tenderness. "I knew you were a strong girl the day I met you," he told me. "You just keep getting ... stronger."

"I only did what you would have done."

He chuckled. "No. I wouldn't have made Jim Prentiss a shirt." Then his face turned serious. His thumb caressed the ball of my hand. "Are you going to be able to do this, Lora? I mean ... you know what I mean. I haven't seen you sew ... since Eva died."

"I know."

"It's not that I miss the sound of that thing, but—"
He looked ruefully at the tear in his nightshirt. "Well,
actually, I guess I do."

I looked down at our hands, at the way his thumb
made circles on my skin. "That's what you said in
your letter. But I guess I don't have much of a choice,
do I? You and Will need shirts, too. I already bought
the cloth."

"I know."

"It's just—" I could hardly say the words. "It's so
loud."

His thumb stopped. He pressed a little, and I
looked up and caught his glance. He looked sad and
concerned, and suddenly I missed the feel of him so
much . . . the way I could bury my face in his solid
chest, the smell of him, the strong warmth of his
arms around me.

"You wouldn't have heard," he said quietly, and
he emphasized each word, as if he wanted me to
understand every one, to hear him. "She was too far
away."

The tears came up into my throat. It was hard to
talk around them. "I should have gone with her. She
asked me to go. She wanted . . . strawberries."

"You can't blame yourself forever."

"But it was my fault."

Eli took a deep breath, and his hand held me tight
in place. "It would have happened anyway, Lora. You
have to believe that. It's the only way to stay sane. If it
hadn't been the ditch, it would have been diphtheria,
or whooping cough, or a rattler . . . It's the only thing

we can do, just believe she was taken for a reason."

I felt the tears on my cheeks before I knew they were in my eyes. "What reason is that, Eli? Why would God want a little girl like that? Why?"

"She was too good to stay."

"Oh, does anyone really believe that, Eli? The good are put on this earth to make us better. Why would God take them away?"

"Didn't she make us better, Lora? Didn't she really give everything meaning?"

I looked at him, and the ache inside me stretched and stretched—it seemed endless, as if it could just go on and on forever and never be soothed again.

"Think about it, honey," he said softly, almost in a whisper. "When you start to remember how she was, the good memories, you'll know I'm right."

That night, as I tried to sleep on the settee downstairs, I thought of those words of his for a long, long time. The moon was high, the sky clear, and it was almost as light in the front room as during the daytime, even with the thin curtains drawn. I lay there with the quilt pulled up around my chin and stared at the ceiling, the even planks soot-stained from the lamp, Eli's bed just above. *The good things.* It seemed truly as if those things had gone from me forever, those tender memories. I felt snatches of them from time to time, but in the last year I'd bolted them down so tight I didn't know if I could bring them up again. I didn't know if anything could survive the memory of seeing her lank hair, darkened with the muddy irrigation water, or the still, cold face of the child I'd loved so hard it was a pain in my heart. Where were the good things? How had I let them fall away from me so easily?

My eyes were dry and burning from staring into the moonlight, wishing I could remember, afraid to try. The things I did remember were so strong they haunted everything I did. Like the sewing machine, and its fatal sound, that horrible *clack clack whrrrr*.

The promise I'd made to Jim Prentiss choked me in the darkness. I felt that bolt of cloth beneath me as a dark presence, a terrible heaviness in the air. I wondered if I could fulfill my part of the bargain.

I didn't know. I didn't know if I could even bring myself to touch the sewing machine again. I hadn't been able to look at it after that day we'd found Eva at the ditch. I'd walked into the house and seen it there, and walked out again. John Zimmerman had been standing on the porch, and I asked him to take it into the attic, and when he looked at me in surprise, I practically screamed at him to get it away from me. I must have sounded crazy, but he went right in to do it, and the next time I went into the house, it was gone.

Just the memory was hard to think on, and as the hours passed I believed more and more that I'd saved us only to bring us down again when I couldn't deliver Jim Prentiss his shirts. The bolt had been under the settee for over a week, and I hadn't even managed to make clothes for those I loved—how would I do it for a near stranger?

The question nagged me. I tried closing my eyes, but I could see the brightness of the moonlight behind my lids. I tried turning my face into the settee, but the air was too close, and I couldn't breathe. And all the time I thought of that sewing machine upstairs, the trunk full of patterns and needles and . . .

Every thought came back to those shadows in the attic, and they grew and grew until it seemed the whole attic might collapse with the weight of them. It was like an itch you can't stop scratching even when you turn it raw. As the night lingered, I had the strangest feeling that those shadows would follow me until I faced them, that those things in the attic were waiting for me, drawing me on.

I didn't know I was going up there until I sat up and threw off the quilt. The night was chilly, the floors cold enough that my bare toes drew up in protest, and I drew my thin nightgown tighter around me. The summer was truly gone; it was time to find my flannel gown, to wear heavy woolen socks to bed. I tried to think of that, and of how the stairs creaked beneath my weight—the seventh one up was warping at the edge; someone would have to fix that. I went upstairs as quietly as I could. Eli's snores were soft and deep. Carefully, I took the lamp from beside the bed and slid open the bedside-table drawer for the matches. Eli stirred once, and I froze, but then he settled back into sleep, and I paused there, looking down on his face, wishing I could crawl into bed beside him and take comfort from his arms.

But those shadows were calling. I padded softly to the corner, where the slat ladder to the attic was built into the wall. I barely made a sound as I climbed it, and I was careful to keep hold of the small hinged door Eli had built into the ceiling so it didn't crash onto the attic floor.

A strong wind whistled through the cracks in the walls and between the loose shingles of the roof. It was dark except for what moonlight managed to find its way through, and the dust was thick, clinging to my hands and to my gown as I crept up. Up there, the smell of the valley was strong, as if the dust layering everything held the nature of the land within it. Sage and cherries, apples and sand.

I set the lamp on the floor and carefully closed the attic door again so I wouldn't wake Eli with the light. It was even darker now, and I was cold to the bone and trembling as I knelt to light the lamp. It hissed to a start, the light came up bright and blinding, and in it, the shadows that held such power in my dreams took shape before my eyes.

I saw the trunk first, shoved up against the wall, the heavy, leather-strapped trunk I'd packed up the afternoon of her funeral. I stared at it, my dread freezing me in place. In my head I heard the heavy *clack clack whrrrr* of the sewing machine.

Slowly, I turned. Its shadow was unmistakable, a big, bulky shape beneath a haphazardly thrown flour sack. I saw the rough glint of black metal peeking from an edge, and I wanted to cry. I could not keep myself from going over to it and pulling back the flour sack, and then I did cry. I cried because, still balled up beneath the footing, was a half-finished pinafore, and a ruffle that wouldn't come right no matter what I did.

I'd had such plans for that pinafore. It was blue calico, and I'd embroidered birds on the bib, blue ones and violet ones because purple was her favorite color. I'd meant it to be a Sunday frock, and now . . . I reached out and touched it, the material stiff with dust. I remembered how it had felt in my hands, how she'd smiled when I showed her the calico, how she'd said, "I love blue, Mama."

All I could do was bury my face in my hands so my sobbing wouldn't wake Eli. I wanted him there beside me, but I knew that this was for me. This was something I had to do alone. Unless I looked at these things again, I would forever be haunted by them. Eli was right; I could not think of the good things until I'd got rid of the bad.

I sat back on my heels, wiping the tears from my face. Carefully, I turned the wheel of the machine, lifting the needle that caught the fabric, and I jerked the pinafore loose of the thread and held it in my lap, caressing it the way I could no longer caress her, touching calico and feeling soft, warm skin, the curl of fingers in my hand.

I clutched the pinafore to my breast and turned around to look at that trunk. Her whole life was in there—gingham dresses and stockings, small boots already splitting from the winter before, a coat, sunbonnets I'd had to fight with her to wear. I'd wrapped them all in brown paper and shoved them away, each one, hardly looking at them, dry-eyed and determined to forget her, to shove away the pain forever if I could. There was a china doll and a cloth dog with a missing eye and a christening dress made from the finest satin and lace. I could picture each one in my mind; I knew each piece. So hard to believe a life could fit inside a trunk. But then, she'd been so young, and her things took up only a corner.

Everything else in the trunk was mine. Things I'd locked away so I wouldn't have to look at them and remember.

The trunk was unbuckled, and it opened easily. There were my patterns on top, folded and stacked in a neat pile, brown paper that crackled when I lifted them. I blew off the fine layer of dust that crept into everything and put them aside. Below that were the embroidered wall hangings—*God Bless Our Happy Home,* the sampler I'd made when I was twelve, a tapestry of spring flowers that Eli had always liked. There were antimacassars my mother had tatted for my wedding trunk, and a carefully wrapped china milkmaid missing her left arm, so there was nothing between her shoulder and her hand on the cow's teat—another of Eva's legacies. She'd broken it at fifteen months and walked around with that arm clutched between her fat little fingers for an hour before I could take it away from her without her sobbing in heartbreak.

I stared at those things, and it seemed there were so many memories in that trunk, things I'd forgotten. I took them out one by one, and there, at the bottom, was her photograph.

It was hidden from my eyes, wrapped as it was in brown paper, but I saw it just the same. The image leapt into my mind with the strength of a precious memory—every detail intact, every moment captured. It hurt as much now as it had the day the photograph was taken, and I realized: This was not how I wanted to remember her.

But it was the image I'd chosen, the one I hadn't

been able to lose. Eli was right—the only memories I'd allowed myself to have were the ones that took her from me, her still body and the dripping hair, and every detail of the moments after, laying her out and ironing the Sunday frock of sprigged calico to dress her in, lifting arms that didn't lift for me, turning a limp body to button up, washing skin that was cold beneath my fingers. And I wanted . . . I wanted so badly to feel her warmth again. I wanted to hold the memory of her squirming in my arms, I wanted her laughter ringing in my ears. Where was the Eva I'd loved? How had I forgotten her?

I kept the photograph wrapped and put it away from me, settling it safely again in the trunk. My fingers brushed the china doll, with her soft golden ringlets and painted blue eyes, a dress of blue silk and lace, and I remembered suddenly when it had come, wrapped in layers of tissue in a big white box, carried lovingly by my mother the whole way from Walla Walla. I remembered the excited glow in her eyes when she handed it to Eva. The box was too heavy, and it slipped to the floor, and Mama caught her breath and looked worried for a moment before Eva took off the lid and tore through the tissue.

Her blue eyes had rounded in pleasure and awe when she looked at that doll, and I'd felt a selfish little ache—a beautiful doll to take the place of the ragged one I'd sewn her for her first Christmas. I was ashamed of my relief and joy when Eva fingered the fine silk dress and touched the blond hair, and then set it aside and said, "Mama, can I go outside?" and grabbed up Lucindy.

I remember trying to make excuses to Mama even though I was smiling inside—"Oh, she loves it. I'm sure she'll play with it later"—but Eva never did. With Eli's help, she named her Anna, and I put the doll on the lowest shelf of the whatnot so Eva could hold her whenever she wanted, but Anna became only another decoration, and plain Lucindy wore out from hard loving.

Hard loving. I had done that once. It seemed I'd loved Eva so hard that when she died it pulled everything out of me. And now I was afraid of loving that way again. And because I was afraid, I was dying, too. Will had been right about that. In these last months, I'd felt joy and spirit and hope seeping away, fading into those sun-scarred ridges. I was afraid of living again.

That was how the healing started, just a single memory at first, of a little girl running out to play. But perhaps that was enough. Sometimes, hope is just a little light.

I turned away from the trunk and saw my sampler lying there on the floor. The words I'd sewn in dark blue thread at twelve leapt at me with a meaning that filled my throat with tears: *The night shall be light about me. Psalms 39:11.*

Words I'd forgotten once. I did not want to forget them again.

I lifted my sewing basket from the trunk and took out a pair of shears. Then slowly, methodically, my hands steady, I cut that blue calico pinafore into little squares. Then I took out her clothes, little dresses and smocks and chemises so small they looked as if they'd been made for dolls, and each one I had a memory of I cut up, too—this Sunday school dress, and this one for when she'd first started to crawl, another from the time I'd caught her sitting up on the kitchen table, her hands full of custard pie. I cut and I cut and I cut, and when I was done I had a pile of them. Enough for a quilt. A mourning quilt to remember my daughter.

I put everything away except for the sewing basket and those squares and the sampler. I closed the trunk lid tight, and put the squares in my sewing basket, and carried it all to the attic door, along with the lamp. I left the other things up there for another day, and left the attic alone with the memories it held. I blew out the lamp and put it back on the bedside table, and smiled at the familiar sound of Eli's soft snores.

Downstairs, where the sampler had been, there was still a nail. Carefully, I hung it again over the settee, straightening it until it was right. In the darkness and the moonlight, I stood back and looked at it. And though the moonlight could not have touched it where it was, it seemed to glow just a little. Then I went back upstairs to where my husband slept, and I sat in the chair beside the bed, pulling an extra quilt over my freezing legs, and there, in the dark hours of the morning, listening to the music of Eli's breath, I started to sew.

23

I was still sewing when the sky outside the bedroom window began to lighten and turn pink, when dawn broke finally in the sky. I'd turned the lamp low so as not to wake Eli, and my eyes burned from straining to see. My fingers were sore from lack of practice; I had different calluses now. But in my lap, trailing off the edge of the chair, was a yard-long piece of quilt made of small little squares, sewn together without method or design, simply because I'd liked the way the blue gingham looked next to the sprigged calico, or because there was poetry and reason in putting the little square of butternut wool from her crawling days next to the piece of apron she'd been wearing when she took her first step. Her life was mapped out in that quilt, a pattern ordered by the way memories fell into my head, and with every square I sewed, she came clearer, closer. Maybe Will had been right about remembering, about how mementos wrote immortality on the heart, because with each stitch, I remembered how Eva had written herself on mine.

The ache was no less there, but it was tempered,

and the horror of her last day began finally to lose its power, though I could not have said why. All I knew was that it felt as if I'd been holding my breath for a very long time, and now at last I could breathe again.

I kept sewing, though I heard Will downstairs. I didn't move from that chair at my husband's side, and I watched my needle flash in the soft light in rhythm with his breathing and did not want to break the spell of it, the quiet peace, the doing again of something I'd missed more than I'd known.

I'm not sure what it was that made me realize he was awake. He didn't move; his breathing didn't change. But I felt his awareness, and I looked up to find him watching me and had the sense that he had been for some time.

"You're sewing," he whispered.

"Yes. I'm just . . . I'm making a mourning quilt."

He tilted his head at me, and in the pink light I saw the softness in his eyes. He reached for the piece dangling over the edge of my chair and pulled it gently toward him, so we were each holding a part of it. His fingers brushed a square of lace-covered satin. "Her christening dress."

"Look at this one beside it—do you remember? That little smocked dress I loved?"

"Turkey red calico." He smiled. "There's a spot there still. I guess you never did get the soot out."

"She was sitting in stove ash. Remember? It was all over her face and in her hair—"

"I remember I made her sit in the woodshed for ten minutes, and when I went to see why the hens were stirred up, she got into the grease barrel. That child was more trouble. . . ."

"She was, wasn't she?"

There was a wistfulness in his eyes that warmed me so I smiled back at him, and then the quietness moved through the room, and I was remembering, and I think so was he. But not the sad things. I was thinking of her baby smile and her face streaked with ash and grease, and how I almost threw out the turkey red calico because it was so filthy, but I loved that pretty smocking. Now I was glad I'd kept it, and I was glad there was a smudge of ash on it to make her real for me, to bring her back.

Eli said, "It's good to see you with a needle again."

"I've missed it."

"So have I. You look pretty that way, bent over that quilt."

More of Eli's poetic words. I'd almost forgotten he could talk like that. I felt the warmth steal into my cheeks.

"It reminds me of how you used to sit up in bed and spread those threads out all over."

"Oh, Eli, you used to hate that."

"Waking up with red threads in my hair . . ." His voice trailed off. "This last year . . . sometimes remembering those things was all that kept me from giving everything up. Remembering how it used to be . . ."

"Wishing it could be that way again," I whispered.

He looked surprised, and then his eyes darkened with that longing look I knew so well, and he swallowed hard. Carefully, he set aside the quilt squares, levering himself onto his elbows—an effort, as always.

His breathing grew raspy, and his hair fell into his face, but when I went to help him, he motioned me away and grabbed the pillows he'd thrown over the side of the bed, stuffing them behind him so he could sit up. He looked out the window then, at the brightening sky, and said, "Get dressed and call Will up. I want to go downstairs."

"Eli, you can't. You can barely sit up as it is. The doctor—"

"Lockwood doesn't have a farm to run."

"Neither do you just now. Will and I are taking care of everything."

"But Will won't be here forever, will he?" Eli turned back to me. "I can't stand to be a burden to you. Your face . . . it's not so sad anymore. I wish I could take the credit for that. I wish I were the one making you happy again."

"It *is* you, Eli—"

"No, it's not. And until now, that's been all right. But not anymore."

"Eli—"

"I want to love my wife again," he said softly. "I want to put those smiles on your face. I can't do it lying here. Now, please, Lora, get dressed. And call Will up."

I shivered at his words, and I did what he asked. I put aside the mourning quilt and I washed and dressed quickly, and then I went downstairs to get Will. He was in the kitchen. I smelled coffee, and salt pork frying. He looked up at me when I came around the corner, and smiled. "You're sleeping the day away. Lucky for you, I make a fine plate of eggs."

I smiled back at him. "They smell good. But just now Eli wants to come downstairs."

Will frowned. "You think he can?"

"It doesn't matter. He wants to try. It's just . . . I can't bring him down here by myself."

"I'll finish breakfast, and then we'll do it."

"He wants to try now."

Almost the same moment I said the words, I heard Eli call, "Lora!"

Will took the pork off the fire. "Guess we'd better get up there."

I did love him for that, for understanding so quickly, for *knowing*. I followed him up the stairs, and when we were there, he said, "Morning, Eli. Lora tells me you want to go downstairs."

"Think you can oblige?"

Will went over to the bed and looked Eli over. "We'd better take the splints off, or we'll never get you down."

"Get them off, then," Eli said, pushing back the covers.

I did it as quickly as I could. His breathing came heavy with pain as I moved them, and I looked at him and said, "No, Eli, this is too soon."

He clenched his jaw and shook his head. "Just do it."

When the splints were off, I stepped back. Will knelt by the side of the bed. "Put your arm over my shoulder," he instructed Eli. "Lora, you get his other arm."

Eli put his arm around my shoulder and grabbed on, and together, Will and I lifted him. It was hard; he was heavy, and I felt him tense and heard the groan beneath his breath as we began to lift.

Together, we tried to pull him from the bed. I was stumbling and panting before we moved him even a few inches. Eli's hand gripped my shoulder so hard it hurt. He was taking deep, unsteady breaths, and his eyes were closed, and when we took him from the bed and his unsplinted legs went lax, he screamed a little, deep in his throat. Will stopped and threw a quick look at me.

"Put him back," I said. "This is ridiculous—"

"No." Eli's eyes were closed. The word came from between gritted teeth. "Keep . . . going."

"Eli—"

"Don't stop. Don't . . . you . . . stop."

"Can you put your other arm under his legs, Lora?" Will asked me. "Like this."

I tried. Eli's legs were like a dead weight, and when I touched them, he made that awful sound in his throat again, then bit it off hard. We staggered to the stairs. I looked down them, so steep, so narrow, and remembered when Will and Harry had first brought Eli up them, how he'd screamed in pain and passed out.

"You ready?" Will asked.

I nodded, though I felt anything but ready. Sweat was breaking out on Eli's forehead, and his breathing had become rapid and shallow. When Will took the first, jerking step, Eli stiffened. His fingers bit into my skin.

"Slowly," Will mouthed to me, but it was unnecessary. Eli was too heavy for me, and slowly was the only way I could go. It was sheer will that made it possible for me to keep my hold on him. My arms felt ready to give out at any moment, but I would not drop him. I simply refused to. Carefully, bending beneath his weight, we took him down. Will's shoulder hit the wall; he was sweating and I was stumbling, and Eli opened his eyes just to close them again. He didn't pass out, though the pain must have been terrible. His better leg dangled from the knee, the other was still swollen nearly straight out, so when the stairs ended at the wall and we had to turn, Will and I struggled to get him past without hitting it.

We nearly dropped him into the chair at the bottom of the stairs. I fell to my knees at his side, trying to catch my breath again, while Eli's arm went limp around my shoulders. Will ducked away and grabbed the small, low table Eli had made of black birch. He shoved it close, and lifted Eli's legs again to lay them over it. Then he ran upstairs to get the pillows that had bolstered Eli's legs in bed, and shoved them over and around. The whole time, Eli was stiff and quiet, his eyes shut tight. When Will was finished with the pillows, Eli opened his eyes. They were bleary from pain, his face had gone ashen, and the sweat was beaded on his forehead.

"Much . . . obliged," he said to Will.

Will shrugged. "It's—"

"No." Eli grabbed his arm hard. "I mean . . . for . . . everything."

In the months Will had been on the farm, I'd never seen him look uncomfortable or out of place, but in that moment, he did. So much so I was puzzled by it. But then Eli groaned, and I leapt to my feet. "I'll get the laudanum—"

"No," Eli said, but there was something in his voice, something odd, and when I turned to look at him I saw he was staring straight ahead and up, and I followed his gaze to the wall. To the sampler I'd hung there during the night.

"You . . . put . . . it up." Words said in breath, a slow sigh.

He was staring at that sampler as if he took strength from it, as if the sight could take away his pain, and suddenly I realized something terrible: that what I'd done all those months ago I hadn't done just to me. I'd taken away everything that made our house a home. I'd created a world of barrenness for both of us. It was not just *my* soul that needed Eva. It was Eli's, too.

I wanted to cry. I squeezed his hand, and when he looked at me in surprise, I mouthed, "I'm sorry," and he clutched my fingers in reply.

"I'm glad . . . to see it . . . again," he said.

Then he passed out.

The next morning, Eli made us do it again. And the next. He lasted a bit longer each time, though never more than a few minutes. We talked about keeping him downstairs, but he wouldn't fit on the settee, and there was no room for the bed, and so, though bringing him up and down those stairs was a terrible trial each time, and I had five little bruises on my shoulder, from his fingers, that were growing into one big one, I did it willingly, because it seemed to give him hope again, just that little bit of looking out the front window over this land he loved, seeing that sampler on the wall. I would sit beside him and sew on Jim Prentiss's shirts and listen to the rise and fall of his breath and be so grateful he was there. And each night I went to the attic and pulled out something else to put up for him: the tapestry of spring flowers he'd liked, then the china shepherdess, things growing here and there like a garden just for him. He never said anything, but he noticed, I knew, because I would see him search for the new thing each morning, and I would see him smile through the pain, and it made me happier than I knew how to say.

The next few days after that, I kept finding things. Little surprises that leapt out at me from nowhere. One evening I went to get sagebrush to stack for the next morning's fire, and I found one of my hens setting clear around the back edge of the barn. I wouldn't have found her but for her soft clucking sounds in the twilight air, and in the dead of winter there would have been little chicks running around, freezing to the ground. I shooshed her off and put the eggs in my wood basket and left her chasing after me, scolding me for taking her unhatched brood away. Such blind faith made me smile—life going on even when there was no chance it would survive. A month ago, it would have saddened me; I was not sure why today it made me hopeful instead.

I found spiderwebs spreading from the corner of the porch to the house, dew glittering in their patterns like fine lace, and a bird's nest gathering dust beneath the stairs, and a meadow owl that whirled out at me one day as I crossed the orchard. I found myself pausing to watch the shift of the wind in the rye grass out toward the river—something I had not done for a long time, for so long I could not remember doing it before now.

I set no store by it; I barely thought about it. But one morning, when Eli was downstairs and I was kneading bread, and I turned suddenly to grab a towel and caught sight of a mallard duck and his mate flying so close by the window I could see their colors, I was stunned by how pretty they were in the light, and when they were gone except for the beating of their wings, I turned to Eli and said, "There're mallards out there."

"Must be that pair that nest out by the ditch."

It startled me that he would know that, that I didn't. A pair of mallards had been nesting by the ditch, and I had never seen them before now. It made me think of all the things about this land I'd never noticed, all the things Eli held close in his heart, and I asked him quietly, "Why didn't I know that?"

He was hardly moving in the chair, and I knew it was because he hurt, and that he'd already been there ten minutes and wouldn't last much longer. But when I asked that question, he smiled and shrugged and said, "I don't know, Lora. Why didn't you?"

I was covered in flour. It was up to my elbows and all over my apron, dusting my face. The bread dough was spreading over the table, sticky and waiting for me to knead it into body and shape, but I let it lie. There was something in Eli's eyes that drew me, little secrets I wanted to understand. I wiped my hands on my apron and went over to stand beside him. "What other things do you know that I don't?"

He reached up and took my hand, covered as it still was with flour, and then he nodded toward the window he faced, the one he stared out the whole time he was downstairs, as if he could drink up the land just by looking at it, and I realized without his telling me and without asking that he knew every curve and wrinkle and plain out there, that he had the grasses memorized, and the way the light fell across the land, and where there were meadowlarks and where the water gathered when the rain fell. The things he knew that I didn't . . . there were so many, more than I could imagine.

"I've been thinking of that field out there," he said, and there was a little strain of pain in his voice. He would be able to bear sitting only a few minutes more this morning. "The one against the road. Maybe we could put wheat in next year, if things work out. Your father's been trying to talk me into it since they were up last year. He's been doing well enough with it. Maybe it wouldn't hurt to try it ourselves."

I squeezed his hand. "I guess not."

"You know, Lora, I think—I know you don't feel the same, but—sometimes I see that sun come over the ridge, and it's so beautiful. This place . . . it has . . . a hold on me. . . ."

"I know."

"Did I ever tell you about the ice caves?" His breath was raspier now, and he was shifting in the chair, wincing, going pale with every movement.

I knelt down beside him so he wouldn't have to look up at me, and he held my hand hard in his, squeezing so his knuckles were white. But I didn't take my hand away. I leaned close to listen to him, because I recognized a story in what he was about to tell me, and it had been forever since I'd heard him talk this way. "No. You never told me."

"Hard . . . to believe." He swallowed hard and took a deep breath, and his voice was steadier when he started to talk. "Down around Mt. Adams, there are all these ice caves. Some collapsed years ago, and there's nothing to show they were even there. But there's one I saw when I first came up here. It was hard to get into. Just a hole in the ground and a sapling to let you down. But the floor was ice, and there was a forest of icicles, and wherever the light hit, there were colors."

"Rainbows in the rock," I murmured, and he looked at me in surprise.

"Yeah, that's . . . how did you know?"

"I saw something like that . . . once."

He looked at me for a moment, as if what I'd said puzzled him, and then he smiled slowly and brought my hand to his mouth, brushing my knuckles with his lips the way he used to do, and just like always, I found myself flushing at the intimacy of it. He laughed lightly before he caught his breath in pain.

"That's what I like to remember about this place," he whispered against my skin. "Even in the middle of a dust storm, I can remember that cave. And Lora, I . . . I know the apples aren't going to be much, but I think about those icicles and I think a place where that could exist is . . . worth being in."

"You keep thinking about your ice cave. I'll be practical for both of us."

He kissed my knuckles again. "This place has got you, too, Lora. More than you know."

I didn't believe him, but I held his hand and stayed close beside him. And I thought that as long as I felt his breath on my fingers, I could forget about how I was dreading the apple harvest, and how the long winter stretched out before me with no way to fill it. I could forget about the money we owed and the things we'd lost. As long as Eli and I were together, I would believe again in wheat fields rustling in a summer wind, and the smell of cherries in the air.

The morning Will and I went out to pick the Spitzenbergs was sunny and cold, with only wisps of cloud in the sky. The garden was empty now, just brown and dying bean and squash vines that needed to be pulled out, the ground turned in readiness for spring. The root cellar was full and my shelves heavy with jars. The apples were all that was left, and there was no point in putting it off longer. I would have to face the small harvest. I would have to start thinking about how we would survive the winter.

Last spring, when the apple buyer had come out, Eli had contracted with him for two thousand pounds, and now every day I expected the man to come riding up to see what a sorry deal he'd made. I didn't know how I would explain to him what had happened, how I would convince him to contract with us next year, too, in spite of everything. Then I began to worry that he wouldn't come at all. He was late—usually he came before we picked—but this time we couldn't wait any longer.

I was distracted with all this, or I would have noticed how quiet and thoughtful Will seemed as we went down to the orchard. I would have wondered on it. But I didn't see it. I didn't think anything of how his eyes seemed to hold me close as I handed him a basket and told him where to start. That study in his expression seemed only passing strange; there was nothing all that unusual in the way he lingered when I was finished, as if there was something he wanted to say. But then he didn't say it, and I turned away and went to the ladder, leaving him to go to his.

The morning's picking went fast, and dinnertime seemed to come up on me without warning. The early mornings coming downstairs wore Eli out; he'd been sleeping until late afternoon, far past dinner, so I'd only packed some bread and some of Lizzie Zimmerman's cheese and a jar of pickles for Will and me to eat out there in the orchard to save us time. When we sat down to eat, he didn't touch his food. He seemed restless, tossing an apple back and forth in his hands, rocking where he sat, staring off toward the ridge, and then at me, as if he were trying to find secrets in the hills, in my face.

"What is it?" I asked finally. "What's wrong?"

He seemed surprised by the question. "Nothing. Eli's getting better."

I thought I understood then, and it made me feel wistful and a little sad. I suppose it was in my voice. "I guess you'll be leaving soon."

"Yeah. Soon."

"I . . . I wish you'd stay."

"Do you?"

"There's still so much to do. We could use your help. It'll be a long time before Eli's walking again."

Will went still, as if he heard a sudden sound in the wind, or saw something to note in my face. "Is that the only reason you want me to stay?"

"No, of course not."

"Why, then?"

"Because you've become a friend to me. I'd hate to lose a friend."

He was quiet, and then he nodded and got to his feet in one lithe, fluid motion, and I felt as if I'd disappointed him somehow. I watched him go to his ladder and start to pick, and I wrapped everything up and put it away in the basket I'd brought and went back to the apples.

I'd thought we'd lost so many apples in the storm that there would be hardly any left to pick. I expected we would be done before the day was close to over. But two o'clock came, and then three, and we were still picking. The baskets filled, and then the few barrels we'd brought out, so that Will even had to fetch a couple more from the barn. I began to feel this slow, startling elation, this certainty that I'd been wrong about the storm. There were more apples than I'd thought. So many more.

I didn't say anything to Will—I was afraid somehow it would all vanish if I did. It wasn't until we were nearing suppertime that I finally climbed down from the ladder and walked among those barrels, counting them, touching the top apples to make sure they were real, that this wasn't an illusion. We weren't done picking yet, and it looked already close to four or five hundred pounds. Twice as many as I'd thought, more than that. I couldn't believe it. I stood there at one barrel staring down into the red of those apples, breathing in their smell, the dust of their skins on my hands, and felt hope again, growing stronger and stronger within me. I thought of how Eli's face would look when I told him, and that image took hold in my heart and my head, so I could not keep hold of my excitement when Will came over to unload the last of the day's bushels. I couldn't keep it from my voice.

"We've got at least four hundred pounds, and we haven't even finished! Four hundred pounds, Will!" I picked one up and laughed at the way it filled my palm, the solid heaviness of it. I wanted to kiss that apple all over.

He smiled; he looked bemused. "Is that good?"

"Good? It's wonderful. I thought, after the storm, we'd maybe get two hundred, but this ... I can't believe this!" I turned it over in my hands. "Look at this. It's so beautiful. Isn't it beautiful?"

"Yeah," he said, "it's beautiful."

There was something in his voice, something quiet that made me stop and look up at him, and when I saw the way he was looking at me, I forgot the apple; I forgot everything.

I had seen a gaze like that only once before in my life, in Eli's eyes. In one stunning, bittersweet moment, I knew Will was in love with me, and I realized that I'd known it for a long time without knowing it—it was what I'd seen in his eyes earlier that day, and on so many other days. I'd heard it in his voice, felt it in his stiffening when I called him a boy. He loved me.

He said, "Lora," softly, and came closer, and then he hesitated. I could have moved away. I could have turned aside, but I didn't. And when he kissed me, I let him. I felt his hands on my shoulders and the heat of his lips and I smelled apples in his hair. The Spitzenberg in my hand squeezed between us, pressing into his chest, into mine, before the pressure was suddenly gone, before he was stepping away again and I was standing there looking at him without moving, and he whispered, "I love you, Lora. I love you. Tell me we're more than just friends. Tell me you'll come with me when I go."

I managed one word, "Will—" before he stopped me.

He pressed two fingers gently against my lips. His hands were trembling. "No—don't say anything. Don't answer me yet. Just think about it. Think about it. That's all I ask. Don't make up your mind right now. Promise? Promise?" He took his fingers away, though he held up his hand to keep me silent, and he spoke so fast, with such conviction, that I listened to him with my heart beating, and the sad knowledge that I would hurt him.

"Think of how good things could be, Lora. Think of the places I told you about. We could see all those places, you and me—there are things I can show you, things you wouldn't believe. I just . . . I've been waiting for you so long, you don't know. You couldn't know. I know how you feel about Eli. I know he's your husband. But you were made for so much more than this, Lora. He knows it, too. He knows you need to go. He can't love you like I can. He'll keep you on this farm, and you'll just wither away. You'll disappear here, Lora, and I can't stand for that to happen. I can't let it. I can't let you just keep on dying."

I felt the tears in my eyes, so sudden I hardly knew where they came from, or why. I forced my voice through a throat that seemed to have closed up. "You don't understand."

"No. Don't talk. Don't say anything. Just think about it. Really think about it, Lora. Promise me you'll do that."

He didn't wait for me to answer. He turned away, walking fast, as if he was afraid I would call him back, as if he was afraid of the answer he knew I would give him. He was halfway to the house when he stopped and turned, and I heard his voice floating with the dust on the wind. "The flowers, Lora! Remember New Orleans! Remember the flowers! I can give you that!"

I looked down at the apple in my hand. Carefully, I put it with the others, settling it in tight, making sure it wouldn't fall. When I looked up again, Will was gone, and I was alone, listening to the rustle of apple branches in the wind.

24

People make choices every day. About what to wear and what to eat, whom to see. Little things, but together sometimes they point you in a direction you can't escape. A decision made once— *Today I'll just watch the sunrise,* something simple—can set your years in stone. *If I hadn't done this, if I hadn't done that, things would be different.* Making a pinafore instead of going with a little girl to pick strawberries, pulling away from your husband one time instead of holding him close, letting a boy kiss you. The consequences of a single moment in time. As I stood there watching the sunset turn the ridges pink and gold and purple and the faint blue of the mountains beyond, I wondered what moment it was that had made Will think I could love him. I wondered what I'd done, what he'd seen in me.

I had a long time to think on it. Will didn't come in for supper, and I didn't call him, but I saw him when the darkness began to fall, striding out to the orchard, his hair blowing in the wind, that too-big coat slumped on his shoulders because it had started to grow cold. I watched him from the kitchen window as he stood under those trees and looked up into their branches, and though I couldn't see his face, I felt his sadness, and my own. I felt his leaving, and I remembered how, when Will had first come, I'd felt Eli's leaving this same way. No, not the same, because though Will had given me so much, it was Eli who filled my heart. It was Eli I wanted.

But it brought to mind the way life turns on you, how it completes itself without your knowing, full circle after full circle. Eli's leaving and Will's arrival, and Eva's living again inside me. Things have a way of working themselves out. I needed to have more faith that they would.

That reminded me of what Will's confession had made me forget: the apples. When I heard Eli moving around, I forgot all about Will in my excitement to tell him. I put Eli's dinner on a plate and took it upstairs, and I couldn't keep myself from smiling like a fool when I saw him sitting there in the lamplight.

He looked at me in surprise, and tilted his head, as if he were trying to see inside me. "You look like a robin stuffed full of stolen cherries."

"I've got a surprise." I sat on the chair and handed him his plate.

"A good one, I hope."

"Oh, I think so. It's the apples, Eli. Will and I were picking today."

He'd brought a forkful of potatoes to his mouth, and now he paused with it poised in the air. "This is good news?"

"There's at least five hundred pounds there, and

we haven't finished picking yet. We won't make two thousand, but I'd guess maybe six or seven. Enough to pay off Mason Albright, and there might be a barrel to trade for half a hog."

He put the fork back on the plate. "Five hundred pounds? You're sure?"

"I think so. Probably more. I was wrong, Eli. I was wrong about the storm. I don't know. I guess I don't really know how to tell from the trees, but I've never been so happy over being wrong about anything."

"Five hundred pounds," he whispered. He closed his eyes on a sigh. "Thank God."

When he opened his eyes again, he was smiling, and there was a brightness there that might have been tears. He put his plate on the night table, and then he grabbed my hand and pulled me into his chest, and though I heard him gasp in pain, I went there. I buried my face in him and breathed deep of his laudanum and comfrey scent, and it seemed it had been so long since I'd been there where I belonged, in his arms, loving him.

"Eli, I was thinking about next year."

His fingers were in my hair, stroking, holding me tight. His voice was a rumbling in his chest. "Yes?"

"Maybe, if the cherries are good, we could add on another room. Just a small one."

He went very still. "An invalid's room?"

I shook my head. "A child's room."

I heard his heart making time with mine, a rhythmic pounding, a harmony in my ears. I felt the press of his fingers in my hair, and then the slow way they slipped down my face to my chin, and he was raising my face to his. The tenderness in his eyes was like a sweetness wherever his gaze touched, a healing in my spirit.

"I might not walk again, Lora. You . . . you know that."

"You don't believe that," I said. "And neither do I."

"It's not going to be easy."

"Oh, Eli," I said with a sigh, "whatever is?"

He smiled at me, and then he kissed me, and that kiss slid into me with such a hot longing that I shivered and clutched him tighter, and opened my mouth so I could kiss him deeper. I wanted him so much then, with that same hunger I'd felt all those years ago, when I'd first looked up to see him standing tall and handsome in my father's yard. And I realized then that this was what I'd been waiting for; I hadn't known how much. I held the desire close and felt it grow and savored it, and when the kiss ended, we sat there together and watched the sky change color outside the window, and I listened to his heartbeat pounding in my ear and thought of how well I knew its sound, how strong I'd always thought it was, how safe. And how I'd almost given it away.

The next morning, the milk and the butter were on the back stoop, but Will did not come in for breakfast. I knew he hadn't left because I saw the shovel leaning against the porch rail the way it always was when he was getting ready to work, and I knew, too, that he was giving me time to make a decision that was already made. Maybe he even knew that. So I took a long time getting ready to go out to the apples. I washed the dishes slowly, feeling the tension build up in me, dreading telling him what I knew would hurt.

When I heard the hoofbeats in the yard and saw Walter McAlester, the apple buyer, riding in, I was relieved at the distraction. I put aside the dishes and went out to the porch to wait for him. He walked over slowly, dusting himself off, taking his hat from his head.

"Mrs. Cameron. It's good to see you again."

"I wasn't sure you were coming."

"I never miss a trip. Had a little trouble coming over the pass is all. But I'm here now."

Behind him, I saw Will coming from the barn, the sun shining on his hair, and my heart seized up so I stumbled over my words. "C-Come on out to the orchard. I'll show you the apples."

"Where's your husband?"

I glanced up at the window. "He's confined to bed just now, Mr. McAlester. There was an accident. . . ."

"I'm sorry to hear that."

"No sorrier than he is," I said. Will came over; he looked up at me, a hard look, as if he was trying to tell things by my face, and I told Walter McAlester, "This is Will Bennett. Eli hired him to help out for a while."

McAlester looked concerned. "A hired hand? Then this is a serious illness? I'd heard something in Yakima, but I'm afraid I didn't put much stock in it. I don't mind telling you I'm dismayed."

"Eli'll be fine," I assured him.

"He's good enough that I'll be moving on soon," Will said, and he gave me a quick look that I tried not to catch.

"Well, that's good to hear."

I was nervous over telling him the rest, but there was no point in waiting. "I'm afraid I have more bad news, Mr. McAlester. I know Eli contracted with you for two thousand pounds, but we had a storm—"

He looked more concerned now than he had over the news of Eli's accident. "A storm?"

"Hail. We lost quite a few."

"How many?"

"I'm afraid there's maybe only five or six hundred pounds."

"That *is* bad news," he said. His forehead furrowed into a hundred tiny lines. "And the rest? Were they affected?"

"Why don't you come on out and see?"

The three of us walked out to the orchard, Will walking behind, close enough that I could feel his presence, and the dread of hurting him was greater than my dread at showing Walter McAlester the extent of the crop damage. When we got to the trees, to one of the barrels Will and I had filled the day before, McAlester stopped. He reached in and pulled out one, and then another, looking them over before he put them back and walked among the apples still hanging on the trees. He was quiet and somber-looking. I walked behind him, tense and nervous, and when he pulled one from a branch and held it out to me, saying, "There's some hail damage here," I stared at him in stunned disbelief.

"Hail damage?"

"That's what I said." He tossed the apple aside, and Will picked it up and frowned at it.

"There's nothing on this apple," he said.

"Look closer, boy," McAlester said. "You'll see it."

Will looked again, and then he held the apple out to me, his fingers lingering a little against mine as I took it into my hands and looked it over and saw that he was right. There wasn't a mark on that apple. We'd lost so many apples to the hail, but the ones left had looked good. I'd been careful to pick only the ones that did and to tell Will to do the same.

I felt again the way I'd felt in Yakima earlier in the summer, staring at a cherry buyer and listening to him cheat me without saying a word to stop it. I told myself it couldn't be, that Walter McAlester was not the same as some nameless agent working for Beaman's, but the apple was clean, and this was the first year we'd contracted with McAlester. I had no more reason to trust him than he did me.

"I won't give you more than half a cent a pound on these," he told me, shaking his head. "You're lucky I'll even take them off your hands, but I suppose we can press cider with them—"

"There's nothing wrong with this apple," I said. I held it out, and my hands were shaking. "There's not a hail mark on it. On any of them."

McAlester stopped. He folded his arms across his chest and regarded me as if he were a teacher and I was some lowly student who had dared to sass him. "Mrs. Cameron, now, I don't expect you to recognize these things. But you bring your husband out here, and I'm sure he'll show you what I'm talking about. I know a gentle lady like yourself is more at home in a kitchen than out here. I appreciate that."

I felt Will tense beside me. He stepped forward. "She's been raising these apples all summer. She knows them better than Eli—"

I touched his arm, and when he turned his eyes to me, I shook my head at him. I saw McAlester's measuring look, the same look that had been on the face of the Beaman's agent, and my anger over the cherries and the apples and every bill collector who'd tried to take advantage of me these last months rose so hot I felt my skin burn.

"There's not a thing wrong with these apples, Mr. McAlester," I said, and I hated that my voice was shaking, that I was shaking, but I went on. "You know it and I know it. I'm not taking your half cent a pound. They're prime Spitzenbergs worth more than that. I can cart them into North Yakima and sell them off my wagon myself for four cents."

McAlester looked at me a minute, and then he nodded. "Why don't you go on and do that, then."

"All right, I will."

I waited for him to turn and go, and I wondered how I would do that, if I could get four cents a pound for them in North Yakima, when everyone and their neighbor had barrels of apples falling on the ground. But I didn't move, and I didn't waver.

McAlester considered me. "They aren't much good to me, but I'll tell you what. I'm a little short on quota this year. I'll take 'em off your hands. It looks like about five hundred fifty, maybe six hundred fifty pounds out here. We'll call it five hundred fifty even, and I'll give you three quarters of a cent for all of them."

"I'm guessing there's seven hundred pounds. How about we call it six hundred fifty even and you pay me three cents a pound."

He shook his head. He started to walk away. "Too rich for me."

Panic made me brave. I called after him, "Six hundred pounds, at two cents a pound!"

McAlester stopped. Slowly, he turned back to face me, looking at me with a considering expression that made me raise my chin higher to face him down. His long, slow nod was about the most beautiful thing I'd ever seen. "Mrs. Cameron, you've got a deal."

It wasn't the best price, but it was fair, and I was satisfied with it. More than that, truly—I was jubilant as he wrote out the bank draft and handed it to me with the words, "Have them at the railroad station on Friday."

I tucked the check in my apron pocket. "It's been a pleasure doing business with you, Mr. McAlester."

He didn't look so pleased. "I'll look forward to dealing with your husband again in the spring, Mrs. Cameron."

He trudged away across the yard, and I watched him go and put my hand in my apron pocket so I could hold that bank draft tight in my fingers. I guess I was half afraid he would turn around again and tell me he'd changed his mind. But he didn't. He got on his horse and rode away, leaving me twelve dollars richer and light-headed from my success.

"You did it, Lora," Will said from behind me, a quiet voice. "You didn't let him cheat you."

I turned to see him. "Not this time. Thank you for

your help. For saying those things to him."

"You didn't need my help. I guess you never did."

It surprised me that he didn't know, that he couldn't see it. For all Will Bennett's far-thinking ways, he was not so wise; he was still very young. "Don't think like that. This whole summer—I couldn't have done it without you."

He paused, and a silence came between us, so I knew what was coming next. It didn't make it any easier to hear when he said, "But you're not coming with me."

"No." I saw him flinch, I saw the hurt come into his clear blue eyes, and I was so sad for him. "It's too late for that, Will. It's always been too late. Probably it has since the moment I met him. I love Eli. I'm not going anywhere."

"I can't let you die here."

"Die?" I laughed a little, a laugh that hurt when I made it. "Oh, Will, do you know, I can smell this land again. I can smell the sage and the dust, and it doesn't hurt—not the way it did. The sunsets look beautiful to me again, and I owe you for that; I hope you know how much. I love you for it. But I'm not . . . in love with you."

He considered me. Then he sighed and looked off to the ridge, and there were tears in his voice, that heavy sound, though they weren't on his face. "You promise me, Lora. You promise me. . . ."

"I'll be fine."

"I like to believe that if a day comes that you're not happy, I'll know it. I'll feel it somehow. And if I do, I'll be back."

"There won't be a need."

He reached out then, and his hand was soft where he cupped my cheek, though I felt the calluses there, the blisters from working this land of Eli's and mine. His voice was soft as a whisper, like a dream. "I know that. But just let me believe it, Lora. Let me believe it for a little while."

Will didn't leave right away, though I expected him to. I guess he knew how much I needed his help, or maybe he found in himself some yearning to stay, some wish finally to see how things worked out. Whatever it was, he was still there a month later, after the apples were long sold, when the ground began to freeze and it became hard to work on the canal.

The things we'd said to each other in the orchard that day were never mentioned again, but I felt them in the way he looked at me, in his lingering, and in a way I loved him more for it, for caring even though there was no need. As the evenings began to come on sooner, he started to stay inside awhile after dinner, and together we would bring Eli downstairs again to sit for a bit longer. Those evenings held a peace I cherished, even more so because I sensed they were short-lived. Will would not stay forever. As the days passed, I sensed him looking more and more to the horizon, waiting for the time to go.

It was a night in mid-November when I felt the fleetingness of time more than usual. The night had come on, but the lamplight held the darkness at bay, and I was sitting close to it, bent over a pillowcase I was embroidering, soft cotton threads in bright colors strewn over the arm of the settee. Eli was finishing the last slice of a custard pie, and the house was warm and quiet while the wind whooshed by outside.

Will came in from the barn in a rush of cold air and dust. He shivered a little as he closed the door behind him. He was holding some strange contraption—a low, heavy frame with wheels attached—and he set it down to take off his coat and then smiled when he turned to us.

"I've been working on something in the barn," he said. "Thought tonight might be a good time to try it out."

"What is it?" I asked.

"You'll see." Will took it over to Eli. He set the frame beside the chair, and his smile was full of waiting and expectation.

Eli looked at him curiously for a minute, and then something came into his eyes, some knowing, and he said, "You think it'll work?"

"Guess we won't know until we try. Come over here a minute, Lora. Help me get Eli to the settee."

I put aside my sewing and looked at that thing on the floor, and suddenly I knew what he was doing, what it was. He had made a set of wheels for Eli's chair.

It was thoughtful and kind, and when I went over and helped him lift Eli into the settee, and then knelt beside him to help, I wanted to hug him tight for such a gift, for what it would mean to my husband. Instead, I met his gaze and I smiled at him, and I saw that lingering sadness come into his eyes in the second before he smiled back at me and looked away.

Together, we lifted the chair onto that frame, and Will lashed it tight. We tested it; the chair moved roughly across the uneven floorboards, but it did move.

He looked at Eli. "You want to try it out?"

Only a few months before, it would have been strange to think that the ability to move across a floor would make Eli so happy—would make me so happy—but it did. We lifted him into the chair, and he laughed as he grabbed hold of the birch table and moved himself from one wall to another, and I laughed with him while Will stood back and folded his arms across his chest and looked proud. Then Will knelt beside the chair to make sure the lashings were tight. "I had to use nails here, so it's not quite as smooth as it should be. There wasn't much else out there."

"What about leather?" Eli asked.

"Leather?"

"There's an awl in the barn. Why don't you go get it and bring it back? I'll show you what I mean."

While Will went back outside, Eli moved himself back to the far wall. He grabbed his shoemaking kit and pulled it into his lap. He looked at me as he moved himself back, and there was a wicked grin on his face. "Want a ride?" he asked.

I laughed, and when Will came breathlessly back, carrying the awl, I was still laughing. And I felt so tenderhearted as he knelt next to Eli and I watched the two of them bent close together while Eli showed him how to cut the leather, and how to use the awl. Dark head against blond, their newly made shirts gleaming white and gold in the lamplight. It raised an ache in me that nearly made me cry. I listened to them as they spoke in low voices, back and forth, Eli first, then Will:

"Twist it like that—no, slower . . . that's right, nice and easy."

"Like this?"

"A little farther down. Now loop it over. Right there's the perfect spot for the hole—see how the doubling gives it strength? Rest the awl like this—"

"Ouch."

"Not so hard. Tap it easier. Slow and steady."

"It's not going through."

"It takes a while. Not everything is a race, Will."

"Like this?"

"That's better. You make more progress when you keep a nice, even pace. Try it again."

I listened to it, life lessons in a simple task, the things Eli could teach Will if only he would listen, and I sat back and watched them and wished it could be this way forever. Then Will fumbled again and handed the leather to Eli, and I watched them pass the strap and saw it for what it was—the passing back of the farm, the handing over—and when Eli popped the awl through the leather with hardly any trouble, and leaned over the side of the chair to weave it through the frame Will had made and fasten it with a stronger, better hold to the chair, I saw how Will sat back on his heels and watched him—and knew what he was seeing: that Eli was not helpless any longer, that he was growing stronger every day. Before long, he would be able to work the farm on his own.

Already, with the winter coming, we hardly needed Will. I saw a thoughtfulness come into Will's eyes that made me feel sad again, as if I'd somehow lost him, when the truth was he'd never been mine at all— at least never the way I'd wanted him.

When the chair was done, Will stayed for a few minutes longer. But he seemed far away. Then he went to the door and shrugged into his coat. He stood there at the door, looking over things, and then he smiled softly and said, "Good night," and went outside, disappearing into the cold wind and the scent of frost.

When I looked back at Eli, he was watching the door. He said, "He's leaving."

"I know."

"Will you miss him, Lora?"

The question held more than just those words, and I knew it. I met my husband's eyes and said, "No."

But I didn't tell him the rest. I didn't tell him that I wouldn't miss Will because he was already in my heart, because I would keep close the memory of our friendship, and the things Will had given me, the life I owed to him. But I didn't need him now. I had Eli again, and it was all that mattered.

Eli nodded, and then he grabbed the table and pulled himself over closer to me. I sat on the end of the settee and picked up my embroidery, and when he said, "I think it's going to snow soon," I said to him, "It'll be a good chance to build some more cherry boxes. We used up about a quarter of them. We'll need plenty more for next year."

He smiled. "Now that is something I can do."

I leaned over, and he pulled me as close as he could with the arm of the settee coming between us. "As far as I know," I said, "there's nothing you can't do."

"I'm looking forward to discovering that again," he said, and then he kissed me hard and long, and I saw in his eyes a wickedness that made me long for the wintertime, and for snow, and evenings spent cuddled together beside the stove, holding each other tight long into the darkness.

25

The next morning, Will was gone. The milk was on the stoop, and the butter, and he'd collected the eggs, but the air was too quiet, and I saw his footprints in the frosted grass, leading to the road.

I'd known the night before that he'd been saying good-bye, but somehow I'd thought I would see him one final time, that my last memory of him would not be the sight of him standing in the doorway, wrapped in a too-big coat with his heart in his eyes. So I went out to the barn, thinking perhaps he hadn't gone, that he might still be there. But I knew he wouldn't be, and as I walked out there, I remembered the story he'd told me, of the hired hand who'd painted the portrait of his master's wife on the barn door, a forever remembrance, and I suppose I expected to find he'd left me my own painted door in the form of a photograph taken in North Yakima, of a young couple who looked like newlyweds, frozen in time, together forever.

But the barn was empty; all that was left of him was an indentation in the straw where he'd slept. I'd thought to find the picture tacked to the wall, but he'd taken it with him, too, and I was glad, because in spite of what he'd told me about remembering, I knew that Will Bennett needed that picture more than I did, that he hadn't yet learned that there were some things you never forgot, memories that didn't need photographs or paintings to remember.

And truthfully, I liked knowing he carried it with him, that when he was far from our land, he would pull that picture from his pocket and remember me, and think of me, and wonder how things were and if the trees were producing that year, and whether I was being cheated over cherries. I hoped he would find his happiness, his simplicity, his freedom—whatever it was he was looking for. I hoped I'd taught him something about what there was to be found. He had certainly taught me.

I thought he'd left me only a memory, but as I was turning to leave I saw it. Sitting on the door to Bessie's stall was an old piece of gray stone that held colors in crystal when you turned it over. Rainbows in a rock.

I put the rock into my apron pocket, and kept it there, and in the months that followed, it was a reassuring weight against my leg, a lesson I remembered.

And when winter was over and spring came again, when the sun emerged once more to turn the hillsides green with larkspur and camas, and new shoots of bunch grass pushed up through the old, shining bright green at the crown, I saw the valley green again with promise and thought of Will again, and the flowers he'd wanted me to see.

I was kneeling in the spring-melted soil at the base of the porch, planting dahlias, when I heard an awkward step on the porch, and I looked up to see Eli standing there, leaning on the cane he was coming to need less and less, smiling down at me.

"What are you doing?"

"Planting dahlias," I said. "For Eva."

He came down the stairs and left the cane there, balanced against the porch, and then he knelt slowly beside me, wincing a little as he did. He reached into the basket beside me and pulled out one of the dirt-encrusted tubers, rolling it in his farmer's hands before he pushed it deep into the soil and covered it over. "It'll be good to see flowers here," he said, and then he reached over and pulled me close so he could lay his hand on my stomach. It was too early yet to show, but it seemed the new soul inside me leapt to his hand, and in his eyes I saw the whole of my life before me, my love for him and my marriage, Eva's death, Will, and this new baby growing strong inside me. The wind blew up dust in my eyes and my nose was full of the smell of this land, and I felt my roots growing in this soil.

It seems strange to say that I saw Eli's dreams again, and I suppose that isn't really what happened. It wasn't Eli's dreams I saw, but my own. Tree branches breaking beneath the weight of climbing children, a house growing room by room, more lop-sided with the years, a place that was never quiet. Eli had said we had to make the land work to make Eva's death mean something, but I knew it wasn't about making the land pay. It was about putting your dreams into it and holding on until it bloomed beneath your hands. Will thought I wanted flowers, and I did. But I wanted them knee-high against my own house. I wanted chubby little hands filled with them, and a vase on the windowsill, and the husband I loved smiling at the sight as he bent close to kiss my shoulder.

I looked up at the house, at the windows reflecting in the sunlight, bright beacons glaring off glass brought all the way from The Dalles, settled into windowsills by hands anxious to please me. I saw dust all around, and a dying oak tree in the yard, and a man kneeling beside me in the dirt, planting dahlias, and the land resonated beneath my feet; I felt its pulse in my toes.

Once, I'd had Eden. I turned my dreams toward having it again.